READER, I MARRIED HIM

Commissioned to celebrate Charlotte Brontë's bicentenary year in 2016, this collection of original stories by today's finest women writers draws inspiration from a line in *Jane Eyre*. A bohemian wedding party takes an unexpected turn for the bride and her daughter . . . A family trip to a Texan waterpark prompts a life-changing decision . . . Mr Rochester reveals a long-kept secret . . . Jane's married life after the original novel ends is explored . . . A new mother encounters an old lover after her daily swim, and inexplicably lies to him . . . A fitness instructor teaches teenage boys how to handle a pit bull terrier by telling them Jane Eyre's story. These tales, and more, salute the lasting relevance of Brontë's famous novel and its themes of love, compromise and self-determination.

READER, I MARRIED HIM

STORIES INSPIRED BY JANE EYRE

EDITED BY

TRACY CHEVALIER

ISIS
LARGE
PRINT

2017

First published in Great Britain 2016
by
The Borough Press
An imprint of HarperCollins*Publishers*

First Isis Edition
published 2017
by arrangement with
HarperCollins*Publishers*

A catalogue record for this book is available
from the British Library.

ISBN 978–1–78541–328–5 (hb)
ISBN 978–1–78541–334–6 (pb)

Published by
F. A. Thorpe (Publishing)
Anstey, Leicestershire

Set by Words & Graphics Ltd.
Anstey, Leicestershire
Printed and bound in Great Britain by
T. J. International Ltd., Padstow, Cornwall

This book is printed on acid-free paper

For Charlotte, of course

Contents

Foreword by
Tracy Chevalier

Why is "Reader, I married him" one of the most famous lines in literature? Why do we remember it and quote it so much? Why have twenty-one writers jumped at the opportunity to take that line and run with it, folding its powerful resonance and sheer chutzpah into their own stories? Is it because of who says it and how she says it, or who has written it, or how we read it — or all of those things?

Charlotte Brontë's *Jane Eyre*, the story of a nineteenth-century orphan who becomes a governess and finds her place in the world, is most memorable for the character of Jane herself. "Poor, obscure, plain, and little", with no family and no prospects, nothing to cushion her from a life of poverty and loneliness except her wits and her self-belief, Jane is the embodiment of the underdog who ultimately triumphs. And who doesn't support the underdog? No matter what our circumstances, most of us see ourselves as underdogs; we can relate to her, and cheer her on.

Despite a childhood of physical abuse (near-starvation at her boarding school) and psychological torment (locked in the "red room" by her cruel aunt), Jane grows up with her self-esteem intact, and throughout the novel proves to be tough, resilient and morally grounded. She catches the eye of her employer, Mr Rochester, a man assumed to be way out of her league. She is as witty and as clever as he, eventually winning his love when she isn't even trying to. She stands up to him too, declaring, in probably the second most quoted line from the book: "I am no bird; and no net ensnares me; I am a free human being with an independent will." Who can resist a character like Jane Eyre?

"Reader, I married him" is Jane's defiant conclusion to her rollercoaster story. It is not, "Reader, he married me" — as you would expect in a Victorian society where women were supposed to be passive; or even, "Reader, we married." Instead Jane asserts herself; she is the driving force of her narrative, and it is she who chooses to be with Rochester. (Interestingly, Jane also inherits a fortune from an absent uncle, but no one ever remembers that detail; it is a *deus ex machina* out of her control and so it means less to us.) Her self-determination is not only very appealing; it also serves to undercut the potential over-sweetness of a classic happy ending where the heroine gets her man. The mouse roars, and we pump our fist with her.

It is also flattering — and memorable — to be addressed directly. How many novels acknowledge their readers? Jane addresses us the Reader throughout, and by doing so brings us on her side. Not only that: the line resonates because of the silent clauses that

2

surround it. What it really says is: "You may be surprised to learn that, Reader, I married him" or, "Reader, I married him, though perhaps I shouldn't have" or even, "Reader, I married him and then we went to bed." We readers fill in those blanks, and doing so involves us in Jane's decision as much as her speaking directly to us does. Her story becomes entwined with us, so that it feels as if we are telling it alongside Jane and her creator. No wonder we remember the line: we seem to have written it ourselves.

The woman who created that line is also a significant factor in its power. Though most readers may not know a lot about Charlotte Brontë, many will be struck by even the briefest outline of her remarkable life: remarkable not for being full of incident, but because it *wasn't*. Or it was, but it was drama played out within an intimate domestic space rather than on a wider stage. Charlotte was one of a trio of sisters who grew up in a parsonage in a remote Yorkshire village on the edge of the moors, who all published novels around the same time, with strong characters and storylines, before dying young. If you visit the atmospheric Brontë Parsonage in Haworth, where I first had the idea to create this collection of stories, you will be struck by what a strange, intense family the Brontës were: a hothouse of creativity springing from unpromising surroundings. Charlotte, Emily and Anne Brontë often sat together in the severe dining room, all writing and talking about what they wrote.

Women just didn't *do* that back in the nineteenth century. Most writers then were men; middle-class women were expected to be decorative rather than active. They were not meant to write novels about obsessive love on the moors (Emily's *Wuthering Heights*), or wives escaping their drunken, abusive husbands (Anne's *The Tenant of Wildfell Hall*), or a headstrong governess who declares that she will marry. That they published at all — at first under the peculiar male names Currer, Ellis and Acton Bell — is miraculous. *Jane Eyre* went on to become a publishing sensation; it was well reviewed, sold well, and Charlotte was fêted by other writers such as William Thackeray and Elizabeth Gaskell (one of the few other popular women writers at the time).

The fact that from such an unlikely background she became a famous, bestselling writer is heartening news for all would-be writers, for all women — and indeed, for all women writers. That is why I have asked women to contribute to this collection — we have even more reason to be grateful to Charlotte for her ambition and imagination, which paved the way for more women to write and be published. "Reader, I married him" reveals not just Jane Eyre's determination, but Charlotte Brontë's too, and it inspires our own.

Twenty-one writers, then, have taken up the line and written what it has urged them to write. I liken "Reader, I married him" to a stone thrown into a pond, with its resulting ripples. Some of the writers have written close to where the stone has entered the water, taking the Jane Eyre story itself and writing it from a different angle: Helen Dunmore from Grace Poole's point of view; Salley Vickers from Mr Rochester's eyes. Audrey Niffenegger places Jane in a contemporary war-torn country in "The Orphan Exchange". Other stories are ripples a little further from the source, including elements from the novel such as the moors setting, or specific incidents, or imagery such as mirrors or animals, or even certain lines. (Look out for "small and plain", Rochester's famous description of Jane.) You do not need to know *Jane Eyre* to enjoy these stories, but if you do, those resonances will make you smile.

Other stories may move still further away from Jane, yet almost all of them address marriage (or today's equivalent of it) in some way, exploring when marriage might happen, or should happen, or shouldn't, or when it ends, or is with the wrong person, or seems to be with the right person but goes wrong. There are at least two proposals in the collection — though we will have to guess at the replies!

For some weddings themselves provide the drama, courtesy of a painful shard of glass in Linda Grant's "The Mash-Up", or a sudden cast change in "My Mother's Wedding" by Tessa Hadley, or a secret liaison during a Zambian bonding ceremony in Namwali Serpell's "Double Men", or a muddy Gothic encounter on the moors in "To Hold" by Joanna Briscoe.

For others, a wedding is only the start of a relationship, the stories moving beyond the traditional happy ending to find out what happens within marriage. Evie Wyld explores a woman's feelings about her husband, set against an austere Canadian landscape peopled with bears, while Susan Hill dissects the fall-out from a famous Anglo-American marriage, and Francine Prose looks at what happens to Jane Eyre and Mr Rochester after they wed. In "The Self-Seeding Sycamore" Lionel Shriver reminds us of what can grow after a marriage has ended.

Always, always in these stories there is love — whether it is the first spark or the last dying embers — in its many heart-breaking, life-affirming forms.

All of these stories have their own memorable lines, their own truths, their own happy or wry or devastating endings, but each is one of the ripples that finds its centre in Jane and Charlotte's decisive clarion call: Reader, I married him.

My Mother's Wedding

Tessa Hadley

It was never going to be an ordinary kind of wedding. My mother didn't do anything ordinary. She would marry Patrick at the summer solstice; it would all take place on the smallholding where we lived, in Pembrokeshire. My parents had bought the place in the seventies from an old couple, Welsh-speaking and chapel-going. Family and friends were coming from all over; all our Pembrokeshire friends would be there, and those of our neighbours who were still our friends: some of them didn't like the way we lived. My mother had dreamed up a wedding ceremony with plenty of drama. She and Patrick would drink Fen's home-made mead from a special cup, then smash it; the clinching moment would come when they got to take off all their clothes at sunset and immerse themselves in the pond while everyone sang — Fen would wave myrtle branches over them and pronounce them man and wife. Mum had spent hours puzzling over her notebook, trying to devise the right form of words for her vow. She could whisper to horses (she really could, that wasn't just hokum, I've seen her quieting a berserk half-broken young gelding when grown men wouldn't go near it), but she struggled sometimes to find the right words for things.

Patrick wasn't my father, needless to say. My father was long gone: from the smallholding and from west Wales and from the lifestyle. Dad had short hair now; he worked for an insurance company and voted for Mrs Thatcher. From time to time I went to stay with him and my stepmother, and I thought of those weeks in High Barnet as a tranquil escape, the way other people enjoyed a holiday in the country: with their central heating, and their kitchen with its food processor and waste-disposal unit, and the long empty days while they were both out at work, when I tried on all her trim little dresses and her make-up. I never mentioned Mrs Thatcher when I got back to Wales. I didn't like her politics any more than the others did, but I loved my dad. I didn't want to encourage the way everyone gloated, pretending to be shocked and disappointed by how he'd gone over to the dark side.

Patrick wasn't the father of my two half-siblings, Eithne and Rowan, either. Their dad was Lawrence, and he was still very much in our lives, lived a mile down the road — only he'd left Mum around the time Rowan was starting school, went off with Nancy Withers. And on the rebound Mum had had a fling with Fen, who was her best friend's husband. But that was all over now and Patrick was the love of her life and someone new from outside our set; all those people from her past — Lawrence and Nancy and Fen and Sue and all the others, though not my dad or my stepmother — would be at her wedding because that

8

was the kind of party they all liked best, where everyone had a history with everyone else, and anything might happen, and there was opportunity for plenty of pouring out their hearts to one another and dancing and pairing up in the wrong pairs, while the dope and the drink and the mushroom-brew kept everything lubricated and crazy. Meanwhile, the ragged gang of their kids would be running wild around the place in the dark, wilder even than their parents dreamed, stealing Fen's disgusting mead and spying on what they never should have seen — and one of them would almost inevitably break an arm, or set fire to a tent, or nearly drown. (Once, at a different party, one of the children really did drown, but that's another story.)

And I wouldn't know what to do with myself, because at seventeen I was too old to run with the kids, yet I was still holding back — too wary and angry and sceptical — from joining in with the adults. I was pretty much angry about everything, around that time. My mother came draping herself over my shoulders where I was trying to learn about photosynthesis out of the textbook for my Biology A level. "Janey, precious-heart, help me with this wretched vow thing, I can't get it right. You're the one who's clever with words. What should I say? I've put 'I promise to worship the loving man in you,' but then I have this picture of Patrick flinging it back at me if ever anything went wrong. Because of course I know what can happen, I know about men, I'm not going into this with my eyes closed."

"Mum, get off," I said, trying to ease myself out from under her. "I can't possibly make up your wedding vows. It's inappropriate."

"You're such an old stick-in-the-mud," she said fondly, squeezing my shoulders tightly and kissing the top of my head, her auburn hair flopping down on to the page. Her hair is like Elizabeth Siddal's in Rossetti's paintings and she wears it either loose or in a kind of rope wrapped around her head, and actually her looks are like Elizabeth Siddal's too, and she wears the same drapey kind of clothes. But I was the one who knew who Elizabeth Siddal was, and that Rossetti buried her with a book of his poems and then dug her up again to get them back; I knew all about the Pre-Raphaelites and Rossetti and Burne-Jones and the rest, and I didn't even like them all that much. That was the way life was divided up between me and my mother. I knew about things, and she was beautiful.

I couldn't imagine Patrick flinging anything back at anyone. Patrick had the sweetest temperament. He was much younger than Mum, only twenty-six, closer to my age than hers, and he was loose-limbed with messy pale hair, and sleepy grey eyes as though everything in his life had been a dream until he woke up and saw my mother — in the wholefood cooperative in the village, as it happened, when they both reached out for a paper sack of muesli base at the same moment. He'd come out to west Wales to stay for free in a friend's family's holiday home for a couple of months, to finish his PhD thesis on the theology of Julian of Norwich (I knew who she was too). He'd run out of grant money and

10

told us he'd been living for weeks on end on nothing much but apples and muesli base. "It's very filling," he said cheerfully. Mum thought he was otherworldly like the Celtic saints, but I knew he was just an intellectual. All his experience had been in books and he'd never properly come up against life in its full force before: he fell for the first real thing he laid his eyes on, like an innocent in a Shakespeare play. There was a girlfriend back in Oxford — another theologian — but she didn't stand a chance against that rope of auburn hair. He'd abandoned the thesis, too.

We loved Patrick, Eithne and Rowan and me. Eithne and Rowan loved rambling with him around our land, finding out how he'd never done anything before: never swung out on a rope over the river or ridden a pony bareback (or ridden any way at all), never seen anything like the dead crows strung up along the fence wire of the neighbouring farmer who hated us. I loved talking with someone who knew things instead of being experienced. Experience was etched into the leathery, tanned faces of all the other adults in my life; experience was like a calculating light in their eyes when they looked at me. Patrick and I sank deep in the sagging old sofa which stank of the dogs, while my mother cooked vats of curry for the freezer, and he told me about Julian of Norwich, and I was happy. This doesn't mean I was keen on his marrying my mother.

I kept saying it would rain on the wedding party because it's always raining in Wales (that's another nice thing about High Barnet). We ought to make plans for the rain, I said, but my mother just smiled and said she knew it was going to be fine, and then it was: the day dawned cloudless and pure, yellow haze gleaming in the meadows, hills in the distance delicately drawn in blue. I had to hold on very firmly, sometimes, to my conviction that everything could be explained in the light of reason; it really did seem as though Mum had witch powers. She could smell if rain was coming, her dreams seemed to foretell the future, and her hands could find the place where a horse was hurt, or a child. People said her touch was healing — only I didn't want her touching me, not any more.

She and I worked together all that morning, defrosting the curries and loaves of wholemeal bread and the dishes of crumble we'd cooked with our own apples and quinces, mixing jugs of home-made lemonade. Fen drove over with plastic buckets of mead and crates of bottles in the back of his flatbed, along with a suspect carrier bag: he was in charge of the stronger stuff. Sue had sent the wedding cake, soaked in brandy and decorated with hearts and flowers cut out in coloured marzipan. "You don't think it's poisoned?" I said. "After what you did to her?"

My mother only laughed. "We've forgiven each other everything. Anyway, Sue started it — when she slept with your dad, while I was still breastfeeding you." I pretended I knew about this, just to prevent her telling me more.

Then I sorted out sleeping bags and blankets for all the guests who were going to stay over. Patrick helped me haul the old mattresses up into the hayloft in our barn, built of ancient grey stone, older and more spacious than the farmhouse. When we stood at the open loft window with the sweet air blowing around us — it was tall as the loft itself, gracious as a church window, only without any glass — we could see ten miles, all the way to the glinting fine line of the sea.

"Are you sure you want to go through with this?" I said daringly. "I know Mum's overwhelming."

I expected him to reply with the same dazed absent-mindedness I was used to, as if he were under her spell — and was surprised when he looked at me sharply. "I suppose you think she's too old for me," he said.

I made some joke about cradle-snatching.

"She looks great though, doesn't she?" Patrick went on uneasily. "For her age."

So he wasn't so otherworldly after all! I didn't know whether to be triumphant, or disappointed in him.

Our guests began to arrive in the afternoon. The party grew around the outdoor fireplace Lawrence had built in the meadow years ago, when he still lived with us. Lawrence was handsome, big and ruddy-faced with thick black hair and sideburns and moustache; he made his living as a builder though he'd been to one of the famous public schools. He was in charge of barbecuing as usual, and we brought out all the rest of the food from the kitchen, to keep warm beside his fire. Fen — not handsome in the least but wickedly funny, tall and stooped with a shaved head and huge crooked nose — started doling out the drink. I wouldn't drink, and they all thought it was because I was a puritan, controlled and disapproving; actually the reason was rather different. A year ago at another party, when no one was looking I'd helped myself to too much mushroom liquor from the bottom of one of Fen's brews, and since then I'd been accompanied everywhere by a minor hallucination: hearing my own feet scraping on the floor like little trotting hooves. Nothing disastrous, but enough to scare me.

Patrick had scythed along the top of the meadow that morning and smells of fresh-cut grass and roasting meat mingled together. Swallows came darting and mewing among the clouds of insects in the slanting yellow light. When the Irish band turned up, Mum and Patrick danced the first dance alone, then everyone else joined in; the warmth seemed to thicken as the sun sank lower. The kids had found our old punt in the long grass and taken it out on the pond; it leaked and they had to bail it frantically. The sounds of their distant shouting and laughter and splashing, and the dogs barking at them, all came scudding back to us across the water. I thought that my sister Eithne must be down at the pond with the others, until I caught sight of her at the heart of the dancing — and she looked as if she'd been drinking, too. There was always trouble at our parties (my little hooves didn't begin to count, in the scale of things), and this time the trouble began with Eithne.

She was fourteen, and her face was expressive enough when she was sober, with her big twisted mouth and bright auburn hair, and the funny cast in one of her hazel eyes like a black inkblot; she was wearing her pale old stretch-towelling pyjamas to dance in, and had her hair done in several plaits that bounced around her head like snakes. Eithne had all sorts of mystery illnesses; I used to get mad because I thought Mum kept her home from school on the least excuse, or if she just thought the teacher wasn't being spiritual enough. So Eithne could hardly read or write; she didn't know basic things like fractions or the date of the French Revolution — probably didn't know the French Revolution had even happened. But she'd always been able to dance like a dream, the same graceful easy way that she could ride and swim.

While Mum and Patrick were drinking out of the wedding cup, which Nancy Withers had made specially, Eithne came snuggling up next to me. I felt her shivering. "Have you been at Fen's mead?" I asked her. "You'll make yourself sick."

"I don't care if I die," she said.

"You won't die. You'll just be throwing up all night."

Mum promised to love the holy wanderer in Patrick, and Patrick promised, because he could quote poetry, to love the pilgrim soul in Mum. They lifted the wedding cup between them and smashed it down against the stones of Lawrence's fireplace, then kissed passionately. Eithne said it was disgusting, and that she was going to bed.

"I told you you'd make yourself sick," I said.

Then when she'd gone, Mum and Patrick were smooching together for a while to the sound of the band, until Mum suddenly had one of her intuitions.

15

She pushed Patrick away and went running up towards the house with her skirts pulled up around her knees so she could go faster. And somehow I must have half-shared in the intuition because I went running up after her, and as we left the meadow behind and came round the side of the farmhouse we could see Eithne standing framed against the last of the light, in her pyjamas, in the barn's hayloft window — which wasn't really a window at all, just an opening into the air, fifteen feet above the ground.

"Ethie, take care!" Mum called out. "Step back from the window, my darling."

"I love Patrick," Eithne said. "I don't want you to marry him."

And then she stepped forward out of the window into nothingness, flopping down like a doll and landing with a thud on a heap of rubble overgrown with nettles. Mum ran forward with an awful cry and picked her up, and I really thought my sister must be dead — but by some miracle she wasn't hurt. (Mum said afterwards it was because she'd fallen with her limbs so floppy and relaxed.) Cradling Eithne in her arms, she told me to go and tell Patrick to wait for her. "I've got to deal with this," she said. And she carried Eithne into the house and lay on the bed upstairs with her, soothing her, making everything all right. This is the kind of thing that happens at our parties.

Everyone including the band had drifted down the meadow to stand beside the pond. The kids had pulled the punt out into the grass and now everyone was waiting for the finale, when Mum and Patrick took off their clothes and walked into the water. Patrick stood at the edge by himself, looking doubtful. The sun was going down behind the row of beech trees that marked the edge of our smallholding, and its light made a shining path across the water's surface, motionless as glass. I don't know what made me do the mad thing I did next; perhaps it was the last kick of my year-long mushroom hallucination. Instead of giving Mum's message to Patrick, I put my arms around his neck and kissed him. "Mum's not coming," I said. "Marry me."

"Janey says Patrick ought to marry her instead," Fen announced to everyone, booming, waving his myrtle branch.

"Marry me," I said, louder.

"Where is she, anyway?" Patrick looked around him helplessly.

"Marry her, marry Janey instead," they all called encouragingly, maliciously: Lawrence and Fen, Nancy and Sue, and all the rest.

The fiddle player started up the "Wedding March".

And I pulled my dress over my head and stepped out of my knickers and unhooked my bra, not looking at anyone though I knew they were all looking at me, and I waded naked into the pond water along the shining path, up to my knees and then up to my thighs, feeling the silt oozing between my toes, not caring about the sinister, slippery things that touched me. It was such a risk; it would have been so humiliating if Patrick hadn't come in after me. I waited, not looking back at him, looking ahead at the sunset glowing like a fire between

17

the beeches, while he stood hesitating on the brink. I heard them all singing and I felt the first drops of rain on my skin, like a sign.

Luxury Hour

Sarah Hall

It was the last week of the season and the lido was nearly deserted. She arrived at the usual time, changed into her suit, left her clothes in a locker and walked out across the chlorine-scented vault. The concrete paving had traces of frost in the corners and was almost painful on the soles of her feet. Light rustled under the blue rectangular surface. She climbed down the metal ladder and moved away from the edge without pausing. In October, entering the unheated pool was an act of bravery; the trick was to remain thoughtless. The water was coldly radiant. Her limbs felt stiff as she kicked and her chin burned. At the halfway mark she looked up at the guard, who was sinking into the fur hood of his parka. Nothing in his demeanour gave the impression of a man ready to intervene, should it be necessary. She took a breath, put her head underwater, surfacing a few strokes later. She was awake now, her heart jabbing. She turned on to her back, rotated her arms. The clouds above were grey and fast. Rain later, perhaps.

She swam twenty lengths, by which time she was warm and the idea of autumn seemed acceptable, then rested her head on the coping and caught her breath.

The pool slopped gently against her chest. Light filaments flashed and extinguished in the rocking fluid. In summer it was hard to swim, hard to find the space; the pool was choppy, kids bombed in at the deep end, and the water washed out over the edges, soaking towels and bags. Barely an inch between sunbathers. Not many came after early September. But the old couple with rubber caps she always saw on quieter mornings were in the next lane, swimming side by side: her chin tipped high, his submerged. She followed in their wake. They nodded hello when she reached the end, and she smiled. She climbed out. Her breasts and thighs were blotched red with the chill and exertion.

In the changing room she tried not to look at her midriff in the mirrors, the crêping and the sag. She showered and dressed, and went into the poolside café. It was busy as usual. There were prams parked between tables, people working on laptops and reading books. The debris of muesli, pastries and napkins was strewn about. On the walls were photographs from the thirties, pictures of young women diving from the high board, now dismantled, or posing with their hands on their hips. The grace, the vivacity of another era: dark mouths, straight teeth, a kind of ebullient confidence. The scenes looked pre-industrial — open sky, birds in vee formations overhead. The five-storey civic building opposite the park hadn't been built. London had not yet arrived.

The man behind the counter leaned away from the growling espresso machine and predicted her order.

Latte?

Yes, please.

There was an immaculate row of silver rings in his bottom lip.

Bring it over.

She took a seat by the window, in the corner, and watched the old couple emerge from the lido. Their stamina was far greater than hers — an hour's swimming at least. They stood dripping and chatting for a moment as if unaffected by the smart breeze. The woman's legs were thin, but strung with muscle. Her belly was a tiny mound under the swimming costume. The man had a buckled torso, a white beard. There was a vast laparotomy scar up his abdomen. They were the same height and seemed perfectly suited. She wondered if they'd evolved towards their symmetry over the years. The couple parted and went towards separate changing rooms. He walked awkwardly, favouring one hip. In the pool he swam well. Occasionally she'd seen his sedate, companionable breaststroke morph into an energetic butterfly.

There was no one left in the lido. The guard rested his head on his hand, eyes closed, the whistle attached to his wrist hanging in the air. The surface of the pool stilled to a beautiful chemical blue.

Her coffee arrived. She opened a packet of sugar and poured it. She shouldn't be taking sugar — the baby weight was still not coming off — but hadn't ever been able to drink coffee without. She sipped slowly. The pool was hypnotic; something about the water was calming, rapturous almost. Time here, after swimming, always felt inadmissible to her day. She would linger, ignore her phone. Often she had to race round the shops to be back in time for the sitter. "Luxury hour", Daniel called it, as if she were indulging herself, but it was the only time she had without the baby.

After a while she went to the counter, paid and left. She began to walk through the park. The breeze was strengthening, the leaves of the trees moving briskly. There were some kids playing cycle polo on one of the hard courts, wheeling about and whacking the puck against the metal cage. Dogs bounded across the grass. She passed the glass merchant's mansion and the old glassworks, both hidden under flapping plastic drapes and renovation scaffolding. She'd hated the city when she and Daniel had first arrived. She'd missed the Devon countryside, the fragrance of peat and gorse, horses with torn manes, the lack of people. But it was what one did — for the jobs, for the culture; London's sacrificial gravity was too strong and it had taken them. Discovering the park had changed everything, and the nearby property was just about affordable.

She passed through the rank of dark-trunked sycamores. Beyond was the meadow. Its pale brindle stirred in the wind, belts of grass lightening and darkening. The field had been resown after a local campaign by the Friends of the Park. For a century it had been a wasteland — the horses used for pulling the carts of quartz sand to the glassworks had overgrazed it. Dust, cullet and oil from the annealing ovens had polluted the soil. Now it was lush again; there were bees and mice, even city kestrels — she'd seen them tremoring above the burrows, stooping with astonishing speed. There was a dry, chaff-like smell to the meadow after the summer; the grasses clicked and hushed. The enormous, elaborate spider webs of the previous month had broken apart and were drifting free.

A man was walking down the scythed path towards her. She stepped aside to let him pass but he stopped and held out his hand.

Alex.

She looked up. For a second she didn't recognise him. He had on a tie and a suit jacket. The planes of his face came into focus. The heavy bones, the irises, with their concentration of colour, no divisions or rings. He was a little older, his hair darker than she remembered, but it was him.

Oh, God, she said. Hi.

He moved to kiss her cheek. She put a hand on his arm, turned her face too much and he kissed her ear, awkwardly.

Hi. Do you still live around here?

Yes, I'm over on Hillworth. Near the station.

Nice area.

Yes.

The wind was throwing her hair around her face, tangling it. She hadn't properly washed or brushed it in the changing room. She moved a damp strand from her forehead. It felt sticky with chlorine. He was looking at her, his expression unreadable.

I've been swimming.

At the lido?

She nodded.

Wow! It's still open? I must go there. Is it cold?

It's OK. Bracing.

Had he forgotten? The cold water never used to bother him. She ran a hand through her hair again, tried to think what to say. Her mind felt white, soft. The shock of the real. Even though he'd said he was going, she'd expected to run into him and had, for a time, avoided the park. After a few months the expectation had lessened, and the hope, and she had reclaimed the space. Then the baby had come, and life had altered drastically. She'd assumed he'd moved away for good. His face was becoming increasingly familiar as she looked. The shape of his mouth, too full, voluptuous for a man, the fine white scar in the upper lip.

So, where are you these days? she asked.

Brighton.

Brighton!

I know!

He smiled. His teeth. One of the front ones was a fraction squarer, mostly porcelain — the accident on his bike. She had liked tapping it, then the tooth next to it, to hear the difference. Heat bloomed up her neck. These days she could not remember things — where her purse was, which breast she had last fed the baby on, the name of the artist from her university dissertation. But she could remember his mouth, and lying so close to his face that the details began to blur. She felt as if she might reach out now and touch the hard wet surface of his tooth. She put her hands in her coat pockets. Around them the grass was swaying and hissing. The silk webs floated. A bird darted up out of the field, flew a few feet and then disappeared between stalks.

He was studying her too. Probably she looked tired, leached, aged, the classic new mother, not like the woman who had come up to him in a low-cut swimsuit and asked to borrow change for the locker.

I'll pay you back tomorrow.

I might not be here tomorrow.

Yes, you will.

So confident, then.

She hadn't applied make-up, there was no point most days really, and her mouth was dry and bitter from the coffee. At least the long coat hid her figure.

Did you go to Burma? she asked.

Myanmar, he said, quietly. I did. For eighteen months. Well, officially to Thailand for eighteen months, but we went across the border most days into the training camps.

I thought you would.

Now it's not such a problem getting in. Tourism.

She nodded. She was not up to speed on such things any more; she'd lost interest.

Was it difficult?

She was not sure what she meant by this question, only that she imagined privation, forfeit, that he had made the wrong decision.

Sometimes. We had a decent team. A lot of them were more missionaries than medics really, but on the whole the quality was good. I don't know whether we helped really. The students qualify, then get arrested for practising.

He shrugged. He glanced towards the north end of the park.

So it's still open?

Yes. Last week before winter closing. You should go before it shuts.

For old times' sake. She did not say it. Nor, *why have you come back?*

He glanced at his watch.

I have a conference. I'm presenting the first paper, actually. I have to get to Barts.

Oh, great. Congratulations.

Hence the suit, the tidy version of his former self. He shrugged again. Humility; the duty was clearly very important. There was a pause. She could barely look at him; the past was restoring itself too viscerally. Since the baby she had felt nothing, no desire, not even sorrow that this part of her life had vanished, perhaps for good. Daniel had been understanding, patient. She couldn't explain it: breastfeeding, different priorities, the wrong smell. Now, that familiar low ache. She wanted to step forward, reach out. *Compatible immune systems*, he had once said, to explain their impulses, *that's what it really is.* For something to do she took her bag off her shoulder and rummaged around inside. It was a pointless act, spurred by panic; she was looking for nothing in particular. But then, in the inside pocket, she found the season ticket. She held it out.

Here. It still has a couple of swims. They won't check the name when they stamp it, they never do.

He took the pass.

You should go, since you're here.

That's so thoughtful of you. God, I do miss it!

He was grinning now, and she could see in him the uninhibited man who'd never cared about the cold, who'd plunged into the pool without hesitation and swum almost a length under the surface. She could see his damp body on the bed in his flat, those stolen moments, the chaos of sheets, his expression, agonised, abandoned, as if in a seizure dream. She could see herself, holding the railings of the bed, fighting for control of the space they were using. Walking quickly home, ashamed, electrified, and holding her swimsuit under the kitchen tap, so that it would look used. Luxury hour.

She still swam, in October. Perhaps he was impressed because his interest suddenly seemed piqued.

So, Alexandra. What's your life like now? Are you still at the gallery?

No. I'm married.

Ah.

She looked at him, then away.

To Daniel?

Yes, to Daniel.

Any children?

There was nothing to his tone other than polite conversation, the logical assumption of one thing following another. Or perhaps a slight wistfulness, some emotion, it was always hard to tell. The wind moved across the meadow. The grass rippled, like dry water.

No. No children.

He nodded, neither surprised nor sympathetic. She looked at the meadow. As if it could be as it was before.

It was suddenly harder to breathe, though there were acres of air above. The lie was so great there would surely be a penalty. She would go home and the house would be silent, her son's room empty. Or the baby would be screaming in the cot, and he would turn to ash when she lifted him up. The baby would be motionless in the shallow water of the bath while the minder sat on a stool, waiting.

He was speaking, saying something about his engagement to a woman from Thailand; her name was Sook, his family liked her, they had no children yet either. He was holding the season pass. He looked contented, established, a man in a tie about to give an important paper. Everything had moved on, except that he was here, and this was not the way to Barts. She reached out and touched his arm. He was real, of course he was.

You should swim, she said. Will you swim?

He looked at his watch again.

Yeah. Why not. I reckon there's time, if I'm quick. What shall I wear? Will I get away with boxers?

I have to go, she said.

Oh. OK.

It was too abrupt, she knew, a breach in the otherwise civil conversation between old lovers that should have wound up more carefully. But already she had turned and was walking away up the path. His voice, calling behind her:

Bye, Alex. Lovely seeing you.

She kept walking. She did not turn round. At the edge of the meadow she stepped off the track, put her bag down, and crouched in the grass. He would not follow her, she knew, but she stayed there a long time, hidden. From her bag came the faint sound of ringing. She was late for the sitter again. She stayed crouched until her legs felt stiff. Embedded in the earth, between stalks, were tiny pieces of brown glass from the old works. The wind had lessened, the rain still holding off. She stood. If she ran back to the lido maybe she could catch him. She could apologise, and explain, tell him that she'd been afraid, she'd been angry and hurt that he was leaving; she'd had to choose, as he'd had to choose. The baby was a complication, but she could tell him what the child's name was, at least. They could exchange numbers. They could meet, somewhere between Brighton and here. Or she could just watch him swimming from the café window, from the corner table, behind the blind pane, his body a long shadow under the surface.

Grace Poole her Testimony

Helen Dunmore

Reader, I married him. Those are her words for sure. She would have him at the time and place she chose, with every dish on the table to her appetite.

She came in meek and mild but I knew her at first glance. There she sat in her low chair at a decent distance from the fire, buttering up Mrs Fairfax as if the old lady were a plate of parsnips. She didn't see me but I saw her. You don't live the life I've lived without learning to move so quiet that there is never a stir to frighten anyone.

Jane Eyre. You couldn't touch her. Nothing could bring a flush of colour to that pale cheek. What kind of pallor was it, you ask? A snowdrop pushing its way out of the bare earth, as green as it was white: that would be a comparison she'd like. But I would say: sheets. Blank sheets. Paper, or else a bed that no one had ever lain in or ever would.

I am a coarse creature. No one has ever married me and I have not much taste for marrying. I like my porter, and there's no harm in that. I am quick with the laudanum too. My lady takes it flavoured with cinnamon, and I keep the bottle under lock and key because sometimes she likes it too much. This little pale one won't touch a drop of anything. Won't let it sully her lips. Doesn't want to be babbling out her secrets in that French she's so proud of, as if anyone cared to listen. The little girl speaks French as pure as a bird.

I sweat and my stays creak when I move. I have good employment and I am respected by everyone in the household, not least Mr R. He's a sly one, a fox if ever there was, and my poor lady was no vixen. All she ever had, and I will swear my Bible oath to it, was a weakness.

Violent? Not she. Not my lady. Mr R brought Dr Gallion here to measure her skull. She was tied firm to a ladder-back chair and she did not resist although her eyes rolled. The doctor undertook the palpation of my lady's skull prominences. Here, he said, this is the bump of Amativeness. A propensity to Combativeness, do you see here, sir? His hands roved over her head and everything he discovered was to her detriment. He went beyond prodding at her bones to observe the way her hair grew low on her forehead, which he said showed an animal disposition. It vexed me. It was because she would not speak that he called her animal, but she could talk when she liked. She spoke in her dreams, when only I was there to hear her. If she preferred to be called mute I did not blame her. Downstairs, the pale one, chatter chatter in French with the little girl, scribble scribble on whatever piece of paper she could get, as if words were all anybody needed.

What I hated most was the way she made herself milk and water, a dish of whey for anyone to drink at, sip sop sip sop, when what she truly wanted was to be a blade through the heart of us. I knew it but the rest were dumb and blind. The old lady loved the sip sop. As for the little girl, she was taken by her, like a baby taken for a changeling.

My poor lady's skull showed an enlarged Organ of Destructiveness. Dr Gallion passed his fingers over the place and repeated the words. He nodded and Mr R nodded with him, the two gentlemen solemn together now while my lady bent her head and her hair slid over her shoulders. The doctor had loosened it from the knots and coils she wore, the better to get at her.

In such a case as this, the doctor said, it would be wise to shave the head entire, the more clearly to see how the organs display themselves.

I rubbed oil into the bristle that sprouted from my lady's scalp, so that it would grow more quickly. She was bewildered at the loss of her hair. She would raise her hand as if to touch the knot that sat at her nape, and find it gone, and then her hand would waver. I would give her a little laudanum and she would rock herself and seem to find comfort in it.

The pale one thinks she has the measure of us all. Up and down the garden she goes in the shadows of evening. She ticks us off in her steps. The old lady. Mr R. The little girl. The guests who come and go. She would tick me off too but she only knows my name. She asked it and they told her: Grace Poole.

I am a strong creature with a pot of porter. I receive excellent wages. I am so turned and turned about that if I saw a snowdrop push its way out of the earth I would stamp on it.

She was brought here to dig the frippery out of the little girl, so that the child might take her proper station in life.

Less noise there, Grace.

I can make a noise if I want. They know that. I have not yet lost my voice. If I spoke out I'd tell the pale one a story she wouldn't soon forget.

Long ago he married my lady and they were Mr and Mrs R. Amativeness is what the doctor called it. This was long before the snowdrop raised its head, but the creature with the porter was already here. Me. Fifteen was I? As old as my tongue and a little older than my teeth. I was a lovely flashing bit of a girl then. I could stop men of thirty dead in their tracks as they ploughed. I made the air so thick around me they seemed to wade or drown in it. I was Grace Poole.

I stopped him dead in his tracks. I did not care for my lady then or know her. She did not come downstairs. They said she was nervous. To me she was a foreign land where I never wished to go.

Grace Poole, he said to me, and I saw him tremble. Is that your name?

I tilted the water I was carrying so that the jug rested on my hip. I said nothing. Let him look, I thought, and I shall look back at him.

I had an attic then. A slip of a room all white with sunlight and almost bare, but there was a bed in it. He was older than me but not by so much. He had married

34

young and they said he was unhappy. I thought of nothing then except having him.

I dare say he had never lain down on such a bed in his life. We had to put our hands over each other's mouths so as not to cry out.

Grace Poole, he said when I released him. Grace Poole. It was the most beautiful thing I had ever heard: my own name. No one heard and no one came.

No man likes a big belly. I carried mine to a place he procured for me. He told me that he would provide for the child and give it a station in life, and I would come back to Thornfield. It was more than I expected. He was a fox because it was his nature, but he kept his word about the child. I did not resist when it was born and taken by a wet nurse, to go far away to a better place.

I took a fever when it was gone and the room stank so that even the nurse who tended me held up a handkerchief over her face, but I did not die. I pitted and spotted and what got up from the bed was no longer the old Grace Poole but the beginning of the creature you see presently. I grew as strong as you like. I came back to Thornfield and took a taste for nursing, as perhaps he had foreseen.

I did not want anyone to look at me. And there she is, the pale one, bursting with it, every inch of her chill little flesh shouting: Look at me.

She will never stand before him as I did and look back at him, and make him come to her. She hunts in another fashion.

So I came to nurse my lady here. She would not eat so I fed her from a spoon. She would not speak so I learned her gestures and what they meant. I brushed her hair, which was thick and soft and long enough to touch the ground when she sat. It took an hour sometimes to brush her hair, to plait it and coil it into the knot she liked. When it was finished she would put up her hands to touch it and she would be satisfied. She liked her laudanum flavoured with cinnamon and not with saffron, which was what they gave her at first. Another thing she liked was a bit of red satin ribbon which she would wrap around her fingers and rub against her cheek as she rocked herself, and at those times although she never spoke she would hum and I would think: Perhaps she is content.

Each morning: porridge with cream and syrup, so that even a little of it will fatten her. Sometimes she will take a dish of tea; other times she will dash it from my hand. But no matter how fiercely she smashes china, she never touches me. There has been long discussion over whether or not she should take meat. It is heating. It inflames the passions. She is allowed only a very little beef. I make broth for her myself, out of bones she likes to crack with her teeth when they are cooked so that the marrow is ready to drip out of them. She will eat toast sometimes, as long as it is cut so fine it splinters to pieces if the butter is hard. On the days when she puts her lips together and will not swallow, I know better now than to persuade her. I take out my two packs of cards and make them flicker down into heaps over and over. It soothes her.

But now here we are: the old lady, the snowdrop, the little girl, Mr R, my lady and the creature with the porter. Me. The little girl has come back from France and she does not know me. She peeps and cheeps about the house with her high French voice and her dancing slippers. In the kitchen they say that she is the child of a French opera dancer that Mr R has kept in France. Some say that the opera dancer is dead, others that he has tired of her. They are used to me going in and out without partaking of the conversation, as I fetch and carry my lady's food and drink. They call me Mrs Poole and none of them will cross me. Richard the footman visited London when he was a boy and he says he would rather have charge of the entire menagerie at Exeter 'Change than be left alone with Mrs R as I am. All I will ever own is that my lady has her ways.

If the pale one had not come to this house we should all have kept on safe. The little girl did not know me. I was content with that. I liked to see her flutter about the house in her lace and silk, and dance in front of the mirror. I was no more the Grace Poole who laid herself down on the narrow bed in the sunlit attic than I was Mr R himself. I rose up from childbed another woman and I am that woman now. I have no child but I have Mrs R. Let the little girl skip where she wants and peep out her French phrases and grow up to a suitable station. But this pale one has come here, loitering in our lanes and uncannily stealing what does not belong to her. And now here is my lady disturbed night after night, murmuring and rocking. No one knows what senses she has. Sometimes I see thoughts whisk in her eyes that I would never dare to see the bottom of, and I know that Mr R will not come here again and face her.

Mr R knows that I will never leave her. We should have been safe, if that one had never come here. Of course she wants my lady gone. She spins out words in her head like a spider. She will have us all wrapped tight. I see him walking in the garden, and her walking after him, so sly and small and neat that you would never think twice of it. She calls my lady a madwoman and a danger, and he listens. She says these words and he listens, in spite of all the years I have kept my lady safe and she has never troubled him. She wants my lady gone.

She may marry Mr R. She may take him for all that there is left in him. She will never stop him dead and make him tremble all over, as I did, before he ever touched me. She can do no harm to the little girl. With her bright black eyes and her dancing feet the child will go where she chooses, and by the time she is fifteen she will turn the air around her thick with longing. We will all be what we are again.

But you could put your hand through Miss Eyre and never grasp her. I know what she is. There she sits in the window seat, folded into the shadows, watching us. She has come here hunting. I have seen how she devours red meat when she thinks herself alone. She wants my lady gone. She will have my lady put away like a madwoman. Her hair cut again, her ribbon taken and nothing to comfort her. The doctors will measure her skull with callipers.

The pale one may hunt but she must not touch my lady. I read in my Bible with my good candles burning late. St Paul says that it is better to marry than to burn, but there is marriage and there is marriage. Sometimes it may be better to burn.

I will make my lady a custard, which I can do better than any cook in England. I will sit on my stool beside her and hold the spoon to her lips. Sometimes I chirrup as if she were a bird, to make her open her lips. She holds her red ribbon in her lap and her eyes meet mine and then she does open, she does take the spoon of custard into her mouth and she does swallow.

Dangerous Dog

Kirsty Gunn

In a way, I could start this short story with a dream I had last night in which I was attacked by two rogue Labradors who'd seemed sweet at first but then turned mean. This was at the gates of the park where I normally go running, and the Labradors went for me right there, one biting my hand, holding on and not letting go, the other mauling my clothing. I could start with that, I suppose, because the same park features heavily in the story I want to write and it works as a nice "gateway to narrative" — a phrase Reed has taught me and the kind of thing I come out with now as casually as terms like "core muscles" or "aerobic as opposed to muscular fitness", which have been a natural part of my professional vocabulary as a fitness trainer and personal body-development coach.

So yes, I could start with that dream, with me reaching down to a pair of dogs who were sitting just outside the gates to the park, just reaching down to pat their soft black heads — and wham! Just like that they were on to me, one with my hand in its mouth, the other grabbing on tight to the hem of my jacket. "Hang on a minute, you two," I heard myself say, "this isn't what you're supposed to do. You're Labradors, for goodness' sake." At which point, hearing myself speak, I woke up.

Of course everyone knows about dreams like this, about Jung and Freud, those dream counsellors with their unconscious-world this and their myths-and-meanings that. And sure, we all know about the biting-dog dream: that it's about either sexual repression or confidence. Or fear of sex. Or too much, or not enough. Whatever. So I suppose it could be that the dream itself might be a little short story if I wanted. It's starting the writing classes that got me thinking this way. You, whoever you are, are reading now because you like reading, you're used to it — even something like this, a short story from a writing class — and you're used to thinking of life in a fictional sort of way; you probably write short stories yourself. But for me, finding meanings in the day-to-day, using them to create a written piece of work . . . It's weird and it's exciting. Now I think back on so many things that have happened to me and find shapes in those things, patterns . . . Like how come I went through most of my adult life in and out of relationships when I know I've got my own ways of going about things, always have had, so why should I be surprised they didn't work out? Of course it comes of being a professional athlete, my mother used to say, as well as having my own business and telling people all the time: You've got to do this, you've got to do that.

And here I am, still doing those things — giving the aerobics and weights lessons, signing up new clients for training, etc. etc. — but also taking writing classes, and everything changed for me because of that. And maybe it's what the dream was telling me — reminding me of that connection between life and art. Who knows. All I can tell you is that when I started this particular exercise — the title we were given: "Something that really happened that has far-reaching consequences" — I just thought, first off: Hey, get the biting dogs in, Kitty. Start with that.

The class I go to isn't strictly short story writing. It's "Life Writing" with various approaches to prose. We, to quote the course leaflet, "draw from material that has occurred in the student's life and from that fashion stories and non-fiction articles — 'prose artworks' — that both transform the original and stay true to its shape and turn of events". Amazing, right? That a class could deliver that kind of result with a bunch of men and women in their thirties to sixties, taking two hours of night school per week to "hone their writing skills"? Well, that's Reed Garner for you, that one man. He developed the course and teaches the whole thirty-two weeks' worth of it, and he knows what he's doing because he is an American short story writer who himself writes from life, creates those "prose artworks", and though no one here has heard of him he's quite a big name in the States, with stuff in the *New Yorker* and collections of short fiction and has won big prizes over there too — all this information I have at my fingertips, now, you see, and can write about with such authority and ease. I also know that he has taught at Princeton and Yale and is Visiting Professor of Short

Fiction at St Hilda's College, Oxford, which is where my mother used to go. So, hey. I guess I was bound to feel a connection. Because my mother was a big presence in my life, I must tell you, massive, and my dad, too, and I miss them both more than I can say.

Still, even with all these credentials running from him like water, he's a teacher who doesn't make a big deal of that. From the outset he said, "Guys, we're all in this together. Just because you're starter-writers and I've been doing it longer doesn't make me your professor any more than it makes any of you a student. You'll be teaching me easily as much, if not more, than I'll ever be able to show you." And then he did this thing with his hair — he has super-long hair that's white as white because of being part Native American and he has to keep flipping it back to get it out of his way — flipping it back and then with one hand gathering it up and twisting it into a pretty little rough ponytail or bun, talking all the while. "So teach me," he was saying. "I'll be paying attention to you all."

For my part, I couldn't listen hard enough, pay attention close enough . . . "Reed Garner. Just say his name out loud, Kitty," I used to murmur to myself as I was walking home, those first few classes. Not even thinking about going for a run or working out. Just going over ideas about fiction and prose and Reed Garner, saying his name. One day he cycled past me as I was in this kind of daydream and when I lunged out of my thoughts to shout "Hi!" he nearly fell off his bike, took a sort of tumble to avoid hitting me, but then went on his way.

Already that feels like a long time ago, when we sort of crashed into each other like that on the street ... But I know it's got nothing to do with my "gateway" and "Something that really happened that has far-reaching consequences", so I'd better get on with all that now.

Well, I was running, as I do every morning, through the park, coming back around seven, getting to the front gates, and there up ahead I saw, seven o'clock in the morning, remember, a gang of kids, teenagers I thought at first but more like in their early twenties, and they were laughing at something, a shouting and jeering that sounded like a crowd — though I saw when I got closer that there were only four of them. The thing they were all looking down at was a dog, a pit bull terrier, with a black, flat expression in its eyes. Its ears were back, and its head down, its tail level, and it was pretty unhappy, twitching and twisting on a chain because those kids were tormenting it. One was bent over and jeering at the dog and poking him with a stick to make him mad and he was spinning around and snapping at it. Another was yanking on the chain. "Nah, Rocky!" one of the kids sneered at him, and tickled his balls when the chain was pulled back so tight I could see the little dog was nearly choking. "Yah, pussy!" the kid said, and made to kick him when his friend released his grip.

Now I may be a personal trainer and strong, but actually I'm quite small. And I may be super-fit, I am, but I wouldn't describe myself as brawny. Still I hate to see a dog being taunted — any animal, but dogs especially. Perhaps that's because I'd always had dogs as a kid and my parents, when they were still alive, used to take in strays and mutts, "orphan anything", my mother used to say — I was an orphan myself, you see, and my mother and father took me in — and I'd always thought I'd have a dog one day, when I quit the personal training . . . Anyhow, when I saw those kids, well, young men really, they weren't kids at all, when I saw them taunting that little dog so that he was snapping and growling and starting to look as if any minute he was going to slip his chain and make a lunge and then there'd be trouble . . . Well, I saw red.

Professor Garner — just joking: I mean, Reed — says we must never use clichés in a story. "Do anything to avoid 'em, kids," he says, in his American way. Yet sometimes, like just then, it seems there is no way around them. Because I did . . . see red. We'd been reading *Jane Eyre* in class, as part of a study of "the intersection between Life Writing and Fiction", and looking at how that novel by Charlotte Brontë seems for all the world to be just the story of a particular woman's life, a study of Jane, and not the usual kind of fiction with a plot that has been figured out in advance to make it seem exciting. The red room in that book — it's there towards the beginning when Jane is being punished by her terrible aunt — and the idea that it might surround a person, that colour, might make her see things in a particular way . . . well, that detail stayed with me. All that opening section, actually, because I related to it, maybe, with being an orphan too and my parents only adopting me when I was four so I can

46

remember that other part of my life, not in detail, maybe, the orphanage or "home", as people always called it, but I can remember my mother and father walking towards me that day they came to collect me, and my mother getting down on her knees in front of me and opening her arms and I ran towards her . . . And I can remember, too, exactly how I felt, being held in her arms that first time . . . So yes, the early section of *Jane Eyre*, it stayed with me, how it must have been for Jane to have that terrible aunt and not someone like my mother and what it must have been like, growing up so alone . . . And "seeing red", well, altogether it seems a likely expression for me to use — cliché or not — when that book had been so clearly in my mind.

I saw red with what those kids were doing. So instead of walking on, I went straight up to those boys, young men, whatever, and said, "What on earth are you doing?"

Let me tell you, that was a moment. A moment, right then, of silence. Then one of the men said, "Fuck off, bitch," and the one beside him, "Yeah. Fuck off," and then someone else said, in a low and dangerous voice, "Get her, Rocky. Get her," and the dog turned.

Now again, as I say, I'm not tall and what do I know? And I'm not brawny in any way and I'm not confrontational with strangers, but neither do I believe anyone is inherently mean, human or animal, boy or dog . . . I just don't believe it. It's like bodies. You can be overweight or your tone can be shot to hell or you've got no endurance, no core strength . . . but I can work with you on that. Take my classes and you'll see, straight away, how together we can improve things. I'm saying all this as a kind of metaphor, I guess, as a way of showing that I wasn't about to walk away from that situation, even though the boy who held the dog lengthened the chain and the dog lit out at me and someone said, "Get her, Rocky," again, but then the boy with the chain pulled it back just in time, so that nothing happened, even though the little guy's teeth were bared and his eyes like a shark because he was ready to get me all right, he'd been commanded.

"You're being very cruel to that dog," I said then. "How old are you all, anyway? Twenty? Thirty? You should know better. Here . . ." and at that point I got down on my knees, just like my mother got down on her knees that day at the orphanage, and the little dog looked at me, and his expression changed. His ears went up. He put his head to one side.

"Look at him," I said to the boys, for now I could see that they were just boys, I'd kind of made that up about them being twenty or thirty, just to flatter them, because they wanted to be very, very tough. "Look," I said again, from down there, though one of them was lashing some other chain he had, and another was muttering over and over in a dark low voice, "Fuck, fuck, fuck, fuck, fuck," just like that, and another turned to spit.

"Look," I said again, for the third time. And then I put out my balled fist and the dog stretched his head towards me. Then he stood up, took a step or two, his head still tilted to one side, while all the time I kept my fist in front of him, quite steady. Then he let out a little whimper and sat down again. He had a lovely face. His eyes, which had been black and scary-flat like a killer fish, were now full of thoughts and interest. He gave a little bark, like a puppy. He was really just a puppy. He put out his head towards my hand and smelled my hand all over and then he licked it. And I opened my hand then to let him sniff my palm and then, when he'd done that, too, I gave him a little scratch around his ears and fondled his muzzle.

"There," I said to him, and sort of to the boys as well. "There, you see? Everything's all right."

The boys kind of shuffled, reassembled slightly. The one with the chain just let the chain hang.

"You see," I said, "you think you've got a mean dog here, boys. But" — I wasn't looking at them as I spoke. I was just looking at the dog — "he's not mean at all."

"He should be fucking mean," said one of them, the one who had been swinging a length of chain attached to his jeans, though he wasn't swinging it now. "He should fucking be."

"But he's not, Steve," said the guy holding the actual dog chain. "Look at him. He's a pussy. He's a mummy's dog."

"My old mum wouldn't be seen dead with a dog like that," the third boy said. "She wouldn't be seen dead."

"His name's not even Rocky," I said then. "It's Mr Rochester. Little Roc, for short, because look, he's only a puppy . . ." By now the boys could see that the little dog was wriggling with pleasure, tail wagging, only wanting to play. Not the kind of dog they'd thought he was at all. "He's named after a guy I've been reading about in this book about someone's life," I said. "That guy is a bit like this little dog of yours. He may seem all tough and mean but really . . ." And I gave Little Roc a lovely rub all over his haunches and down his back. "Really," I said, "this little guy wants — like all of us want — like you boys yourself want" — and by now I had the puppy snuggled up right by me, his eyes closed with pleasure — "someone to give him attention and to love him and to love them back."

"Hah!" they all went then, the four kids, and snorted like young ponies.

"You be some crazy bitch," one of them said, the third one again.

"Well, this book I've been reading, that I was telling you about, *Jane Eyre* . . . She seems crazy too, I suppose, but her story is not so different from Mr Rochester here, this little guy, not so different from all of you, too, I reckon. Listen . . ." I said then, and I stood up — and I still can't believe I did all this, spoke that way to total strangers, acted so cool and so assured, because all the time, let me tell you, my heart was beating, it was going like bam, bam, bam as though those boys could hear it because, remember, this was seven something in the morning, inner London but in a park, there was no one else around — and I started speaking then, like it was all prepared. I told them about my life and about Jane Eyre and the writing classes and about my mother and father and how I missed them — and really, this is the heart of the short story, the reason Reed said I should write it in the first place, because I had a central "incident" or "pulse

moment", as he calls it, the unexpected bit coming —
bang — just like in *Jane Eyre*, you might say, a certain
thing happening that's like — whew! — this doesn't
seem like real life, but it is. And I said then, "Listen,
boys. Why don't you let me have this dog? I can see he's
not yours. And you don't know what to do with him."

"That's the truth," one of them said.

"We didn't even want the fucking dog," said another,
right away, but looking at me as he spoke, and then
saying, "It wasn't my idea, you know."

And then someone else said, "Yeah, Keith. She's
right. You didn't know what you were going to do with
him. None of us did."

And so the conversation went on. And Keith, for he
was the one who'd taken on Mr Rochester in the first
place, told me he'd promised to look after the dog for
someone who didn't want him but might be able to sell
him on, but that if Keith took him off his hands, he
could have the money, if there was any. They'd only got
him the night before at the pub and someone there had
said that the guy who had been interested wasn't even
around. They had the choke chain, a bit of food in a
bag, but no bowl, nothing to feed him in . . . All this
came out, bit by bit, as the boys started telling me their
story, why, that same morning, after being up all night,
roaming around with a dog they never really intended
to have, it was a good thing I'd come upon them,
walking out of the park from my morning run . . . And,
as for me, well, seeing some young men with a little
dog, and leaving, after the conversation I had with
them, with a pit bull terrier on a chain — one of the

most dangerous dogs in Britain, all the papers say, with the most attacks on babies and toddlers, getting mauled in dog fights, all of it, you name it — it just shows how interesting life is, in stories and out of them. Because not only did I leave that morning with Mr Rochester on his little chain, but by the time I left I'd told his previous "owners" pretty much the full plot of *Jane Eyre*, and though all four of them thought it sounded "pretty fucking lame", they agreed that the scene in the red room had its merits. "Yeah," Steve said, quietly, as though to himself, after I'd finished telling that bit, "my gran used to put me in a room like that."

Anyhow, I've gone on and on, and Reed gave me, he gave all of us, a word limit and I need to start counting words now. But the reason I wanted to get it down as a story for class is because it was due to the events I've described that my life went into a change position when I came upon Mr Rochester that day. That was the "incident", the "pulse moment", you see — Reed said that straight away when I told him after class about what had happened to me in the park that morning. "This is all a story, Katherine, a great story with a pulse moment that kicks the whole thing into life. I think you should write it all down sometime," and then we arranged to meet the next day and have a dog walk together because it turns out he was a pit bull man himself, he used to have one when he was a boy. "Let's go for it," he said, referring to the dog walk idea and doing that thing with his hair that I like so much, twisting it back with one hand so that he looks diffident and shy.

And change, yes, change. Because now the story is done and I'm still training, of course I'm still doing all that, but I'm writing more, too, and reading, and Mr Rochester is a total peach and we take him to the park, twice every day, Reed and I, and we sometimes run into the guys there — Steve and Keith and Dave and Kevin — and they take a look at Mr Rochester then and I might tell them a bit more about his namesake because they occasionally ask after "Jane" and what else went on in that book and apparently, it's written all over me, Reed says, I "could bring fiction to troubled kids in a new way".

And Reed? You've probably guessed. I married him. We decided that pretty soon after he said "Let's go for it" about the dog walk but also meaning the idea of the two of us together. He said the whole thing lit up for him, as it did for me, the second I told him about my meeting with a so-called "dangerous dog" and the boys who gave him to me and what we talked about that morning, the boys and I, and what happened then, and what happened next. After that, as he said, it was just a case of writing it down.

To Hold

Joanna Briscoe

Reader, I married him because I had to.

You see, we did in those days. There was no glimmer of a choice.

My hand in marriage was requested by the boy with the triangular Adam's apple and a shuffling thirst for a girl. He was the lad who worked for his parents' motor garage on a yard beyond the village, and I hadn't expected his offer after a lifetime of nods, three conversations, one dance and no kiss with him. But he knocked on our door and asked my father, who postponed his answer, crimson-necked. Using half an excuse, he told Dougie Spreckley to wait.

As my parents' only child — no further births; no boy to help with the rough work; no man's wages to soften old age; only one womb available for the grandchildren they already treasured — I was aware that all hope lay with me, though they never said it, and the knowledge made me swallow a rise of nausea. They were good parents.

It was Mr Tay-Mosby with his Mosby Hall who was the bright dream on the other side of Gibbeswick.

The Hall lay along the Oxenhope road, behind park walls, vegetable garden abutting the moors. He had shown the Hall and gardens to me when I was a girl, just as he had taken me once to the fells and Tarey Carr beyond, where the bogs slumped and beige fogs sickened when the winds weren't screaming.

The espaliered walls, the choke of cabbages, ended in a gate that led straight through to where the gorse was webbed with nests and the merlins soared to Gibbeswick Fell. Tay-Mosby hiked daily through the tussocks accompanied by his dog, Ranger Boy, surmounted the head of the waterfall as he chopped at thorns with his stick, walked by the beck to where the quarry was, the Pennine Way, the views further west to witch country.

He contemplated me as I grew. I was only aware of his appraisal as a blush inside me, because he wouldn't look at me with his eyes. He turned away with a statue's indifference if he ever spoke to me, yet he watched me too; my skin knew it.

My mother was flustered by him, and mentioned him repeatedly; my father merely nodded his approval. I was fifteen when I understood their hope that I might one day have a chance with John Tay-Mosby, though he was as old as a father, and the shock of the realisation was so much worse than the terror of the blood when it first came out of me, worse than the killing of baby birds by Dougie and his friends, worse than seeing my father bang his head against the door because the beet crop's roots grew cysts.

You're so pretty, they said, pretty as a picture, bonny as the day, smooth down your frock, stockings at sixteen. I was the picture; my parents were the frame. Mr Tay-Mosby looked at me by not looking at me.

"Will she have me?" Dougie said to my father, to silence. "Please. Sir?"

"Will you — will you — shall we be married?" Dougie stumbled to me, his neck bulge so close it blotted out the clouds behind him.

In my surprise, I couldn't answer. I was nearly nineteen by then; I was taking my teaching certificate, and they were scrimping and dressing me, and it was for Mr Tay-Mosby's benefit as I was nudged towards him. All points led towards the Oxenhope road. By prettifying me, they wound me in shrouds that went over my mouth, but not my eyes.

My mind shot along that road. The garden. The tussocks beyond.

"Yes. I will, then. Thank you," I said to Dougie, and wanted to hurt myself, but beyond the Adam's apple was not the sky, only the stick of Tay-Mosby.

The rumour of my engagement to Dougie Spreckley was put about the village, and my parents waited for Mr Tay-Mosby to emerge from the Hall with his own offer, but John Tay-Mosby wouldn't marry *me*, though I could see him considering it, fighting with himself then resisting, as my parents rose and fell with the currents from the Hall. He would take aristocracy, or something close to it. I knew this. He did.

My wedding night, it was like a wound that was scab-crusted and could only be broken with battering,

Dougie pounding and belabouring, all concentration tight in a face like sinew, his eyes closed, and though I cried out and so nearly begged him to stop, so nearly, I knew that if I didn't let him through that night, he would never get there. I would be unable to face the hunger in his stranger's eyes again, his trembling hips, the jolting spine on top of me. I would cry out, or be sick, or tear in two. So I let him ram through the scar, scab, skin, and he got there and all was warmth and blood and death and soreness, then the searing pain subsided.

We had to live with my parents at first, because there was no money, though I hoped to escape that village with its frost-shattered houses like kennels straggling along the Keighley road, its sinking farms and cottages. The babies came, and when they were old enough, I went to Hessenton to teach in the mornings, and there she was.

Mary Lewthorne. It was as though I recognised her the first time I saw her, her face a heart on a stem in a grey teaching dress, her very being so serene, yet complicated, and complete. She would have been my dear friend if we had been at school together as children, instead of working there as adults, but the friendship was as sudden and as fast as those forged by girls.

The babies were dears, and naughty good children, and they became my companions. We talked when we didn't play, and I snuffled up their scenty skin, and I loved them like little otters. Dougie looked after us well enough, but we barely knew each other better over the years, and I wasn't sure how much there was to discover. I married a man who never read a book, and he married a woman who never watched a game. I sank my face into the washing of my little ones to breathe them in, but I touched his smalls with the ends of my fingers. He tried, and then he didn't try. I pretended, straining to feel the love for him, but I didn't, and it was my private sin, my sorrow. I could hardly look at him or taste him, with his bobbing neck, his few words. He tired me; he bored me. He was not a bad man. I could almost like him.

We moved into our own place outside the village later: a little cottage with a midden, so beaten by the winds, so sleet-cracked, the rains came in and the drains croaked when the storms poured down from Gibbeswick Fell. John Tay-Mosby tightened when he saw me, and pretended he hadn't.

I taught at the school just a few hours a week, and there, there and on the fells, I felt most alive.

"There's a world outside here," Mary Lewthorne said when we sat in Hessenton, and she showed me. She had lost her husband young, had a room in an older widow's house, and worked every day to make her living, using her big, twisting mind. We found each other where we could, along the ginnel that led to the paths that led to the fells, and chattered like the fastest starlings.

My poor husband Dougie Spreckley went to work one day, as he always did, but that morning he was run over by an apprentice backing towards the mechanic's shed in his father's garage, and they mended his legs while his lungs bubbled, but it was infections that later killed him in the hospital, and left my three without a father. I said my sorries to him when we buried him, and wept for what wasn't, and couldn't be.

John Tay-Mosby began courting me with improper haste, seeing no reason to wait. He was between wives, the first having produced the heir and back-up, a Scottish land-owner's daughter rumoured to be her successor. This time, he visited. My parents knew nothing of it. He offered me his company, dining and protection, and I resisted. He gazed at me this time, his eyes like the mud puddles on Tarey Carr. He stood as upright as his stick in his rain-coloured shooting coat, his taste for moorland game shining pink on his lower lip, and I said no, and thank you, and no. No.

Reader, I married him because I liked him.

I did not desire him. Robert Briley, serious and considerate, was a teacher at the school in Hessenton along with Mary Lewthorne, and he visited me to offer his help after Dougie died, and when we were married, we moved into the town. We needed more money than I could ever make, but I didn't want John Tay-Mosby's riches; my children needed a father, and they found a good and an interesting man in Robert Briley, my husband. We were safe again. Wives in Gibbeswick had eyed me askance when I was widowed, though I had the stains of three children on my dress and their tugs

60

on my hair and was shabbier by the week. Robert was my friend and theirs.

Mary and I stole conversations between lessons, between days and nights, every moment with her treasured, even the times when we clashed and tangled and cried, then tried so hard to start afresh. But how could you love a woman as I loved her? She lined my existence because she lived inside me, and at night as Robert slept, there were the colours of her, the fragrance, the smooth shell of skin behind her ear. When we could escape town, no one else on the moors on wet days, she walked with me in all the winds, which had names, and by the stream sources, among the curlews, the peregrine nests. She showed me the sandstone and the thorns and waterfalls: all the pretty places where the toadstools grew in dark secret; the drowning ponds, sphagnum, fairytale growth in tree shadows.

She touched my temple first. After that, her hand was on my face all night, every night until I saw her again, and all my body desired was her fingertips on me once more.

We could talk, Robert and I, read books together, and guard those children as they grew to be tall, healthy things, the joy of their grandparents before they died. We closed the curtains on the dark after the evening's supper and chatted, and when he slept, I dreamed of hiding in a bower, a nest, with my three young, and her.

It was as the children grew older and there was a slackening to the days' bustling routine that he began, from time to time, to look at me differently. He had a deep understanding of me as I did of him, and he saw, more clearly, the screen that lay between us, but he was too much of a gentleman to fight me.

I tensed at night. My body no longer wanted children; it never wanted him inside, and his clean smell made me stiffen when he was near me, though I tried.

"I saw you today," he said finally.

"What?" I said, and all the colour in my body seemed to leach at once. Mary and I had grown more careless over time, taken to meeting in the alleys behind school when the sleet was too vicious and the hail was running flat over the moors.

He raised one eyebrow, and walked out of the room. And then he kept watching me, his sadness a stain on the house.

He and I scarcely spoke of it again, but he divorced me in the end, when the children were off and happy. I protested and tried a little, but in my most hidden thoughts I understood what it was about me that had driven him away. I wanted to die of the shame, though I was older, and the disgrace did not hurt as terribly as it would have done in previous years.

So Mary and I had our dangerous walks at night where no townspeople could catch us, along the old quarry tracks, the pony beatings, the tunnels between the gorse; or the other way, over the scarred fell tops where the wind might tip you into the air, but the race to her was faster.

Reader I married, married, married him.

John Tay-Mosby asked me outright to become his wife soon after my divorce, no preparatory courtship, no hawk gaze on the horizons. I said yes, I would. Yes, I will *marry* you. He was old by then, half-sprightly, half-bowed, with a cluster of cooks, nurses, day-help to serve him, and oh he was the merry gentleman with a twinkle in his eye, the naughty-boy lord of the manor to be flirted with and pampered and wiped down.

We were married in the chapel on his land, no parents left to witness the event they had frocked me for, and later in the evening, I turned to him, and said, smiling at my feet, "Our real marriage must be on the moor. Where we were all those years ago, Tarey Carr where you took me."

He laughed. "I have a bed that the scurrilous eighth Edward is rumoured to have owned," he said in the game-fed tenor that seemed to emerge through his nose. "Although I suspect that is apocryphal. But it's a fine bed with a superlative mattress."

"I want Tarey Carr, the heather flowers and the skies. It's a warm evening."

He laughed. The guests had gone; the staff had retired to leave us to our pleasure. I began to walk that way, through the garden gate past the vegetables, out past Gibbeswick Fell, and he had to follow.

"This is madness."

"It's what I want."

I turned my back on him, and only looked once to see he was following me, stumbling with that stick, the modern version, Ranger Boy and Ranger Son long dead. I brought him round the fell towards the marshes of Tarey Carr, where he had shot golden plover.

"You're beautiful," he said the one time I looked at him, and he followed me.

"Even now?" I murmured, but I didn't turn.

I thought of Mary as I walked. The way she traced her finger over me for lingering minutes, how I kissed her curves; her beauty, her contradictions, her gentleness. My legs softened as I thought of her, even after so many years. Oh, that I could live with her in the bracken: me, her, my children, who were grown, always visiting. I loved her as you shouldn't. We both knew. We knew what was to be and what was not.

I saw two girls once in town, much much younger than me — decades, an age — holding hands. Quite openly on the causey, just like that. I never forgot them. They were young ladies, not the foreign young women you sometimes saw arm in arm, but young women in love, and they made me want to cry.

I lay down on our marriage bed.

"This is insanity, my dear," he said, but I pulled him down on the sheet of sweet asphodel covering the rocking watery ground of Tarey Carr beside me, and stroked him, and he moaned a little and closed his eyes.

He became excited, at once, soft and hard, but not hurting, not that scream that the marsh had swallowed so many many years before, and I curved over him, a cat, in the evening-scented breeze, to perform our marriage rite, our vows, and he was grunting like a

64

small animal, a calf whose vocal cords were not formed as I pressed into him.

"Do it," I said, arching further, and all the delightful little mud fountains sprang up around him, like points of a crown, springs of a bed, and I cat-lay all over him, a puma, moor beast, stretching over his length. "Do it, then," I said, pressing against him, into him.

Do it as you did when all I had was a young body.

"Marriage is one flesh, you said it then."

I ground into him, and the calf vibrations deepened, and all our bed's mud swelled over us, like the breaking of a membrane, the tear before the gush, but it was cool, and I pressed myself into him, his face, his body, covering his fowl-eating lips that were blackening with marsh, my hair falling over him as my hair had fallen on him so long before, when I was a girl, but in long strands and hooks then, curled by my mother, mud-knitted. I stretched and rubbed myself against him, splashed by swamp-scented Tarey Carr, almost covered as I lay over him with my weight. "Happy, my dear?" I said, his own long-ago words slipping on the air as it chilled. Sheep's breath was loud beside us. His voice was a dying bittern in the mud. The sky darkened, his skin the colour of where he lay beneath me.

We two curled together on our marriage bed, my husband growing cold as the wind gathered and the cows nodded unseeingly. Reader, I married him.

It's a Man's Life, Ladies

Jane Gardam

My maternal grandmother, Gertrude, was born in the lonely seaside village on the northeast coast of England where most of her family had been born, worked, idled and died since the days when, so it was said, bad girls stole away at night from low parts of the town around Fisherman's Square to lie with the seals under the darkness of Hunt Cliff after sunset.

Back then there was still talk of babies born with webbed feet and whiskers, though nobody had ever seen one. My grandmother, Gertrude, did once strike us all dumb by saying that her toes tended to stick together and were long as flippers if she did not curl them up. Looks were exchanged. When I knew Granny she was old but she did have some whiskers which she used to remove one by one with silver sugar-tongs. I have inherited the sugar-tongs, though not the toes and whiskers.

Once, I told my best friend at school about the seals. It was when we were paddling around in the pools in the cliff's shadow. The shadows were sometimes dappled rather in the shape of seals at rest and I said, "My granny got a baby down here, but it died," and

Mary said, "Where d'you get that sort of fancy from?" and I said, "They go honk-honk together and fling about and later there's a baby. With flippers. Someone said."

"I don't believe you."

"Ask our maid," I said. "And there's a bit of shawl at home made of seal-cloth. They made them up to cover the faces of the babies if they died. Most of them did. There was one baby died in our family, called Bertie."

"Did he have flippers?"

"They never said."

I used to imagine my solemn and ever-bewildered grandmother (she could be bewildered by a boiled egg) going honk-honk at the sea's edge, the white lacy water running, and then just sitting for long, long hours at home. Just sitting. She and her two busy sisters.

Granny's big topic was her lonely childhood ("I was born to be lonely") while her older but still lively sisters, my great-aunts Fanny and Beatrice, who sometimes trembled out of sheer exhaustion and old age, would say, "Well, you never kept *busy*, Gertie. You *will* spend your time just *sitting* alone. Here — take this wash-cloth."

But Granny Gertie pleaded tired legs.

"How I wish," she would say, "that I had strong legs, or none," and my aunts would exchange a dire glance.

Every Wednesday afternoon I would be sitting at the kitchen table of the three old sisters. It is the one where I am writing now. I can see the marks where they used to screw down the mincer to mince the meat for the cottage pies. They would leave me a sixpence there to pick up on my way home from school. I would go on doing my homework while poor old Granny Gertrude — the youngest, silly sister, the only married one — rambled on and wept.

The black-leaded shining grate in that kitchen raged and blustered towards the spread of woollen washing hung up or draped about on clothes horses to dry. The woollens were either the family's or those of the lodgers upstairs. The lodgers' undergarments (twopence for a bodice, threepence for socks) were never displayed and certainly never washed alongside the undergarments of the family and the maid, because of the proprieties. I used to try to guess which pearl-buttoned vest or Liberty bodice or flannel belt belonged to which lodger. Or to which aunt, or to the sturdy maid Charlotte, or to my gran.

The long-term lodgers in my great-aunts' house included a Miss Gowland who worked in the Middlesbrough post office counting out postage stamps, a Mr Shaw and old Mr Hennessey, who was somehow connected to Lord Nelson and therefore like royalty along this old-world coast where the sea was king. I never saw him.

My great-aunts gave the household a breakfast, midday dinner at weekends, a full high tea daily and a traditional tea with cakes and scones (extra one penny) on Sunday afternoons. All were provided with clean sheets, pillowcases and towels every Monday, a bright coal fire in bedrooms in winter (plus a scuttle of clean coal) and were always welcome in our own family sitting room (which was usually empty because the

69

family were cooking) at any time. There would always be a bowl of fruit — "lodgers' fruit" — for them, books, the parish magazine, writing materials and even a wireless set labelled "Please Ask Advice". It had a dangerous-looking bottle of purple spirit beside it to coax it into life. All this for seven shillings and sixpence a week.

During one of my sixpence visits, Aunt Fanny, the oldest, chinless great-aunt, came downstairs and into the kitchen with streaming eyes. She had been summoned after his afternoon rest to Mr Shaw's bedsit, the fire making a keen blaze, the sun on his polished shoes. Mr Shaw was a little uncertain in the head. He was heir to one of the nation's ironworks six miles away but could not be at his own home because of his funny habits. On this occasion he had summoned his landlady to ask her to reduce his rent from seven shillings a week to six and sixpence.

Down in the kitchen everyone fell silent. I went on with my homework. Aunt Fanny walked into the scullery to tell Charlotte of the fiscal changes upstairs and consequent drop in her own weekly wage from eight shillings a week to seven. My gran, Gertie — "the silly one" — said only, "Oh, I was so lucky to have had a husband to look after this side of things for me for all those years."

"Willy was hardly ever at home," said Fanny. "There never was any money."

"He always was away at the Pyramids or somewhere," said Aunt Bea, "giving great parties ashore to half the Merchant Navy. They say there's a

William Helm silver cup presented annually for golf to this day—"

"It was Piraeus," said Granny.

"Wasn't it Antwerp?" said Fanny.

"Not for golf," said Granny. "Not golf." (She had her own story, but nobody listened.)

"There's other Merchant Navy widows very comfortable in this town. Very comfortable indeed," said Fanny. "There's Mrs Armitage. She's got a daily maid and a cleaner for the rough and a nice house and a weekly hair appointment. And your wonderful Captain's left you penniless. I don't know why he ever married you. Or anybody. Or why ever you chose him."

This was quite true. The Captain, as he was always called, hated life ashore. His one particular hell was to be without a ship on our family summer holiday in a rented cottage on the moors. He would be the only man, for we went there off-season at a third of the price. Photographs of us with panting dogs and the grinning Charlotte and Thermoses and sandwiches showed him sitting like a thundercloud and face of pastry-white, a hand on each knee and in his naval uniform. When the orange envelope came to order him to Middlesbrough dockyard, he would give the telegraph boy a ten-shilling note and we would all be on the doorstep to watch him go, with his little bag (packed by Granny), towards the perils of the deep. He would sing out goodbye and "It's a man's life, ladies" and — no backward glance (Granny with wet cheeks) — pass into a blessed forgetfulness of home.

My mother, Kathleen, the Captain's eldest, left school at twelve though she had won the Latin prize and her brothers at private schools were always bottom of the class. After the Captain's rather early death (not at sea but in Cardiff in a household unknown to us) it seemed kind to Granny to move back to the two sisters' house next door, the house where she had been happy. She found consolation there, kindly and quiet, especially in the afternoons when everyone slept, the lodgers not coming home until their high teas, Mr Shaw sometimes bringing in a bag of sweets for himself, or the *Evening Gazette*. For me there was a lovely certainty about these afternoons. The sixpence was always waiting. After high tea Miss Gowland got out her knitting and Mr Shaw wrote his memoirs. The sixpence was the only money I had of my very own until my marriage. My grandfather was gone by then and was thus spared embarrassment.

After tea on Wednesdays I sometimes read to my great-aunts. Their eyesight was growing poor and there were no plans to find money for spectacles. The smelly maid, Charlotte, had tried to read to them — something easy like John Buchan's *The Three Hostages*, but she had been allowed to go back to grinding the last of Sunday's roast for shepherd's pies after she had called it *The Three Ostriches*. Once or twice Great-Aunts Fanny and Bea tried reading aloud, something more dramatic, like poetry shouted to the skies — Fanny making an alarming Blind Pew in *Treasure Island* — but Granny and the rest of them disliked books about foreign places.

It had been a surprise to my grandmother to hear from another merchantman's wife that a captain was allowed on a long voyage to take his wife and family with him. The Captain looked evasively at the ceiling but, to everyone's surprise, off she went with him on his next trip. Yes, Granny said afterwards, there had been storms and the sailors had given her black looks because taking a woman on board was said to be unlucky and yes, one or two poor sailors had fallen overboard and oh dear, yes, she'd heard her boys beginning to swear like the crew. "There goes another bloody Dreadnought," Bobby had sung endlessly from his bunk. When she had got up to tell him he mustn't, the Captain had said, "Leave him be. All the swearing disappears once you're home." And it had been true and people should know how good the Captain could be with children.

Her sisters sniffed.

Granny was pure and without guile. When her sisters told her not to talk about her home life when at sea she said, "But I don't have anything else to talk about."

When I was about to go away to university in London, where I knew nobody, I was suddenly smitten with love for my grandmother. The Captain was long gone. Fanny and Beatrice were long gone too, and Charlotte, and some others much more precious still. I was leaving the cocoon alone and for the very first time, and it struck me how strange it must have been for a man like Captain Helm to be chained hand and foot by three old landladies and a host of people he had never heard of.

However had he and my granny met? I asked her once.

"Well, we were next-door neighbours. We were very lucky. We were all born, the three of us, in Fisherman's Square and I'd better pass over what went on *there*," said my grandmother. "Then old Lady Newcomen of Newcomen Hall took up religion and saw angels pointing and that, and she had Newcomen Terrace built for deserving working people. She built this great swathe of terrace rising up from the marshes where the old monks of Guisborough, long since, used to breed rabbits, then down to the sea. And she interviewed a big number of people round here and our own family got the chance of this house, and your grandfather's family got the one next door and the two of us met — just us two children looking through iron railings. And I think we just liked each other's faces.

"But, you know, Willy was shipped off as a cabin boy out East straight after we got privately engaged. To China. And it took three years, and there was no postcards nor telephone and he got shipwrecked off Malaysia or China or somewhere and because he was youngest they lifted him off first in the breeches-buoy and dropped him down in this heathen place by the China Sea where they eat dogs and cut heads off and he was right as rain and didn't want to come back."

"And when he did — did he remember? Did he remember you, Gran?"

"Yes, and I never thought anything of it and we stayed engaged. We'd been engaged since we were thirteen."

"But they couldn't marry yet," said Aunt Fanny. "They were still just sixteen. They were only privately engaged between their two selves. It was years more before they went in the horse and trap to be married in Kirkleatham Church. He'd failed, you see, to get his captain's ticket. He tried five times and he failed every time, and they went crying along the beach. Yes — the Captain cried on until Gertie said, 'Willy, *I'll* teach you,' and do you know she had him word-perfect in no time, and next time, he passed. Your granny, it turned out, was no fool."

"Was it wonderful, Granny?"

"Was what wonderful?" She looked wary.

"When he got his captain's ticket."

"No. I just made him get down to working at it. I think I surprised him."

"And being married, was that wonderful? I mean, what Alice Bigley called 'the life upstairs'?"

"Who is Alice Bigley?"

"A girl at school."

"And she shouldn't have known about that, still at school," said Aunt Fanny.

"Some of us had special lessons with the vicar," said I. Gran suddenly flushed red as roses. "I expect you had your own adventures, Gran?"

She gave us all a terrible glare but later she told me privately, "I had quite an adventure with Mr Jackson, you know. He taught me netball. The nuns asked him to. You must never tell Fanny and Bea."

"Of course not."

"Well, he found I was very good at it, sports, I mean. He gave me a free private lesson on a Saturday afternoon. 'Three o'clock now, Legs. Saturday afternoon,' and I never answered but I always went. I used to wait on Yearby Bank behind the field-gate up there. 'Legs', he used to call me. No nice men ever saw a girl's legs then, you know. Until they were married. And not even then, sometimes. Sometimes they just cut a hole in their petticoat."

"Ought you to be telling me this, Gran?"

"Yes. Of course. Nothing much happened. I did cut a hole in my petticoat once but I still don't know why. Nobody noticed, not even Mr Jackson, but he brought a bicycle sometimes and that was wonderful. It was called a penny-farthing. So tall! I had to be lifted up on it. Under my arms and dropped down on the saddle slowly and he gave me a push and away I flew and I used to scream and shout and catch flies in my open mouth and one day I came off in a field and . . ." A vague look and a silence followed.

"I'm terribly sorry, Granny — so very sorry," and I tried to put my arms round her.

She looked amazed.

"You shouldn't have married Grandad."

Now she looked outraged. "But he was quite a catch, dear. He was a gentleman. I never was so sure of anything when we were in those next-door houses in Newcomen Terrace. Sometimes I think girls of that age know best and yet that's when they are thought to be so silly. Your mother was born nine months from the wedding night and I was told I should have been embarrassed but I somehow never was. Just lost in joy."

"But then off he went again and you couldn't go with him?"

"Oh, it was all right. I sat saying my prayers whenever he was on the Russian run. That's when he took to the whisky. And he got torpedoed, you know, in the Irish Sea. Three times, and then the OBE from the old King. But it only came by post, for some reason."

"He lost his ship three times," said Aunt Fanny from the shadows. "It sounds like carelessness to me."

"I think of him still on the sands," Gran said, "when I think how it's still the same sands and the same sea. All those years, and not able to touch each other."

I said, "Didn't you even *mind*, Gran? There must have been someone else you could have married."

"Oh, I was lucky, you know, to get anyone. I was what they called 'an old bride' of twenty-six. Of *course* I married him. Everyone needs to keep something private from their family."

Since First I Saw Your Face

Emma Donoghue

My fellow boarders at Benson's are mostly cure-seekers, come to Wiesbaden in search of lost health. Two consumptives, an anaemic, half a dozen digestive cases. Mr Christopher Benson himself (withered legs, wheeled around by his valet) is the gentle lord of this house of invalids.

"No, I'm perfectly well, as it happens. It's a natural pallor," I tell his sister-in-law (nerves), who's just arrived from Berkshire as September begins to cool.

"How convenient for you, Miss Hall," says Mrs Mary Benson with a tiny smile. "You could claim to be on the verge of fainting at any moment. In the middle of a dinner party, say, or an interminable tour of a gallery."

I shake my head. "The former, perhaps, but in matters of art I'm tireless. For some years now I've been working on a study of the Madonna and Child motif in German painting and sculpture."

This sister-in-law has witty eyebrows, I notice now, as they soar.

By the second day we're Ellen and Minnie, because, as she points out, watering places are known for their delightful suspension of the rules of etiquette. Thirty-one, and not pretty by any measure: dumpy, snub-nosed, straight dark hair. But a lively conversationalist, despite her shattered health. Her clergyman husband is director of a Berkshire public school, and something of a scholar, preparing a monograph on St Cyprian, a third-century Bishop of Carthage.

Minnie reports pressure on the sides and top of her head; trouble with appetite, sleep, memory; the ground seems to rise and fall beneath her. A devouring sort of lowness. A screwed-tightness, so that her shoulders ache as if she's bearing an invisible yoke.

Having lodged so long at the Bensons', I thought I'd no patience left for symptoms (the perennial topic in Wiesbaden). But somehow I keep listening to Minnie Benson.

Dr Malcolm has prescribed her a complete reprieve from the whirl and clamour of modern life. Prayers by her bed at a quarter past eight; bathe; dress; breakfast; read; walk; rest; luncheon; tonics (cod liver oil, iron, quinine); sew; walk; rest; dine; a little music; to bed by ten, with a dose of chloral hydrate for sleep.

But it doesn't sound to me as if it's modern life that's done the damage. Minnie's given the headmaster six children in eleven years, and her health collapsed after the last.

"Small wonder," I tell her. "The womb is our Waterloo."

That makes her laugh. "Is that why you've never gone to war, Ellen?"

Spinsterhood has more than that to recommend it.

80

Over breakfast Minnie opens her children's letters. They're an accomplished, verbose crew, churning out a weekly magazine on their father's sermon paper. "At our house," she explains, "one must ask for the toast in rhyme."

I smile, as if I find these family habits charming.

I can tell she's touched that I've got the six children straight already. The elder boys, away at school: Martin, at eleven, in a fever of excitement about the Peruvian Indians; Arthur, her earnest favourite, who toils over his writing till the sweat breaks out in drops. The four youngers, at home with Minnie's mother and their nurse: Nellie the bossy prankster; Maggie the shy one, whose stories pile catastrophe on catastrophe; little Fred, five, and (just eleven months) Hugh. *Baby's got two teeth now, and Fred's still afraid of the tiger skins in the hall*, says the letter Minnie reads aloud. *We and Papa — (for Papa is not we)*, Maggie adds in parentheses — *went out yesterday*.

"How very . . . analytical, for seven," I comment.

She passes the letter to Mr Benson, as a specimen of his niece's shockingly spidery hand.

"Who is Lady Abracadabra?" he wants to know.

"Occasionally I pretend to go to bed early, then come down as an Arabian princess, swathed in silks and flowers, with a pair of golden wings and a trumpet, and I lavish them with little gifts." A reminiscent smile, as Minnie rubs her knee through the silk. "I tore a sinew last year playing Three Knights A-Riding."

"Does my brother write often?" asks Mr Benson.

She shakes her head. "Edward's hours are so crammed with work. He does send the odd note with loving wishes and prayers for me to overcome my besetting sins."

I say nothing, and sip lukewarm tea.

I've never had such a friendship. Like trumpets in the distance, when I wake up every morning.

More intimate details emerge, as we stroll under the lime trees. A chronically tender abdomen; pangs in the bosom as if Hugh were still a babe in arms instead of long weaned and staggering after their beloved nurse.

We discuss the strange, idle existence that is convalescence. "There's nothing I can do except try my best to get well," complains Minnie, "but Edward won't believe I'm trying hard enough."

Dr Malcolm says she needs a holiday from her life. Only a prolonged separation from her bustling family will allow her nerves to regain some tone.

I think: Me. What she needs is me.

"Even before I fell ill, I was a failure as a wife," Minnie volunteers. "I'm untidy and always late. I draw up schedules, then fall prey to spontaneity and read the children Dickens for hours on end while Fred strokes my hair. My accounts get in such a muddle, I have to borrow from my mother behind Edward's back. He and I bicker, and I can't obey as I should."

"Reprehensible," I say, in such a deep boom that she laughs into her hand.

My mornings are taken up with giving sketching lessons to Benson's pupils, so Minnie sees a lot of the other boarders; there's a Mrs Mackenzie, for instance, a bore, but Minnie claims she has a good heart.

The afternoons are all ours. We read poetry to each other, or take long jaunts by carriage, squeezed together on the tiny seat. Our walks in the woods are leisurely, because Minnie stops for every bird, or interesting moss, or to practise her German on a passing farmer's wife. I never say no to anything she proposes; I never tire.

In the evenings, in the little parlour, I play for the boarders. Minnie has a sweet alto that illness has done nothing to muddy. I teach her an old lyric from the Bard's day.

> Since first I saw your face I resolved
> To honour and renown ye;
> If now I be disdained I wish
> My heart had never known ye.

She and I sit up well past ten, and I promise not to tell Dr Malcolm.

"I like you exceedingly, Ellen," Minnie whispers, her eyebrows mocking the schoolgirlish adverb. "I knew I would, the moment I set eyes on you. Your perfect, pearly features: like some Gothic angel floating over the toast rack."

"Chalky, I've been called," I say, summoning a chuckle. "Peaked, wan, ashen, whey-faced . . ."

On the stairs, each of us carrying her candle. "I have a secret dread," Minnie whispers.

I freeze. Bend till my ear's by her mouth.

"I may be . . . in that condition again."

So the headmaster took advantage of her before he let her limp off to Germany. Couldn't he allow her three years between births, at least? The woman can't bear it, not this time. I press her plump fingers.

In a half-sob, she asks, "Is it wrong to pray that it should not be so?"

As the weather gets crisper, Minnie grows a little stronger every day. Her headaches are less violent and don't last as long. I encourage her to try all the delicious German cheeses. She accuses herself of a *weakness for luxury*, but I'd call it the simplest acceptance of what each day offers. A soft chair, a book, an orange: why live at all if we can't enjoy that much?

"A French lady is visiting," she hisses in my ear before she sits down at the breakfast table.

For a moment I'm confused — three of our number being from Bordeaux — and then I catch her meaning. "*Deo gratias*," I intone.

No seventh child prodigy, then; or not this year, at least.

She reads aloud from today's packet of Bensoniana. Martin's just finished the three volumes of Carlyle's *French Revolution*. The girls have been playing secret games with their dolls that the boys mockingly call — from the single line they've overheard — How Sweet Are the Affections of These Innocent Babes. Nellie writes to her mother in Dog Latin, *Darlingus superbus*, and defends herself against a charge of kicking Fred in the nose during a game of Sieges: *I only put my foot against his face and pushed.*

That makes us all hoot.

In my room, I look at myself in the tarnished glass. *Pearly.*

We visit the synagogue, to satisfy our curiosity; boil eggs in the hot springs; go to the opera and smirk at the bad acting. I glimpse this woman as she could have been if she'd never come under the patriarch's chill influence.

The two of us are taking exercise in the elegant Walking Room at the Kurhaus, peeking into the Casino, poking fun at the greedy faces of the gamblers. But suddenly Minnie's voice goes flat. "Every letter from home gives me such a pang, Ellen, I can hardly bear to slit the envelope."

"Has your husband been losing his temper again?"

She nods. "With Maggie, for asking the butler what he'd do if there were a revolution. Edward forgets to be patient with petty faults, such as untidy eating. He does love the children," she goes on after a pause, as if I'd said otherwise. "Every morning he reads aloud to them from the Greek Testament while he's shaving."

Heaven spare me such love.

"I suppose I feel for them because I married him when I was only a child in understanding, just eighteen. Or should I say, Edward married me?" she wonders. "He was thirty, and my cousin. He'd picked me out seven years earlier."

"When you were . . . eleven?" I am incredulous.

"He was impressed by my recitation of one of the *Lays of Ancient Rome*. He told my mother I was a *fine bud* and he'd make me his wife if I bloomed accordingly. He was so handsome, intellectual, pious, absolute . . ."

On the evidence of the photograph on her dressing table, the man's distinguished-looking, at best, with drooping, reproachful eyes.

"Edward shaped me. I read what he prescribed. He taught me arithmetic, doctrine, architecture, geography, metre, German," says Minnie. "When he took me on his knee and proposed, I only cried and tied a knot in my handkerchief, but he took that as a yes."

I'm appalled.

All this happened long ago, I remind myself. Her voice has the fatalistic cadence of a legend.

November winds: we lock arms as we walk, so our ballooning skirts won't push us off the path.

The bonds draw tighter. We talk about it but indirectly, eyes on the lashing treetops. Minnie calls what's happening a *kindling*, a *fascination*, a *yearning*, a *restless tingling*.

I say less. Perhaps because — I suspect — I feel more. If I were to put words to it, we'd be in deep waters indeed.

We've driven two days to reach this tiny chapel, to stand side by side before the altarpiece. (The tedious Mrs Mackenzie wanted to come along, but I told her the carriage was too small.)

86

The Madonna's dressed all in red, an unusual colour for her, and her hair flows free, more like a Magdalene's. The Infant on her lap, scarlet roses blooming all around them, but one huge white one beside her to symbolise her purity. "See the goldfinches?" I almost touch the paint; the pastor clears his throat behind us.

"Usually she only has eyes for her son," Minnie observes, "but here—"

"Yes," I say, gratified by her quickness, "the two of them are looking in different directions."

"Almost as if the baby wants to wriggle out of her grasp."

"Or she out of his."

Minnie laughs under her breath at my sacrilegiousness.

Our room at the hotel is barely bigger than the bed. We draw together the moment the candle's out, her head pillowed on my breast. A restless night, no sleep. So wild a fusing, I can hardly bear it.

On our return, Minnie finally draws up her chart of Expenses to Date, and is horrified to find it comes to almost ten pounds. By return of post, the headmaster excoriates her.

"The ridiculous little presents for the children — they only cost a few shillings! And my sealskin coat was specially recommended by Dr Malcolm to keep out the cold," she wails. "But I suppose Edward has a right to be cross about our trips. The driver, the room, the tips . . ."

"Does he expect you to pass a winter in the Rhine Valley and see none of its greatest works of art?"

"Not the whole winter," she corrects me. "He wants me home by December."

Next month. Like a horse kicking me in the chest.

The man writes to say he's been offered a most prestigious position: Chancellorship of Lincoln Cathedral. "The cloistered life, instead of noisy boys. It would suit Edward so much better," says Minnie, frowning over his diagram of the house and grounds.

"A step to greater things," says Mr Christopher Benson, spreading his marmalade thin. "Mark my words, my brother will be a bishop one of these days."

"This pays just half his current salary, mind you," Minnie murmurs.

I press my lips together so as not to burst.

Her husband accepts the job, of course. He expects her back by Christmas, for the last festive season in their old home. He must think she has nothing to keep her here. Does he not understand her at all?

Minnie loses all the ground she's gained since September. Sick stomach, difficulty swallowing, generally prostrated. Every morning, she wakes and wishes she were still asleep. "I feel as if I am in mourning for I don't know what. Like a deep well, and I can't climb out."

At my prompting she appeals to Dr Malcolm.

He writes to the husband himself to say that the news of this great move has brought on a relapse, and to counsel patience.

If you insist on my premature return, Minnie writes, at my dictation, *I only fear you'll find me a poor incapable creature, entirely unfit to be your helpmeet in the years ahead.*

A reprieve. Minnie rallies, and starts to eat better. She comes to my room almost every night.

I've done no work on my book for months, and I find I care not a whit whether it ever sees print. I enjoy this Christmastide more than any I can remember since I was a child.

Minnie's extraordinary progeny write to say they're mounting theatricals of the *Hunchback of Notre Dame*, and Fred's founded a museum for his collections of butterflies, eggs, fossils and coins, which his mother may see if she wears a hat like a proper lady visitor.

They're getting along perfectly well without her. They have their grandmother, their nurse, each other.

But Minnie broods. "When school's out, and they're all at home with their father, Martin's stammer gets worse, and if I'm not there to intercede—"

"Like your namesake," I point out. "Mary, shielding sinners from the wrath of God."

Her smile is sorrowful.

When it's dark we wrap up well and go to the market to see the lit-up, spinning *Weihnachtspyramide* with its rows of carved figures. Back at the boarding house, we help make hundreds of star- and bell-shaped biscuits, and a gingerbread house.

Minnie and I sit up drinking too much mulled wine. "I've never been responsible for my own life," she says, staring into the dying fire.

"You were passed from mother to husband like a parcel," I point out.

"He's a great man, and I'm not worthy of him. I married him out of awe, respect, cowardice, even," she says, very low. "Not love."

I gather up her hands and kiss them.

On Three Kings Day, the garlanded tree is taken down, and Minnie bursts into tears over a note from Fred that says *We miss Lady Abracadabra*.

Then she opens the one from her husband, which commands her to come home.

"I feel literally torn in two," she cries. "I've neglected those who are dear to me."

It comes out in a growl. "Am I not dear to you?"

"How can you ask that? I've enjoyed Wiesbaden — enjoyed you — so much. Too much. But I owe it to my children, to my husband . . ."

I open my mouth and it all spills out. "The man's a nit-picker and a prig. It's a case of natural incompatibility: a free spirit yoked to a Puritan. A marriage that ought never to have happened."

Face in her hands. "What's done is done."

"Done by trickery! He got a little girl into his power before she had a chance to contemplate any other future. He's overstrained a highly intelligent woman to the breaking point by domestic care and ceaseless childbearing."

"Ellen—"

"Tyranny, I call it." I fish up a phrase from the Divorce Court reports. "*Mental cruelty*. And now he chooses to cut his income in two, and orders you back to run his household on a fraction of the resources, with a wrecked constitution . . ."

Her face is screwed up like paper. "I've been asking God—"

"I say Love is God." The words come up in my throat like shards of glass.

She and I hold each other, then, so tightly our arms will be bruised tomorrow.

The rains of February, chill and interminable. Minnie almost boasts of her tossings and turnings, dizzy spells and pukes.

I go to Dr Malcolm. "Just until Easter," I suggest. (Beg.) "Until the weather warms and we see a few roses in her cheeks."

"Miss Hall," he says, not unkindly, "why do you think Mrs Benson came to Wiesbaden?"

"To get better."

He corrects me: "To be restored to what she was, only more fit to take up the great work of wifehood and motherhood again."

My mouth twitches. "You said she needed a holiday from her life."

"The very definition of a holiday is that it ends. There comes a moment when only a sharp tug on the reins will work the final cure."

"She's not a donkey!"

"I've known women recover overnight, in the event of a child's illness, a husband's bankruptcy or death, as if the crisis has produced a miracle," he adds.

I shut my eyes for a moment and savour the image: Edward Benson struck down by an apoplexy over his notes on St Cyprian.

We walk arm in arm below trees barely stippled with green. Under all her softness, I'm coming to realise, Minnie's as hard as nails. "I did marry him, Ellen."

"Stop saying that. As if for a moment I could forget."

"There's no going back. I mean . . . no going back on that vow, no turning back time."

"Don't pretend you would if you could!" What mother would wish her own children unmade? And such children, too: the fusion of his cold brilliance and her fire.

Two tears, a pair of perfect plumb lines down Minnie's face. They make a Pietà of her. "I married him and there's no getting away from that."

"You're already away," I roar. "The hardest part is over." I play my last card, like some sweat-soaked gambler lingering too long at the table. "You're here, aren't you? With me. All you have to do is stay."

Minnie steps back, to fix her glossy eyes on mine. "Ellen, I'm going home."

I avert my face. Did I ever have a chance? She grew up already belonging to him. Six hoops of steel grapple them together. *How Sweet Are the Affections of These Innocent Babes.*

92

"But I have an idea," she says softly. "Edward's offered to pay the expenses of a travel companion. What if it were you?"

I flinch. "What good would it do me to deliver you over like some hostage?"

"We could take our time, and see some pictures. A little European tour of our own. And there'd be no need for you to rush off, when we got to England. Couldn't you stay a while?"

So Minnie imagines me tucking myself into the household? I'd have to make myself indispensable and learn Bensonian ways. *Might I trouble mine host / For another slice of toast?*

Salt, wet shame at the back of my eyes, and the worst of it is, I nod. Hope is flaring up already; is the man oblivious enough to let me into his house, to allow me the best part of his wife? "Write and ask him," I say hoarsely.

Our musical evenings always end with "Since First I Saw Your Face". "What? I that loved and you that liked," Minnie sings sweetly:

> Shall we begin to wrangle?
> No, no, no, my heart is fast,
> And cannot disentangle.

The headmaster's — no, beg pardon, the Chancellor's answer comes by the end of February. He believes Mrs Mackenzie would be a more suitable companion.

So he's not that blind, then. I could pluck out the man's drooping eyes.

Minnie claims to be sorry, so terribly sorry. (Not sorry enough to say no to him, though.) I've been an entertainment, I see that now. One of the winter pastimes of Wiesbaden. All part of her cure.

She keeps singing in the evenings, right up until the last one, when her and Mrs Mackenzie's trunks are packed. I only play the piano, which can be performed in any state.

> I asked you leave, you bade me love;
> Is't now a time to chide me?

The Lady Abracadabra sings the couplet vivaciously, that fount of spirit always bubbling up in her.

> No, no, no, I'll love you still
> What fortune e'er betide me.

And me, how am I to be cured? I would so much prefer not to *love her still*; to let this fever fade from memory. *Vita brevis, ars longa*: painted or carved Madonnas endure longer than real women. I'll remind myself of that, next time, if there ever is a next time.

Note

For this story about Mary "Minnie" Sidgwick Benson's time in Wiesbaden (1872–3), I drew on the voluminous Benson correspondence, a retrospective diary Minnie wrote in 1876 and studies of the family by E. F. Benson (Fred), A. C. Benson (Arthur), Brian Masters, David Williams and Martha Vicinus, as well as the sole biography of Minnie, Rodney Bolt's *As Good as God, as Clever as the Devil: The Impossible Life of Mary Benson.*

Almost nothing is known about Ellen (or possibly Elizabeth) Hall apart from her relationship with Minnie. That seems to have ended when Hall visited the Bensons in England after Minnie's return, and Edward asked her to leave.

In 1883 he was made Archbishop of Canterbury. The Bensons had no more children, and Minnie continued to "fall in love" (her phrase) with one woman after another. The last of them, Lucy Tait, moved in with the family in 1890, and shared a bed with Minnie from Edward's death six years later until Minnie's in 1918.

Reader,
I Married Him

Susan Hill

There was nothing they did not say about me, no name I wasn't called. I was abused to my face and behind my back.

But there was truth among the lies. They said I was ambitious, hard and ruthless and would stop at nothing to get what I wanted.

They did not know what that was, of course. How could they? They thought it was simply the King, and the title, because they could never have understood my desperate need to acquire something they had always had and taken for granted, as their birthright. And that was security. Financial. Social. Domestic. Marital. Security was all I ever longed and struggled and schemed for, because since very early and forgotten childhood, I had never had it, and my deepest, my driving fear through it all was that I never would.

Security.

Did I achieve it?

If I did, it was through men, not through my own effort. I realise now that it was always an illusion. Even after that final, dangerous, all-or-nothing throw of the dice, even when I should have felt safe at last and overwhelmingly secure, I knew at heart that I was not. Loser had lost all.

But I am running ahead. I always run ahead now.

Poverty begot the insecurity, of course, and shame came out of it all. As I grew out of childhood, which does not understand any of this, I became aware that my father was dead and now we were poor. Genteel poverty is the worst of all, because of the contrast. My mother had aspirations. She had some small talents. She could not see herself as poor. But she had to do something about it, use the small talents, and so she embroidered things, modest little nothings, cushion covers and tray cloths, and sold them at a Women's Exchange Shop. They made very little money. But if there is nothing truly shameful about doing business with a talent for something as genteel as embroidery, my mother's next attempt to make frayed ends meet was not only a financial disaster, it was a social one. My face burns, even after all these years, when I remember. We had moved into a house converted into apartments and my mother sent around cards, asking the other tenants to dine — and pay for the pleasure. Few came, the cost of the food was more than they paid. We were obliged to go and live with Aunt Bessie. She had been watching and waiting, knowing that everything would go wrong, ready to welcome us.

I loved her. She was better than a mother. She was as dear to me as any woman could be, and she never let me down, even when it was the very thing she should have done.

But even she could not get rid of the shame and insecurity.

So I went to a ball, and why else does a young woman of nineteen go to a ball but to meet a young man?

He was twenty-seven, a naval lieutenant who had his pilot's wings. He had gold epaulettes and a dashing moustache.

For my part, I had style. I always had style, with or without money. I had a way with me. I discovered that soon enough.

He danced with me. He liked me. He even kissed me.

I had style. I had confidence.

I had an evening wedding, wearing white velvet, with a pearl-embroidered bodice.

I had a husband.

I was secure.

Was he in love with me? Was I in love with him? I have not the slightest idea. I knew I excited him, I know that I was excited, and flattered. I knew excitement and flattery led to marriage. And I wanted marriage.

When I made those promises, I meant to keep them, I really did. I meant to try, I really did.

After all, I was secure. Why rock the boat?

But the boat was already holed below the waterline. I found that out the moment he took a bottle of gin from his suitcase on arriving at our honeymoon hotel in Virginia, where liquor was prohibited.

If poverty and shame had toughened me, I was still a little soft-centred.

Marriage to an occasionally violent drinker baked me hard.

I went on trying, all the same. I left. I returned. Tried harder. Left again. In the course of it, I discovered that I had something that could attract the attention of other men and that was my escape route.

I did not go back again.

Oh, don't look at me like that, with scorn and the advantage of hindsight; look at me and judge me from a time when women had so few options. It was much harder for us then. I was a divorced woman. I lacked security again and worse now, I lacked respectability.

So, to hang with it. I looked elsewhere, loved and was loved, seduced and betrayed. I should have been more careful of my reputation. That came to matter, years later and far more than I had bargained for, when I thought I had buried my past, and they exhumed it. Now I still believed in marriage and craved security, but I craved respectability more. So that is what I sought.

Reader, I . . .

No white velvet, candle-lit church, society column report this time. A register office and a blue coat.

I had broken up his dull marriage, but did I love him?

I was very fond of Ernest. He was kind. Good company. He had a respectable history, money though not riches.

Did he love me? I think he did.

At the least we suited each other and we were content. Is that happiness?

We moved to London and up in the world. I entertained with purpose. I had style and that impressed him. I was secure and felt it, in a way I never would again. If only it had remained there.

But then, introduced by mutual friends, we met. It was a private weekend though it still felt rather awkward. Formal. I was to learn before long that that was normal. It never quite goes.

I had a bad cold.

Ernest was beside himself, as excited as a child. He revered, admired, respected — what is the exact word for the way an Englishman views royalty, especially his future monarch? All the people we had come to know were the same but I, as an American, could never fully understand, let alone feel that way. If I had I might have trodden more warily. I had been raised to respect other people's cultures but I could never believe, as I think my husband truly did, that different blood ran in his veins and in that of all royalty. And so, although naturally I was polite — I had been taught my manners — I broke protocol, I spoke before I was spoken to, said what I thought, was forthright. And it did not seem to shock him; on the contrary, he seemed to find it refreshing. The Prince liked straight talking, because he never got it.

I understood little of this at first, and later I scarcely thought about it. On that weekend ours was a casual, social encounter and, as I wrote to Aunt Bessie, it was most unlikely that we would meet him again.

I forget who it was warned me that "Royalty offers friendliness — but never friendship." They were right. I certainly saw the ruthlessness with which he could sever even a close and longstanding relationship that had become boring or that he wanted to replace with something new and more amusing. I was warned.

But you see, what came my way was so much worse.

Everything was my fault, of course, everyone knew it, everyone blamed me. No one blamed him. But I was not the one who fell in love. I did not lose all reason, control, proportion; I did not throw away everything, *everything* else for . . .

For?

The world well lost for love?

He never doubted it.

Lost? No. It was not lost; he gave it away, he rejected and abandoned it. He turned his back.

He abdicated.

And all for love.

He abdicated the ultimate status. He abdicated Title. Country. Friends. Family.

Respect. Reverence. Deference. Safety. Security. Security.

And all for love.

Think about that.

I do, every single day, though it has become easier. For years after it happened there was no room in my head for anything else, it was so shocking. It was, it still is, unimaginable.

Yes, but he did it, and for me. If I had been ruthless then, if I had turned my back on him, if I had clung instead to the security I enjoyed with Ernest. Who was still my husband.
If. If. If.

David was cowardly about getting rid of those he no longer wanted, always making others speak, write, reject, on his behalf. If I had made my husband take every phone call and pass on the message that I would never speak to him again, what would he have thought?
What was I? Weak? Flattered?
Yes.
I did not care about the status and the deference. That is God's truth.
The title I might have had? HRH?
A little. He cared about it more.
Did I care about him? Want him?
Yes.
No.
Did I love him?
Yes.
But never in the way that he loved me, obsessively, to the exclusion of everyone and everything else. He made life difficult. He thought nothing of the trouble he caused, nothing of how I had to pacify Ernest, when he

turned up without notice at our flat and stayed until two in the morning. As it went on the obsession grew. He became possessive. He once said, "I want to inhabit you, have all of you," and that was terrifying.

I loved his company. We were easy together. I adored dancing with him. I was interested in what made him tick.

I was puzzled by him.

"Sometimes I think you haven't grown up where love is concerned." I wrote that to him and it was true. He never grew up. He was always a child. A boy.

I felt sorry for him — indeed, for all of his family. That is no sort of life, you know.

I am old now and David is dead. I miss him dreadfully because he became my whole life. My only life. We spent so many years together in exile, and every, every time I looked at him, I saw a man who thought the world well lost for love.

He clung to me. He followed me everywhere. He would look around a roomful of people and if he did not see me at once, there was panic in his eyes, like a child who loses sight of his mother.

He telephoned me day and night, sometimes half a dozen times. He neglected everything else for me. He filled the flat with flowers, and I love flowers. He spent his fortune on jewels for me, and I love jewels. But what are gifts? Was he trying to buy me with them? I did not love him more because I loved his flowers and his diamonds.

People who are so comprehensively in love often want to dominate and overpower, but David was far too weak a man for that. Yet out of his desperate passion, careless of everyone and everything else, he also parted me from what I knew and loved, everything familiar and dear and sure. He took the ground from under my feet, and I had not been sure of firm ground for so very long. The only thing left to me was Aunt Bessie, my link with childhood and my growing up. With America — those other worlds. David became very fond of Aunt Bessie.

What he did was the very last thing I ever wanted but no one believed me then or does so now. He was the King and greatly loved. He had the world at his feet and the people held him in their hearts and he threw it all away. He gave up the throne for me. Can you imagine how that made me feel? Yet I wonder if he had ever really wanted it. The work bored him; he hated the stuffiness and the pomp that surrounded it. He would not miss any of it.

But it never crossed his mind that when he gave it all up, he would also lose what he had always cared most about, until he met me — his family and his country. England was his home and so much besides. And knowing it, how could they have behaved as they did? They barred him from their hearts and from returning to live at home. They gave him a royal title with one hand, and refused one to me with the other, knowing that that would hurt and demean him most of all.

He loved his mother, dearly, dearly, but she never believed it. He spent his life trying to win her approval, but he never could. What he did for love of me was the hardest blow of all for her. How did I ever find myself coming between such a mother and son? How was I ever so blind and foolish as to involve myself in any of it?

His mother blamed me for everything. I was the scheming adventuress. The gold-digger. They believed I only wanted him because of what else I would get at the same time. They never understood that I wanted neither.

Be careful of what you wish for. But I was not the one who wished for it.

And love?

I came to love him because I was all he had, because he loved me, because we were trapped together, because he was a child, because he had lost everything else, because . . .

Was that the right sort of love? No. Was it enough for me? No.

Ernest left because there was no other way out — Ernest, that good, loyal, loving, unimaginative, put-upon man.

The night I sat and listened to the wireless, hearing David explain that he was abdicating because he could not face being King without having the woman he loved at his side, I wept more bitterly than I had ever wept. It was the worst night of my life. I had nothing left, no husband, no home, no reputation. I had only this man who clung to me so desperately, and the hatred of half the world.

We were sent into exile and led futile lives there.
If I had known . . .
But in my heart, I think I had known too well.
Be careful what you wish for.
Was he happy? Was I? Did we make the best of it?
Yes.
No.
Everything comes at a price, especially love.

I wore couture. Pale blue crêpe and a halo hat.

I am going out to walk in the garden with the dogs. I love their sweet, ugly, snuffling faces. They are all I have to love now and they love me in return.
If I die before them, who will love them so well? If they die before me, I will have nothing.
How little any of it seems to matter now.
Even this . . . that Reader, I married him.

The Mirror

Francine Prose

Reader, I married him.

It turned out the sounds I heard coming from the attic weren't the screams of Mr Rochester's mad wife Bertha. It wasn't the wife who burned to death in the fire that destroyed Thornfield Hall and blinded my future husband when he tried to save her.

After we'd first got engaged, he'd had to admit that he was already married, and we'd broken off our engagement. He'd asked me to run away with him anyway. Naturally, I'd refused.

But later, after we were properly married, he insisted that it hadn't happened that way. It turned out there had been no wife. It turned out that it had been a parrot, screaming in the attic. The parrot had belonged to his wife. She had got it in the islands, where she had also contracted the tropical fever that killed her. She'd died long before I came to work for him as a governess. That was never Bertha, in the attic.

Mr Rochester couldn't bring himself to get rid of the parrot. He had the servants take care of it, because his wife Bertha had loved it, and because it was pretty. But its cries drove the whole household mad, so they shut it up in the attic. He was sad the parrot died in the fire — but no one said the parrot had set the fire, the way they said his wife did.

And the madwoman who sneaked around the house at night, *ripping up the wedding veil* in which I was to be married to Mr Rochester? Attacking one of the guests! That was not his wife either. That was a lunatic from the village who somehow got past the servants and stalked the dark house, wreaking havoc.

At that time I was very principled, very sensitive about being lied to, perhaps because I'd been called a liar at an earlier point in my life.

I said I remembered that when Mr Rochester and I almost got married the first time, several trustworthy people had testified that his wife was still living. Upstairs.

He said, Obviously, they got it wrong. Was I calling him a liar?

Reader, you are probably thinking that nothing like this would ever happen to you. If you were pretty sure that a man's wife had still been alive when you met, and that she'd gone mad, and that he had her shut up in the attic, and that she died in a fire, you would probably stick to your guns. You might not marry him, after that.

If you're wondering why I did, possibly you are forgetting what he said to me in Chapter 27, the speech that goes on for pages and pages, during which he says everything that a poor orphan governess could possibly want to hear, everything that *every* woman wants to hear: pages and pages of passionately confessing to the growth of his obsession with me, the history of his love.

"I used to enjoy a chance meeting with you, Jane, at this time: there was a curious hesitation in your manner: you glanced at me with a slight trouble — a hovering doubt: you did not know what my caprice might be — whether I was going to play the master and be stern, or the friend and be benignant. I was now too fond of you often to stimulate the first whim; and, when I stretched my hand out cordially, such bloom and light and bliss rose to your young, wistful features, I had much ado often to avoid straining you then and there to my heart."

Even if I'd known how things would turn out, how could I resist that?

And of course we eventually had our dear son, who was also named Edward, and whom I cherished and loved very much. And I think my husband did too, especially when the injuries he'd sustained in the fire were corrected, and he was finally able to see our child.

Mr Rochester and I went into couples therapy. I'm not sure that I trusted the therapist, Dr Collins. But since Mr Rochester knew everyone in the area, since he was the lord of the manor, in attitude and in fact, I let him pick the therapist, though I knew I probably shouldn't.

Dr Collins assumed we were there to talk about how we were coping with my husband's blindness, but that wasn't the problem, at all. In fact we had found a doctor who said he could restore much of my husband's sight.

It turned out: I had some crazy ideas about a mad first wife trapped in the attic.

The doctor produced a document saying that Madame Bertha Mason Rochester had died in Jamaica some years before I came to work as a governess for the man who was now my husband.

That seemed like a strange thing for a therapist to do. But it settled things, you could say. We moved on to other subjects.

It seemed to me that in therapy sessions my husband and I talked entirely too much about my history and my problems and not enough about whether or not the first Mrs Rochester was dead or alive before I met my husband. I don't believe we talked enough about who sneaked into the house that night and slashed my wedding veil to ribbons.

Though maybe I was just being stubborn. I'd always been a stubborn girl. Stubbornness and anger had extricated me from many unfortunate places.

At some point, during these early days, my husband took me to a petting zoo not far from where we've rebuilt an updated Thornfield Hall. (Fortunately, my husband had excellent insurance, and there was my long-delayed inheritance from my uncle.)

At the zoo there was a parrot.

My husband stood me a bit roughly in front of the parrot's cage, put his strong masculine hands on my shoulders and said, Isn't that what you heard, Jane?

No, I said. Actually, it wasn't.

Soon after that, my husband told the therapist there was something he wanted to mention. A story I'd told him about my past. I'd been locked by some evil people in a room where my uncle had died, and I'd been terrified by the idea that I'd seen his ghost.

Did the doctor think that a young person who so powerfully imagined something like that was likely to grow up into a woman who imagined that someone had stolen into her room and slashed up her wedding veil? Wasn't it possible that I could have done it myself — sleepwalking, it could have been?

The doctor asked me if I had a history of sleepwalking.

No, I said. But, mostly to make conversation, I did mention that it was very common among the girls at Lowood, the hellish school I'd gone to, where they punished the girls so cruelly and severely.

I should never have mentioned Lowood. That got my husband started.

Did Dr Collins realise that Jane had gone to a school where the girls were so badly abused that several of them died? Couldn't that sort of experience have affected a person forever?

Well, of course it had affected me. It would affect anyone. But Mr Rochester and I had chosen to agree that my marrying him would be the happy ending, the reward and the consolation that would make the past recede forever.

I couldn't understand why my husband would have wanted me and a therapist to think that I was unstable, possibly even mad. I'd seen the film in which Charles Boyer does something similar to Ingrid Bergman, but there was an unsolved murder and some hidden jewels in that film, and there wasn't anything like that, not with us.

Maybe my husband was still annoyed by my stubborn refusal to agree that the screams I had heard were the voice of a parrot. It would have been in my interest for it to have been a parrot, because it had turned out to be in my interest that his first wife had burned up in the fire. I would be lying if I didn't admit I felt a bit guilty about how I'd benefited from her death. So I should have been eager to think she'd died of tropical fever in Jamaica.

Ultimately, I couldn't understand why my husband would want the mother of his son to have the reputation of being mentally ill. Unless this was part of an evil pattern, an elaborate psychosexual drama that my husband was playing out.

Marry someone, drive her mad, burn the house down, marry someone else. Repeat.

An alarming prospect, but what could I do?

Reader, I'd married him. We had a child. I would leave if things got much worse, or if our boy seemed to be in danger.

114

Yet regardless of how stressful our marriage was, I would say that Mr Rochester and I did a pretty decent job of co-parenting Little Edward.

Our son was growing into a happy, healthy child. Sometimes I thought that's why my husband kept me around — as a first-rate governess he no longer needed to pay.

I practised passive resistance. I chanted these words inside my head: It was not a parrot. It was not a parrot.

The eye doctors kept their promises. My husband was seeing quite well, even without his spectacles. I was grateful and happy for him, and at the same time unnerved by those moments when he looked at me, and I thought: He doesn't like what he's seeing.

I took pride in not being a vain girl. But now I was letting my appearance go, as if that was what he expected.

We continued in therapy where we discussed my life as a series of traumas that absolutely *had* to produce a severely damaged adult.

Around the time Little Edward turned two, he began to cry a lot. We took him to the doctor, who pronounced him perfectly healthy. Then we took him to see a well-respected child therapist, Dr Grey, who, unlike Dr Collins, seemed to think that I was not a borderline lunatic but rather a plucky, resilient woman who had sailed quite bravely through a difficult early life. She said Little Edward wasn't disturbed or depressed; there was nothing wrong with him. He was anxious and sad at times, but so was everyone, at times. We should wait and see, she said. She believed it would pass.

That was what I thought, too.

Dr Grey also said in her opinion my husband — could she call him Big Edward? — had a strain of depression in *his* make-up and perhaps in his family history.

I believe that was the last time we consulted Dr Grey.

Little Edward kept crying.

One day, my husband said that he had hired a governess to help with Little Edward. Someone who might cheer him up, make him more independent and less neurotically and morosely attached to me.

That was a big surprise! I thought I was doing a good job with Little Edward. I thought he'd grow out of this crying phase, as the therapist predicted. And I wasn't really aware that he was so neurotically and morosely attached to me.

But my husband had already hired a vaguely pretty but slightly resentful and sullen-looking young woman to help me with childcare and with educating Little Edward.

Having been a governess myself, I would have felt like a traitor to the sacred sorority of governesses and former governesses if I'd told my husband not to hire an out-of-work governess, not to give the young woman a job.

She sat on the uncomfortable couch while Mr Rochester and I sat on uncomfortable chairs. She told my life story as if it had happened to her. Being orphaned, passing into the care of a cruel aunt, a witch out of a fairy tale, then to a school where so many poor orphan girls suffered and died, and then to work as a governess for a man she fell in love with, but he was married to someone else. His wife lived in the attic and screamed like a parrot and stole into the house in the middle of the night and shredded our new governess's wedding veil.

Mr Rochester said, "There was no wife. That screaming you heard was a parrot."

I looked at the new governess and wondered about the future. My future, to be more specific.

I felt as if I were someone else: a visitor from the future, looking into a mirror.

A Migrating Bird

Elif Shafak

Winter, in this forsaken town, carries itself like a sultan, ceremonious and controlled, sending emissaries of howling winds and messengers of thunderstorms weeks before to let everyone know that it will be arriving soon. Not this year, though. This time winter descends in a day, if not in a couple of hours, as if determined to catch us unawares. Early in the morning we wake up to a piercing chill, and by midday entire streets are canopied by a white mantle. In the afternoon, the snow, no longer falling in soft flakes, comes down in thick flurries. Those of us who have been able to get to the university now realise we are trapped on campus until the roads are opened again.

My feet crunching in the snow, my boots as heavy as the sand buckets used for fire protection, I make my way to the canteen frequented by students, staff and assistants. I am surprised to find it filled to capacity. It seems as if everyone thinks this will be the best location to wait in until the weather calms down.

There, at a corner table, I see a stranger occupying my usual seat, invading my space, surrounded by my friends. The first thing I notice about him is his hair —

wavy and brittle, a blond so pale that, in the anaemic light from the window, it appears almost silver. Amidst people who all have skin and hair of different shades of brown, he looks like a drawing in a colouring book that a child has forgotten to fill in.

As I approach the group, the stranger leans over a notebook and says something that I cannot catch over the noise. My friends clap and laugh. By the time I reach them, the laughter subsides, though their faces are still beaming.

"Ayla, come and join us. We have a visitor; he is learning Turkish!" says Yasemin, whom I have known since first grade.

Why an outsider would move to a place everyone is trying to get away from is a mystery to me. Well, maybe not everybody is eager to leave. I certainly am. Ours is not a fabulous university. Not even the dean cares to pretend otherwise. I cannot help but suspect that while I am wasting time here, my real life awaits elsewhere.

The visitor, having turned towards me, says with a notable accent, "*Merhaba, benim adim Gerard. Senin adin ne?*" My friends chuckle. We adore it when foreigners bend over backwards to utter a few words in Turkish. We will do anything to assure them they are speaking beautifully, even when we don't understand a word they say.

Except, I am not smiling. Gerard has extended his hand towards me, waiting.

I don't shake hands with men. My family is religious, very religious. Since the age of eleven, long before I started bleeding, I have worn a headscarf tied tightly under my chin — a detail impossible for anyone not to see, and yet somehow Gerard has missed the message. Still I nod politely in a clumsy attempt not to offend him. Realising his mistake, he pulls his hand back. A shade of pink creeps up his cheeks, which are spattered with freckles, like the cinnamon powder we sprinkle on hot milk on such bleak days as this. I have never seen a man blush before. And that, more than anything, endears him to me: his vulnerability. To make it up to him, I smile and say my name, "Ayla."

"Ay-la," he repeats in an anxious echo.

I sit with the rest of the group, careful to stay on the fringes, looking sidelong at Gerard. Everything about him is pale — his skin, his knuckles, his grey-green eyes speckled with hints of amber. He is simply too light for this part of the world. Strangely, he invokes in me a desire to protect him, though from what or whom, I cannot tell.

When I was a little girl, my mother, determined to cheer me up after I had my tonsils removed, gave me a chick that had just hatched. All day I held the dainty creature between my palms, too terrified to move, listening to its tiniest of hearts drum in its chest. I lived with an intense fear that a cat might swallow it or someone would sit on it. So profound was my terror that in the end the chick had to be taken away. This pale foreigner reminds me of that yellow ball of down. I want to cup my hands around him, without touching, just to make sure he is safe.

The next day, the snow already turned into a muddy slush, Yasemin finds me after the first class. "What do you think is the Dutchman's real aim?" she says, displaying the mistrust she feels towards people she does not share the same surname or roots with.

"He told us. It's an EU-supported programme. He's an exchange student."

"Yeah, I bet." Yasemin clucks her tongue. "The EU doesn't want to let Turkey in, so why would they send their students over?"

"Aren't you exaggerating?"

Oblivious to my objection, she carries on, "Did it ever occur to you he could be a missionary?"

I pause. "You think?"

She nods fiercely.

Once again, with that same childhood trepidation of being unable to protect the fragile, I try to say something in his defence. "He's clearly into languages. He's going to be a linguist."

Yasemin scrunches her nose in disbelief. "Or a spy."

"What would a spy do in this town?" I protest.

"You never know!" she says, and repeats in hearty agreement with herself, "You never know!"

Then we both fall quiet because we see Gerard sitting alone on a bench. When he catches sight of me he raises his arms in the air, as if I have pulled a gun on him. I understand. He is not going to try to shake my hand ever again. Now it is my turn to redden.

Slowly, slowly Gerard and I begin to talk, to get to know each other. I start to look forward to seeing him again each morning. Yasemin, whose eyes are as sharp as a hawk's, and whose temperament is no less fierce, warns me. "What are you doing, Ayla? Have you lost your senses?"

"He's my friend. And you've got a dirty mind!"

"He's a man. A non-Muslim man to boot. People will talk. Your father—"

She doesn't need to complete the sentence. She can just leave it like that, as though it were an unwrapped candy no one wanted to taste.

"There's nothing to worry about," I say firmly. "I know myself."

Yasemin shrugs — a gesture to make it clear that were I to tumble down some day, she won't be the one lifting me up.

Later in the semester, when we have become good friends, Gerard makes me promise I will always correct the mistakes he makes in Turkish. "Don't be too kind. Otherwise, how can I improve myself?"

Under that easily bruised skin and blushing face, he hides a strange confidence — like an underground city within a city.

One lunch break, he and I reminisce enthusiastically about the day we first met, weeks ago, the snow, the cold, the canteen. I explain to him how his hair was the first thing I saw, a roiling of silvery foam over a dark sea of bodies. Laughing, he says his hair is yet another thing he inherited from his mother, alongside his bad teeth, poor eyesight and incurable sentimentality.

"Whereas when I first saw you," Gerald adds, "I mistook you for an angry soul."

"Why would you think that?"

"You were frowning. A lot. Angry people scare me."

His words, so unexpected and so sincere, shake me to the core. Seeing the change in my expression, he pulls his chair closer to offer sympathy, careful not to touch. "But then I got to know you better, and I understood how flawed my first impression was."

We sit in silence for a while. I cannot bring myself to tell him that I know all about angry souls, as my father happens to be one of them. Baba was a difficult, cantankerous man back when he used to frequent clubs of ill repute, tales of which reached our ears, though we feigned ignorance; and he remained just as angry after he repented of his ways and turned to religion. With or without God, he is always incensed.

As if he reads my thoughts, Gerard asks me about my family, my parents in particular. He questions me about faith and God, gingerly, as though treading in murky waters, afraid of saying the wrong thing or making the wrong move, but unable to resist the temptation to proceed just the same. Such is his timid insistence that I find myself revealing things I never thought I would share with another person — least of all a stranger.

Grandma is the most pious person under our roof, yet the way she lives her faith is different from Baba's. I start telling her about Gerard, little by little, so urgent is the need to open up to someone.

"Don't bind your heart, my lamb," Grandma says.

"Because he is a Christian?"

"Because he is a migrating bird," Grandma says. "Here today, gone tomorrow."

Spotting in her words a thread of hope, I cling to it. "But you don't mind that he comes from another religion. I mean ... if he's serious, he could always convert, no?"

A look of dismay crosses her face. "Your father won't like such talk."

"But you are older. You are his mother! He should listen to you."

Grandma's smile doesn't reach her eyes. "Only Allah can soften your father's heart, and He will, we just don't know when. Until that day comes, we must wait and pray and not do anything to make his blood boil."

Even though it is spring, there is a creeping chill in the air. I shudder as if it were I with old bones.

The next morning I try to give Gerard a wide berth, but it doesn't work. Before the afternoon is over we are talking and laughing together again. People look at us. A blond European and a headscarved girl walking side by side — close enough to whisper secrets — is surely not a sight to miss.

At nights in the bedroom I share with my sister Fatma, I rack my brains to find reasons not to like Gerard. He has a funny way of sucking his teeth after he has eaten lunch, which if I put my mind to it, I know I can find annoying. His skin reminds me of a fence badly in need of a fresh coat of paint. Those freckles, I tell myself, must continue all the way down to his arms, his back. The thought of this, however, rather than being off-putting, proves to be arousing. It dawns on me that I have been trying to picture him naked.

If we ever get married what will our children look like? I wonder. Will they have my dark eyes or his fair hair? Maybe we will go and settle down in Holland, though preferably in a Muslim neighbourhood. Gerard, by then, will have become a Muslim, of course. He will have to change his name.

Fatma has found out. She must have gone through my notebooks.

"Father will kill you," she says.

I rip out all the pages with his name written on it. I destroy the mementos he has given me, silly little presents, and the notes and letters and drawings with his diligent handwriting, each dot on a "ü" or an "ö" a plump blot of ink. I find out that it is possible to erase months in the scope of an hour.

Gerard needs to go home for Easter. Last winter he was disappointed not to see any Christmas decorations around. He tells me about Easter customs, chocolate eggs delivered by the Dutch Easter hare, though carefully avoids any talk of his prophet or his holy book. I listen to everything he says, and I also listen to his silences.

Before he leaves he gives me a book: *The Beloved* by Khalil Gibran. "I have the exact copy," he says. "If we read the same book at the same time, we'll still be connected. And then when we meet again, we can talk about the expert."

"Experience," I correct him.

A loving expression flits across his face, though he holds himself ramrod straight. I look around. There is no one down the corridors. I kiss him on each cheek to say goodbye. Freckles of fire burn my lips.

I was not yet seven when Baba, after squandering all our money with a woman of the night and being beaten by the bodyguards of the club she worked at, saw the error of his ways and decided to devote the rest of his days to balancing out all the sins he had heretofore accumulated. First the ashtrays in the house disappeared, then the empty wine bottles we piled under the sink and sold to gypsy boys over the weekends. Mother was thrilled. No more smells of tobacco and alcohol and cheap perfume, no more dried vomit to wash off the clothes, no more disdainful looks from the neighbours.

Soon after, when I returned home from school, instead of the TV set inside the cabinet, I found a glass vase with plastic roses.

"Where's the TV?" I asked, trying not to let my panic show. There was a programme I was keen not to miss. I had promised a friend who had gone to visit her grandparents that I would watch it and bring her up to speed on it afterwards.

Mother stared at me as if she didn't know what I was talking about. "Your father gave it away."

"When will he get it back?"

"We do not need a TV," Mother said, in the quietest of voices.

I cried. I kicked the vase. I raised as much ruckus as I could. When Baba came home in the evening, though, I was a mouse. Fatma and Mother, tired of listening to my objections all day, exchanged glances. They knew I would never dare to rise up against Baba. Nor would they. Whatever spell of insanity or burst of rebellion, we made sure it would not reach Baba's ears.

He never beat us. At no stage in my life did I remember him hitting anyone. But we were terrified of him. He had a way of looking at you, looking through you, his gaze sharp and formidable enough to make you weep, and if he gave you an earful in this state, it was not words that spilled from his lips, but arrows of pain and bolts of rage. Mother was the most frightened of him, and her fear, like a contagious virus, had passed on to us children.

Following Friday prayers, Mother, her hair escaping from its pins, pulls me aside. Her grasp on my arm is so tight it hurts. Fatma must have told her. "You want everyone to spit in our face? Have you no shame?"

I have nothing to hide. I love him and, even though he has yet to express this, I am sure he loves me too. "He wants to marry me!" I blurt out. "He will convert to Islam!" Right now truth is not as important as courage.

Mother opens and closes her mouth, at a loss for words. "You will stop this minute, you hear me? Or else your father will kill you — and kill me too."

That same night I sleep fitfully but roam around inside a placid dream. There is a man beside me; I don't need to look at him to know he is Gerard. We are in a strange place, not a church, not a mosque, but some other sacred space. He is holding my hand. I notice his fingers are covered in warts and flinch. "How can we be together if you don't like me?" he says. Only then do I see what I am wearing: a long, pearly gown. We are getting married.

In the morning, I wake to a lightness of heart and a clarity of mind. I will tell Baba. But first, I will explain everything to Gerard.

There being no computer at home, I use one at the university to write him an email. Having no experience with boys, I don't know what to say. After much hesitation, I tell him I love him, and I believe he loves me too; upon his return he must convert to Islam. While this might sound frightening, he will be happy in this world, and possibly the next.

Every day for the rest of the week I check to see if there is an answer. Finally a message pops up in my email box. Words from a lost language. He says there is a misunderstanding, and if he's played any role in this he is sorry. He has a girlfriend, and marriage is the last thing on his mind, let alone conversion; he says he's happy to be who he is. He won't be coming back, for he has received a fellowship elsewhere. He will never forget his time in Turkey, and will always remember me.

These days I do not go to the canteen. I avoid Yasemin, from whom I cannot bear to hear another "I told you so".

Like a shutter in a rainstorm, banging against a window, I venture forth, retreat back, try afresh, retreat again. Nothing changes in my life and yet nothing is the same.

Behind the Mountain

Evie Wyld

One of her dreams involves being at the crest of a large wave about to break on a steep sea wall. It is the beach at Deal, flat and grey with a long stretch of pebbles leading up to the promenade. The shoreline is a jumble of barbed wire and the rusting skeletons of beach defences. The concrete is sheer, enormous. The wave, though huge, will break only halfway up the wall, and then she will be dropped by it and churned again into a new wave, beaten against the wall until she is broken into pieces. She thinks of her son, and how he'll take the news, his housemaster calling him out of class, the necessity of his bravery. Her husband will be fine — relieved, perhaps. The part of blameless widower will suit him.

She wakes and is still in Canada and the war is over. And there is her husband next to her, flannel pyjamas against the chill that never quite leaves the house, despite the assurances of the bank that everything is top of the range. Her husband always appears to be wearing a suit, even in sleep. On the boat over, he'd sat out on deck in the sun, wearing cufflinks, shoes shining, sweating. She makes herself touch his back so that he turns, and she smiles and says, "Good morning, darling," to break the spell of sleep, and she watches him reach for a response, roll over and touch her hair, one of his four necessary shows of intimacy for the day.

"How did you sleep?" he asks. The both of them, she thinks, are trying and only failing on the inside.

She runs through the day's errands. Collect the rib roast from the butcher for lunch at the weekend, contact an upholsterer — there is an old mouse hole in the sofa that has split and stretched open so it displays the innards, and if one of their Saturday lunchtime guests moves the magazine stand, it will be exposed. The mouse hole is really the bank's problem — the house came fully furnished, and her husband has told her, *Anything you don't like, we can change.* She will not say, *Take me home to my son.* She will not say, *Reverse time and let me make a different decision about everything.* She must decide on a dessert for Saturday. Send out one of the fortnightly care boxes to Sherborne, and try not to think of the twitching canes of the housemasters.

But first: breakfast. He likes his toast hot, straight from the electric toaster, put in the rack just to make the journey from the kitchen to the table and then straight on to his plate. Of course he has not told her this, and he would never complain of cold toast. But she has seen him pinch a slice between his thumb and forefinger and look crestfallen, as though he has seen his pocket watch fall into a river. This look is instantly masked by the act of pouring tea, and then spreading butter and marmalade on the cold toast, and then the toast is left at the side of the plate, untouched. The first time she noticed, a boiled egg was then eaten without accompaniment; the second time, kippers. Now she has learned that he likes the toast to burn him a little as he plucks it from the rack. And so she waits by the electric toaster until she hears him padding down the stairs in his socks, his shoes waiting for him meekly on newsprint at the bottom of the stairs, and only then will she turn it on. Each time she does it, she wonders briefly if she hates him, then sweeps the thought away like crumbs. He is a good man. She will be a good woman.

On the drive to the general store she passes the town rubbish tip. The garbage dump. Back in England a man in a donkey jacket with a sun-darkened face and a smell about him comes and takes the rubbish straight from their dustbin. At Christmas she pins a pound note in an envelope to the dustbin, and he sings through, *A Happy Christmas*, and she waves from the kitchen sink. That way no one is embarrassed by the smell, or the fact that he has seen the things she threw away and knows something of her life. She had found herself cutting an old pair of stockings into rags, just so that if he were to see them, he would not understand that they had clung to her inner thigh, were worn and stained dark brown at the toe by the leather inner of her shoe, and were laddered beyond repair when the Colemans' terrier tried to get its snout up her skirt. A terrible day. The thought of the dustman seeing was too much.

But it is not the same in this strange place so far away. People's rubbish lies exposed and picked through by black bears and jackdaws on the outskirts of town. Seen from the corner of her eye, she sometimes assumes the bears are cows, and then the great dark mounds of them stretch into standing. Her husband thinks of them as nothing more than stray dogs, but she has misgivings.

At the general store she contemplates a packet of tapioca pearls for a pudding only her husband could like. She imagines the head of the bank and his wife's polite disappointment and this pleases her.

The door opens and there is a woman with dark skin and a peculiar, fungal smell. Her head is hidden beneath bandages. She wears thick wool trousers and a coat made of some sort of hide, and she buys a crate of sandwich paste and one of canned ham, and three bottles of cheap whisky. She responds to the grocer's repeated promptings with grunts and does not look up at him. He asks how she's getting by, twice, and gets a shrug each time in response. She leaves and the grocer and the few other customers watch her go, see her swallowed up by the cold light of the sun, dust motes hanging in the open door.

She puts down the tapioca pearls. She tries to put a name to the feeling she has welling inside of her, reaches for it but it is slippery.

"Old Annie never gets any warmer, eh?" the grocer says to his clerk.

His clerk looks up. "What happened to her head?"

The grocer is pleased to impart his information. He has been hoping someone will ask this question. "Dr Conway has it she was scalped by a bear."

"Scalped, you say, eh?"

"Bear came and caught her in the act of drawing water, head down, and swiped — Dr Conway has it she'll be piebald from now on. She's lucky it didn't take the top of her skull off."

The clerk whistles. "My," he says. "That's a brave bear." They both laugh at the woman who has had the top of her head removed.

She is now holding a jar of black cherries. She is gripping them strongly, afraid that she might drop and break them and cause a mess. Her fingers feel untrustworthy. The shelf is stacked neatly and densely, the space from where the jar came only exactly as big as the jar she holds in her hand. The act of putting the cherries back on the shelf is too great an adventure. She will have to buy it. The bottle would break if she sent it to her son — imagine him opening the box, the disappointment of finding everything soaked in cherry juice, ruined and sodden, glass shards in the maple fudge. He would write her one of his letters, thanking her for the gift, and would not mention the breakage.

They will have to have cherries for dessert on Saturday instead of tapioca, though her husband will baulk at the act of putting one's fingers in one's mouth and taking out the stone, will spit them bird-like into a teaspoon. Dessert. One of the few North American words she has adopted eagerly. To say the word *pudding* makes her feel uncomfortable. The feel of it in her mouth. It is rounded like a backside.

The grocer clears his throat. She is now the only customer in the shop and has been holding the cherries too long. She struggles to control the blush that spiders from her chest, arms herself by tidying her hair, patting it twice, checking her posture.

At the till she is surprised to hear herself ask, "Who was that woman?"

"Old Annie?" The grocer looks at her cherries, picks up the jar and notes down something in his ledger. "This on account?"

She nods. "The woman with the . . ." She again pats at her head.

"Old Annie's our bit of local colour, I suppose you could say." The grocer straightens and lets his gut rest smartly on the counter. "Lives up on an outpost in the mountains."

"What does she do up there?"

"What does she do?" The grocer considers this a while, touches his moustache on one side and then the other. "She's a kinda hermit, I suppose one may say." She has noticed this in reaction to her accent, how the townspeople reach for a more refined cadence around her. It is irritating. Slow.

"What happened to her?"

"A bear did that to her, as I have it," he says, unblinking. But that is not what she means, and she finds she does not have the words to pry further.

"Sam the butcher is her son." He says this as though it explains something. She nods, takes the cherries now wrapped in brown paper, and leaves the shop.

Back in her car she thinks. A woman like that has a son. And the son is the butcher. The young man who pares the flesh from the white bones of a lamb rack for her, but stops short at the parchment chop frills — she has had to learn to make those herself, or serve the chops with naked bone, which she fears makes her husband uncomfortable. She pulls up outside the butcher's and sits for a moment gathering herself. How old is Old Annie? It was hard to tell; with the bandage and the gritty-looking skin she could have been anything from mid-twenties to late fifties. Where is her husband, where is Sam's father? Presumably Old Annie is a widow.

The butcher, Sam, peers out at her, and she takes the keys from the ignition and steps out of the car.

"I've come for the rib roast I ordered last week," she says at the counter, smiling. Sam nods — he is not one for smiling either but, unlike his mother, he makes eye contact. He reaches down into the cold box to bring out a package. There is no blood leak, something she appreciates. A trickle of blood spilled down your wrist is more than an inconvenience.

She buys some chuck steak as well for a stew later in the week, though she doesn't really want the smell permeating the house. He has written it all down in his ledger, but she still stands and tries to come up with some question that does not leave her feeling intrusive. She can't think of one. Instead she asks, "Who supplies your poultry?" as if she cared, but just then the door swings open and it is her, Old Annie.

The butcher nods. "Ma," he says, and she sidesteps to let the woman get to the counter.

Old Annie asks, "You got them bones for me, Sammy?"

The butcher nods. "Out back." He looks at her, standing in the corner feeling small next to the two of them. "'Scuse me, ma'am — I'll not be a moment."

His mother gives a small laugh at his propriety. When he has disappeared out the back, Old Annie says, "I won't keep him long."

"That's fine," she says, surprised to be addressed. "I'm done anyway. Do you . . . live around here?"

Old Annie looks at her; she has her hands on her hips, legs planted far apart, and she is sticking her tongue out to the side of her mouth, tasting her cheek.

"Up over that mountain." She gestures with her head, as if the mountain stands just outside the door. "But you seem new, eh?"

She tries to work out if Old Annie is being friendly or not, and is at a loss. "We moved from England two months ago."

Old Annie sniffs deep and hard. "Long way."

She nods. It is a very long way.

The bandage on her head has slipped, and she can see the scar tissue underneath, still livid.

"A bear," says Old Annie.

She looks away. "Sorry, I didn't mean to pry."

"Not prying. You should know there are bears in these parts. What they can do. This is just a swipe — all it means is I'll be wearing a hat from now on." For the first time Old Annie smiles, and she sees that her canine teeth are sharp and white, and Old Annie looks suddenly not much older than herself. She nods goodbye, just as the butcher comes back out with a package of bones, not neatly wrapped, seeping red into the newsprint.

"That'll keep the dogs happy," she hears as she leaves, but is unsure whose voice speaks it — both are gravelled and deep.

She sits in the car and watches Old Annie cross the street and sling the package in the back of a dark green truck. She moves with the confidence of an animal.

She follows. There are no other cars on the road this morning, and though she catches Old Annie's eye in the rearview mirror, she still follows. They reach the dump and she stops, watches Old Annie drive on, a bear swivelling its head towards her as she goes. Their eye contact is broken. Soon the green truck is a beetle kicking up dust in the distance, the top of the mountain she lives behind a faded pink.

On Saturday when the head of the bank and his wife arrive, she is no closer to tracking down an upholsterer. The mouse hole does not seem to bother her any more, and she even moves the magazine rack out of the way because it is easy to trip over. If they notice the hole they don't mention it. Her husband is caught up with impressing his boss, and politely ignoring the wife. The wife chats loudly in her direction about how wonderful their garden will look in the spring. Mrs Adam, the wife of the last bank manager, *did wonders with perennials*. It feels offensive, like a show of power, this prior knowledge of their home.

Sitting at the dining table, smoothing her napkin over her lap, she thinks of the ringing silence on the other side of the mountain. That is what she imagines, utter silence, even the birds hushed. Would she like that? Will she join the Scotch dancing group?

"Pardon?"

The wife is looking at her expectantly, the boss is now too, because she is not answering. Her husband sips his wine.

"They put on quite a performance at Harvest Festival," says the boss.

She nods and, with no frame of reference, says, "I can imagine they do." She smiles.

There is a lull, and she says, "I met a woman at the butcher's who lives alone in the mountains." She has gestured with her head towards the window, and her husband looks out, expecting the mountain to have moved to their back garden. "She'd been attacked by a bear."

"Ah," says the wife, but it's the boss who speaks.

"Old Annie," he says. "A man-hater. She'd give a dog fleas." His wife laughs.

"What happened to her husband?" she asks, and the wife picks up the reins.

"No one knows — she arrived in town with the little boy, Sam, maybe ten years ago. We all assumed Sam's father died in the war, but you don't get more than a couple of grunts out of the woman."

"The bear took off the top of her head."

"Oh my," the wife says weakly. There is the sound of cutlery on china. Her husband shifts in his seat; she catches his eye.

"Not really lunchtime talk," he says and moves the conversation on to a subject more becoming.

The rib roast is eaten, and after the cheese she brings out the cherries, which she serves with a small jug of cream. It looks an afterthought, she realises too late; it looks as if she happened to have cherries in the pantry.

"I love cherries," says the wife, which may or may not be true.

She has stopped being worried about it. What is the worst that could happen? "Do you miss your son terribly?" the wife asks, and she finds that she cannot answer. Instead she excuses herself, as if she's heard the timer on the oven go, as if there is some extravagant pastry cooking in the oven that will make sense of the cold cherries and cream. There is not and she stands at the cooling oven. What will Old Annie be eating today? Sandwich paste. A tin can of whisky. She takes a bottle out of the cupboard and pours herself two fingers into a teacup. She drinks it and it makes her cough, but she is glad of it. She wonders if her son has tasted whisky yet.

As they leave, the wife leans over and touches her elbow. "Tell the bank to address the mouse hole in your sofa. The Adams never got around to it." There is a note of revulsion. "A better gardener than housekeeper, Mrs Adam."

"It really doesn't bother me," she says, and the wife clasps her hands together and smiles in disgust.

She waits for them to leave, stays in the doorway as her husband walks them down to their car. Her son will be waking, his eyes settling perhaps on the photograph of her and his father kept at his bedside. Old Annie, up there with the bears in the quiet, and Sam cleaving out the back. She feels a thread between them pulled taut for a moment and then snap. Mrs Adam's perennials catch the last rays of the weak sun.

The *China* from
Buenos Aires

Patricia Park

Every day in a classroom in Harlem, Teresa would daydream about food: the smoke-filled steakhouses back home, with short ribs drizzled in parsley sauce, charred provolone, and soft white bread etched with grill marks; the pizzerias with their crimped empanadas and thick onion wedges, instead of the thin, floppy slices here with cheese like chewing gum. New Yorkers, it seemed, could not make a decent pizza *para nada*.

During college lectures on biology and history, her mind wandered back to Argentina as her ears failed to grasp the nasal whine of her professors' unintelligible English. With the other international students she sat through ESL classes where they listened to cassette tapes of slow, crisp, vacuum-sealed speech that they were made to imitate with wide, exaggerated movements of the mouth.

During breaks the students would cluster by country. Initially the Koreans looked at Teresa's face and parted their circle; when she opened her mouth and infantile Korean poured out, their circle closed again. A huddle of Hispanic students referred to Teresa as *china* in the

Spanish they thought she could not understand; she told them in her perfect *porteño* accent, "I'd rather be a 'chink' than an *indígena*." A fight might have broken out if the students hadn't been called back to class. From then on they stopped calling her *china* and started calling her *bicha arrogante*.

After each class Teresa took a graffiti-covered subway to the Upper West Side diner where she worked off the books, peddling fare like "bagels and lox", "pastrami on rye" and "coffee regular". Waiting tables served as a better primer for the English language — in all its uses and misuses — than any of her college classes. After work she would return to the room she shared with two girls from Sri Lanka and China, exchanging no more than a laboured "Hello" and "Goodbye".

Argentina had fallen on hard times. Coming to America during the fat Reagan years had been her father's idea, despite Teresa's protests. Her life was plenty rich in Buenos Aires — she never wanted for friends, boyfriends. At the airport in Ezeiza, her father had kissed her forehead and said, "Better to suffer now while you're still young. Not when it's too late like Mamá and Papá." Her mother had far more practical words: "Don't get yourself into any trouble."

For the scores of Koreans who arrived *por barco* at the port of Buenos Aires, Argentina was only supposed to be a pit-stop to Miguk — literally Land of the Beautiful. They set up shop in Once's garment district and never left. But for the majority of *porteños*, the tens of thousands of Korean immigrants and their native-born children were always, *simplemente, los chinos*.

Three months into her American sojourn, Teresa experienced her first northern winter. This is criminal, she thought each morning as she wound a scarf around her neck and bundled into her too-thin coat. As she stepped outside to face the frost and snow, she tried not to torment herself by imagining the hot summer Buenos Aires was currently enjoying.

Teresa could not find Argentine food in New York, and on one such winter morning she sought out the next best thing: the Korean market in the Queens neighbourhood of Flushing. Growing up, she didn't care for her mother's Korean cooking; like every other Argentine kid she favoured *milanesas* and *sándwiches de miga* and *dulce de leche* dripping from everything. Now, picking through the aisles of red pepper flakes and dandelion roots and Napa cabbage, she was so lost in her thoughts that she did not acknowledge the shopkeeper when he addressed her. He had the same hangdog look as her father: cheeks and jowls drooping, as if defeated by gravity. Finally he snapped, "*¿Jánguk maldo motjaña?*" Can't you even speak Korean?

Teresa bowed her head and shuffled to the door without replying. In Buenos Aires when the shopkeepers on Avenida Carabobo — the main drag of commerce near the Korean churches — would comment on her terrible Korean, she used to quip back in Spanish: *Learn some castellano!* But here when she tried to speak, her mouth grew numb. Her only options were bad Korean, bad English, or the perfect Spanish no one would understand.

Tere, you've grown soft, she thought to herself. Blinking back tears, she nearly collided with a woman who had a baby strapped to her chest and a little boy clinging to her legs. To Teresa's astonishment — she knew so few people in New York — she recognised her: it was Yuna Kim, a girl she knew through their church back home but had not seen since.

"Yuna!" she cried, pressing her lips to the woman's cheek. As she pulled away from the embrace Teresa realised her mistake: she'd forgotten to call her by the term of respect for girls older than herself. "*Oni,*" she added hastily, and Yuna relaxed her pursed mouth.

In her rush to greet someone — anyone — she knew from back home, Teresa had also forgotten that Yuna used to have that effect on her, as though she were being admonished. It was the way her face — fleshier now, as if Yuna had eaten something rich and salty the night before — would reflect its displeasure with a subtle pinch of eyebrow and mouth. "Santa Yuna," the kids used to whisper behind her back.

Yuna's family had not fared so well in their Argentine sojourn. According to the rumours that had circulated in the church courtyard, the Kims' business went belly-up and they were forced to rely on what few connections they had in the States. The story buzzing below that was how Yuna had been hastily patched up in a marriage to a man — older, newly naturalised — who provided the family's passage to New York.

"You got skinnier," Yuna remarked. Her own mid-section bulged, straining the waistband of her Jordache jeans. She used to be *flaca* in Buenos Aires. "You must be homesick to death. Come to my house for dinner."

Teresa was a girl who preferred the certainty of her own solitude to the intrusion of others' bad company. She was arrogant that way, her mother used to chastise her. *You think you're better than everyone else.*

But living alone in a foreign country was humbling; you weren't in a position to choose your companions. It made you long for the familiar. Latching on to the thought of a home-cooked meal, Teresa heartily accepted Yuna's invitation.

In the living room of Yuna's home in Queens, a man was standing on the toy-strewn plush carpet, lifting a little boy up in the air. He effortlessly hoisted the squealing child once, twice, thrice, as if he weighed no more than a paper bag. It was only when he set the boy on the ground to scamper down the hall to his mother that Teresa recognised the man as Yuna's brother, Juan.

In Sunday School Juan had been a small, soft-spoken boy who sat hunched in the corner. In the intervening years he'd grown barrel-chested and developed the compact, stocky build of a soccer player. As Teresa entered, Juan froze — it was clear he hadn't expected to see her. He turned red; shyness shrouded him. Dutifully he brushed his lips across her cheek in greeting. When they broke away, the first word that came to Teresa's mind was *carabobo*: idiot-face.

Carabobo was the nickname kids called each other whenever anyone did something stupid, or anything at all. Juan Kim did not have the face of an idiot, but he had an intense way of fixing his eyes on his subject that suggested autism, or maybe genius. Either way, Teresa had found him rather dull and paid him little attention from the first day of Sunday School until Juan moved to the United States when they were still in high school.

"Where do you go to college?" she asked now.

"I don't," he said, shifting his gaze to his hands; they looked rough to the touch. She was saved from the embarrassment of her blunder when Yuna called them to eat.

To Teresa's disappointment, the meal was not Argentine but Korean — and a far cry from her mother's home cooking at that. Yuna's *bulgogi* was dry and tough. Her *kimchi* was a quick pickle — young leaves tossed in peppery vinegar, lacking the robust-to-the-point-of-funky tones Teresa's mother achieved by fermenting the cabbage in an earthenware jar on the *balcón*.

"Aren't you lucky to be studying here," Yuna said, passing Teresa a platter of *mandu*. To be polite, she took a dumpling from the top but was met with gelatinous resistance as it clung to the one beneath it. If she pried the *mandu* free, its thin, gummy skin would tear and spill its innards. She sensed a mess would only annoy Yuna more. Reluctantly she took both and set them on her plate. "Guess your parents are doing well . . ." Here Yuna trailed off, as if bringing up Teresa's parents' success would call attention to her own family's failure. While Teresa's family business had fared better before the Kims left Argentina, times had changed. Every day buttons and bolts of cloth and coils of elastic for waistbands climbed in price. Sending Teresa to the States was an expense the family could hardly afford, and she had nothing to show for her studies.

She lifted her chin. "I guess I *am* lucky."

Juan was irritatingly quiet during the meal, offering no respite from Yuna's invasive questions about Teresa's classes, her tuition, her living situation, her parents' health. In truth the answer to all of them was "Not good". Instead Teresa answered, "Great. Everything's great."

Her eyes fell on the wedding portrait framed on the wall: a doll-sized Yuna all dressed in white, coupled with a pudgy man who had a face that could have been thirty, or fifty. He rested a fat, proprietary hand on her shoulder. She looked like a child bride.

"It's a shame you don't know anybody who could use some extra work," Yuna was saying. "My husband's opening his *second* dry cleaner's and —"

Teresa nodded at the portrait. "Will your husband be joining us tonight?"

"He's working late," Yuna said curtly, scraping her chair against the floor to attend to her crying baby.

The conjoined *mandu* still sat untouched on her plate. Teresa sighed.

"You don't have to eat that," Juan said. She looked up in surprise; he hadn't spoken since the meal began. His eyes met hers, and this time she did not look away.

It felt like the first genuine thing any of them had said all night.

While Yuna put the children to bed, Teresa washed and sliced the *frutillas* she had brought as a gift. Juan lingered in the doorway of the kitchen. "How do you like it here?" he ventured with more confidence.

Teresa hesitated. Her mother, always conscious of social niceties, used to warn her against airing grievances. *We all have problems*, Mamá would say. *Not just you*. But she was here and her mother was there. And there was something in Juan's expression that made her feel she could be honest.

"Every day they're judging me," she said. "The *yanquis*. The Koreans. The other *hispanohablantes*."

"We don't fit in. Not here, not there."

"Every day I feel like—"

"A fool?"

She nodded. "Exactly."

"It's a luxury to care about what they think. You know you — *we* — don't matter to them."

He was making her complicit in his *we*. "You sound so defeatist."

"It gets easier that way," he said. "The sooner you stop caring so much, the sooner you can start to live."

Fragments of memory were coming back to her of the time Juan performed a violin solo at a church wedding. Initially he'd bitten his lip and rounded his shoulders. But as he began playing the opening bars, his face had taken on the same look of fierce

150

concentration she was seeing now. Perhaps he was not so unmemorable as she had thought.

"I can help, if you'd like," he said.

Teresa understood the imposition of foisting your helplessness on to someone else. But she was overwhelmed by the kindness of Juan's offer. Since her arrival in this country, such gestures were few and far between.

In her effortless *castellano* she replied, "I'd like that very much."

To Teresa New York seemed unconquerable, but Juan demonstrated an enviable fluency with the city's main streets and back roads, its *usos y costumbres*. He did not hem and haw as Teresa did each time they emerged from the subway, unsure of which way was east or west. Juan spoke a fluid street English, free of the textbook parameters and fears of rule-breaking that plagued her own.

They lunched at a *parrilla* in a corner of Queens that Teresa had never been to and doubted she could ever find by herself. Over platters of grilled meat, she asked, "Do you miss Buenos Aires?" The barbecue fumes were mixing with Teresa's floral perfume.

Juan breathed deeply. "Every single day of my life."

"But I thought things were supposed to get better with time."

"You find little comforts where you can. Like this." He lifted his fork. "You learn to savour them."

She followed suit: she lifted her fork to her mouth; she swallowed. "It's good," she said. She did not point out the toughness of the meat, its aggressive seasoning. The meal was not the best *parrillada* ever, but since her arrival it was the closest approximation she had tasted to the flavours of home.

They quickly became an island of two. Together they weathered the remainder of the winter, her first New York spring, the hot flush of summer. What they were exactly — it fell into that nebulous region of grey. For Teresa, Juan had taken away her homesickness. When she was with him, her tongue lapped in the familiar waters of *castellano*. This was the first time she truly understood the word her parents used whenever they spoke nostalgically of Korea: *jiangsu-biong*. Aroma-disease. With Juan at her side, she felt the sweet breeze from back home.

Whatever she was to him, Teresa sensed (in truth, more than sensed) that he wanted more. Though appealingly boyish, Juan had none of the flash of her previous boyfriends: Diego, Rafael, Sergio. She knew her friends from Argentina would think she could do better. Most days she tried to shut those voices out. It was much easier to push away the imaginary disapproval of your peers when they were thousands of miles away.

One autumn afternoon, over coffee and *facturas* at a Uruguayan bakery (the *confiterías* of their neighbours across the river were "good enough" at a pinch), she asked Juan if he still played music.

"I quit that years ago."

"Couldn't you play just once? For me?"

"I don't even own a violin any more."

"But you were so good."

"I *know* I was so good," he shot back. Teresa was surprised by the sudden roughness of his tone, his jolt of angry confidence. "But what's the point? It doesn't *mean* anything here."

"OK, Mr Positive. Forget I ever asked."

Juan closed his eyes and shook his head, as if he were trying to shut out the world. "*Please*, Térea."

Térea. Juan had slipped into a *cariñoso* diminutive she hadn't heard in a long time. These days it was only her father who called her that, his voice sounding tinny and weak in their all-too-brief monthly calls from the communal phone in the hallway.

There was something perversely alluring about seeing Juan rise to anger — to any emotion at all. She was starting to see him in a new light. He had the maturity of a man who had endured.

It was through that same tinny hallway phone one winter day that Teresa's mother, always sensible and collected, called with the news about Papá. "Your father is in the hospital." But then something choked up — her mother's voice? the staticky international wires? — and the phone was quickly passed to one of her elder sisters. "Papá had a heart attack."

Teresa slumped against the wall. "Oh my God. Papá — is he OK?"

"He's stabilised now." The sister's tone was clipped. "But I don't know what we're going to do in the meantime. Every day the price of everything goes up.

You need a *suitcase* full of bills just to buy a bag of rice at the store. We're all doing what we can to help, but we're barely scraping by ourselves."

"Why are you telling me this?"

"To tell you there's no money for you to fly home to see him."

Teresa called Juan immediately after, her voice shaking; he came straight to her. She was racked with guilt. The burden of an overseas education had taken its toll on her father. She told Juan she was done with this godforsaken country. The next morning she would plead her case to the bursar's office, beg for her tuition money back, and hop on the next plane to Argentina, never to return. Miguk was a land that had brought her more harm than good, and life is difficult enough as it is, thank you.

As she spoke, Juan walked to the window and pressed his head against the pane. Cold air seeped in through the cracked-open window. "What is it?" Teresa asked, touching his shoulder.

When Juan turned around, the light struck his profile in a way she had never noticed before, highlighting not the boyishness of his cheeks, but their hard, beautiful edges.

To her astonishment, he let out a little laugh. "Do I even mean anything to you?"

"Don't be ridiculous," she said, knowing it was not the answer he was looking for.

Juan's brow deepened — with anger, with frustration, or maybe some combination of both. In that moment he looked almost like Yuna. "So you're just going to go, like that," he said. "And you're not coming back."

"My father's *sick*," she said. "Sorry for not making this about *you*." But she knew it was more than just that.

As Juan stared at her with that *carabobo* face, she thought back to the first day they had met in New York. She was alone in Miguk and he had taken away her loneliness. But still it did not change what she felt deep down: she did not love him.

It was Juan who broke their gaze. Snapping the strap of his bag, he hoisted it over his shoulder and was out of the door before she could speak.

That night as Teresa was drifting off to sleep, she heard a rustling outside, and an envelope was slipped under the door. The note inside read:

> I feel like a fool about before. I'm sorry. I love you. But I think you already know that.
>
> Go be with your father and your family. I'm selfishly hoping you'll return. But if you do . . . we can't go back to how things used to be. I just couldn't bear it.
>
> I'd rather lose you completely than stay to become nothing to you.

The paper was wrapped around a round-trip ticket to Buenos Aires, departing in the morning, with an open return. She had already taken advantage of too much of his kindness; she knew she shouldn't accept this generous, loaded offering if she could not offer her heart along with it.

But when she opened the door, Juan was already gone.

Teresa's guilt at taking Juan's ticket dwindled on the flight back to Argentina, and all but vanished by the time she touched down at Ezeiza. The Buenos Aires air was hot and languid, nothing like New York's icy chill and frantic energy. Everything was so easy here, so relaxed. There was no linguistic struggle at the *quiosco* for a pack of cigarettes, no more patronising looks because of her awkward English. Already America seemed so far away — she could not imagine ever going back.

Teresa and her mother took turns tending to both the store and her father. Her sisters popped by on occasion, but they had their own families to look after. Papá was weakened from his attack but he still managed to squeeze her hand when she sat at his bedside. On the days he mustered the energy to speak, he would tell her, "You should go back to your studies," his voice cracking into a hoarse whisper. Again and again it broke Teresa's heart.

After another sleepless night, Teresa lay on the sofa as daylight dawned. The morning news was on: the *austral* dropping another 10 per cent, just as it had devalued by more than two hundred since she had left for America. She got up to change the dial, flipping past channels until she landed on a cartoon from her childhood.

156

Settling her head back on a cushion, she sighed happily: she had forgotten the simple pleasure of watching TV in a language she could understand.

Her mother appeared in the doorway. "I just got off the phone with your sisters," she said. "We've decided to sell the business."

"Mamá, you can't! That store is Papá's life."

"The *austral*'s getting weaker. We lose more money than we make." Her mother gave her a hard look. "That business is killing your father."

The high-pitched whine of cartoon voices was beginning to grate, adding an inappropriate comical levity to the moment. Teresa got up and switched the television set off. "But what are you and Papá going to do?"

"Don't you worry about that."

But Teresa knew her mother well enough to know that behind her gruff words she was putting on a brave front. There wouldn't be much — if anything — left over from the sale of the business. Nor could her sisters be relied on to help.

Mamá took a seat on the sofa. In a sudden gesture of tenderness, she patted her lap. Teresa, hesitant at first, curled up against her mother. "I'm so sorry, Teresa." Mamá's tone grew soft. "But there's no money for you to go back to school."

Teresa already knew that. There was no question that she would have to give up her studies. Just as she could read the lines beyond that, to what her mother had not yet said: their roles would be reversed, and she would have to support *them*.

"I didn't like school anyway," Teresa said. "I prefer work."

Any menial job she found here would pay a fraction of her waitress job back home — back *there*, she corrected herself. Teresa did some quick calculations, comparing her future in Buenos Aires to the one she had left in New York. Presuming her diner job was even still hers after her abrupt departure, she could pick up extra shifts that would just cover her own living expenses. But there would be nothing left over to send to her ailing father. Short of being patched up in a marriage to a greying old groom as Yuna had, she had few options.

"Mamá," she asked suddenly. "Did you love Papi from the start?"

She was certain her mother would shoo away the question, but to her surprise Mamá looked thoughtful as she smoothed down the cover of the sofa's armrest. "You learn to," she finally said, "with time. And that produces its own kind of love."

Teresa thought of her mother's uncharacteristic display of emotion about her father on the phone. She thought of Juan's letter, the earnest words he had poured forth, and of her own selfish reaction to his romantic overture. He deserved better than the way she had treated him. He was a good man, one of the selfless ones.

Her mother stroked her hair. "You need a trim, Térea," she murmured.

"Don't worry about me, Mami," Teresa said. "I'll figure it out."

158

She knew that in a few minutes, she would have to rise from the sofa and shower off the previous night, ready to face the new day. But for now she lay in her mother's lap, letting Mami run her gentle fingers through her hair.

That afternoon, Teresa met up with Alejandra and the gang on one of their usual outings. They passed the *mate* gourd back and forth on a blanket in Las Heras park, the sky a lazy blue, the summer air hot and drowsy. She did not want to imagine ever having to leave this.

From there it was on to dinner at the *parrilla*. Teresa's teeth sank into the soft, buttery meat and she almost cried out. Here she was not met with resistance: the *bife* was nothing like the hardened steaks of New York. They passed the Malbec back and forth, each bottle running dry almost as quickly as it was poured.

With her friends she went on to the *boliche*, where she met a tall man with wild bleached hair, wearing a white blazer with the sleeves rolled up. They locked arms and legs and then lips on the dance floor, his soft hands smooth against her skin, his tongue thick against hers.

"Coming up for air?" Alejandra asked as Teresa left the dance floor.

"And this." Teresa held up a tumbler and drained the last of her rum and Coke. "He's hot, no?"

Alejandra looked over at the blazered man, standing expectantly a few feet away. "What about your *chinito*?"

"He's there" — Teresa blew out her cigarette smoke — "and I'm here."

Alejandra nodded in the direction of the man. "Then better not keep Simon Le Bon waiting."

"I won't," she said. "I'll miss you, Ale."

"What, *tonta*?" She tousled Teresa's hair. "You're the one leaving to get ass. I'm staying put."

Teresa kissed Alejandra's cheek and let the man help her into her denim jacket. "You take care of yourself, you hear, *negra*?"

"*Igualmente, china.*"

The sky was a bright blue the next morning when Teresa rolled her suitcase to the entrance of Ezeiza. Her mother had touched her cheek before seeing her off. "Papi always said you were his bravest."

For the fifth time that day, Teresa reached for the back pocket of her jeans, to check that Juan's note was still there. She remembered Juan's first words: *The sooner you stop caring so much, the sooner you can start to live.* Over the din of honking taxis, the shriek of planes jetting for points north, and the thick exhaust of buses, she inhaled deeply.

Savour this, Térea, she told herself. *It will be the last time you breathe in the good Buenos Aires air.*

Reader,
She Married Me

Salley Vickers

It was simply joy at first. So often it is joy "at first", would you not say? It is the "at last" we should judge our human dealings by. Yet who but the Great Judge is able to do that? I do not speak here of God, for about Him I remain a cautious sceptic. No, it is that other exigent imponderable, Death, towards whose kingdom I, Edward Rochester, draw daily closer, whose judgment I am most disposed to trust now.

During those long months, when I searched vainly for Jane, I rehearsed all the blessed times we had spent together. Our first meeting that chilly winter afternoon, when, unaware of my identity, she aided me with the injury sustained from my fall and I teased her that she had bewitched my horse. The time she came in search of me, braving the wind and rain, and on finding me flew like a bird to my glad arms. The many times I found her sitting with that indefatigable knitter, good old Mrs Fairfax (who was always so doubtful over our intended union), a book in her hands and that little burr, Adele, my foster child, idly content at her knee; most speakingly, the recollection of her at the wicket gate, standing beside me in the plain square of blond she had fashioned herself for a bridal veil, when, caught by some impalpable intimation of the coming doom, I delayed our entry into the church. A myriad such images lived on in my memory. And, threaded through them all, the luminous aura of elfishness which had so enchanted me. From our first encounter she provoked in me thoughts of other worlds.

And there were few nights that passed unmolested by stricken consideration of what I might have done differently to avoid that terrible moment of revelation in the church. The shocking breach in the sacrament, the unlooked-for response to the solemn words, "I require and charge you both (as ye will answer at the dreadful day of judgment, when the secrets of all hearts shall be disclosed) that if either of you know any impediment why ye may not lawfully be joined together in matrimony, ye do now confess it . . ." I would give half my life to undo that moment now.

And then the recollections of that night of the final immolation, Thornfield Hall wrecked in a fire which had its own grim fitness. The fire of a passion so long unmet by me that it had finally to erupt into the world, destroying my foolish hopes. I knew there was a fatal logic to the collapse of all I had planned.

I have told Jane I had thought I had lost her for good along with everything else. What I could not tell her, then or now, was that together with the knowledge came a sharp sense of relief. The ruining of those ill-starred prospects was a kind of comfort. It had always been perilously thin ice I was treading.

If you were to ask her, she would say that after the calamity I preferred a life of utter loneliness, that I had hated to be helped in my blindness, that I did not like to put my one sound hand into that of any hireling's and it was only her arrival that induced me to be led back to a semblance of common humanity. I own that it was heaven to hold her slender body in my arms again, to feel the softness of her pale hair and crush in my own surviving paw her child's hand. I never in my life saw such small hands. And when she came to me then, she was tender, oh so tender. And I, no better than the old lightning-struck chestnut tree in Thornfield's orchard, how could that blasted ruin fail to relish the fresh touch of the encircling woodbine?

But I did not ask or expect her to take me as a husband. As I admitted freely, I had betrayed her trust. Why should she give it again to a near-blind cripple whose honour had been impeached by his own folly? And, you see, there was this. I no longer wanted that kind of intimacy with her. The fatality that finally ended my first marriage had changed more than my physical appearance or my outward circumstances.

Let me try to put down as best I can what occurred that night when Thornfield burned.

When, having found my wife's quarters empty, I fought my way up on to the roof, and saw her tall silhouette against the green- and amber-streaked sky, all knowledge that the flames she had started posed a mortal danger evaporated. Suddenly, all that was present to me was the two of us, facing the people we had become on the very threshold of eternity.

She stood there, in her white gown, upright and still on the edge of the battlements. Timbered walls and ceilings were crashing below us, but I swear I recall no sound other than the cracked note of my own voice.

"Bertha," I called. "Bertha, my dear." And I believe, certainly I pray, that she will have heard none of the old harshness and revulsion in my tone, for I felt nothing at that moment but supreme remorse.

She looked so lost, so bewildered, so childlike in her white gown. And the eyes she turned upon me that I had once admired were not those of a raving woman but the anguished eyes of a cornered animal, the whites gleaming her fear in the red glow of the rising flames. "Bertha," I said again, trying for gentleness.

She took a step towards me, her feet pitifully bare, and I saw that she was holding something out, as if it were an offering or a gift. I likewise took a tentative step, mindful that should she take fright and step backward she might fall. But she stood stock still, seeming to wait for me.

I should have known what it was she wanted to show me. A coral, the kind that is given to young babies to jingle and cut their teeth on. A coral that had once been given to our child, born in our first years of marriage.

No one, not even Mrs Poole, not even that fool of her brother, Mason, ever knew of our child. She conceived when we had moved away from her family. We had settled first near their family home, in Jamaica, and I came to find them so unbearable I could see we

164

would have no domestic harmony while they were an influence and nearby. Therefore, I took a house on the far side of the island, on one of the plantations that came with her dowry, and for the two years we lived there, with none of her family to interfere with us, we were all in all to each other.

I was ecstatic when she told me we were to have a child. And I do believe that I attended to her as well as any woman could have wished. I was eager to ensure she had all she desired in good food, in soft clothing, in a comfortable environment and in careful nursing when the birth was at hand.

The birth was not an easy one. Little Clara arrived after many hours of painful labour and my wife was quite drained by the process. Perhaps because of the birth, the child cried unwontedly and was sickly. She was a pale pretty-featured scrap but stubborn-natured with it and she wouldn't feed. We hired wet nurse after wet nurse. Bertha, formerly so comely, so readily at ease with life, became shrill and distraught.

I have heard since that childbirth can send a woman mad but at the time I was on my own in a foreign country with no one to consult. The child was fretful and wasting. And alongside the child Bertha wasted too.

Hers is a superstitious race. She began to declare that the child was not her own, but a witch child, planted in the nursery. Her own sweet healthy baby had been stolen, she averred. And it was true: there was something elfin about the child's form and face. Even a sane soul might have taken her for a sprite or a fairy child.

Soon Bertha became so convinced of her own fantasy that she refused to see the child at all. I thought it best to establish the baby away from home, with the only nurse we had found from whom she would willingly feed. But for all this, Bertha did not recover. If anything, she became more frantic. She began to pace the room at night like a caged panther. Her weeping became histrionic. Often I found her wandering alone, wailing to the moon and stars, her nightwear drenched with sweat or dew, I couldn't tell. Increasingly, for all my greater size, I had a struggle to bring her home. Finally, in desperation, I arranged for us to sail for England, praying that the purer air and more temperate climate would act as a salve to my poor wife's wits. And not having any clear notion what else to do with her, I left our babe behind, with the fervent hope that one day she might join us.

For a while my wife continued in her wild and unpredictable moods. But gradually, with kindly care and the changed circumstance, the fantasy of the changeling child seemed to recede. One day, quite humbly, she asked for Clara by name and I had to explain that we had left her in Jamaica, assuring her nevertheless that she was "in the best hands". She begged tearfully for me to send at once for our child, but before I could arrange for the nurse to bring her to us a message came to say that little Clara had died of swamp fever.

From that day my wife's madness returned. At first, overwhelmed with grief, she let me approach her and I had some hopes that our shared sorrow might act to revive our former love. But soon a persistent fury set in, most often directed against me for parting her from her babe, but also against herself for failing her as a mother. I consulted private physicians from London. Discreet men who could be trusted to hold their tongues came to offer their diagnoses. But none of their medicines seemed to heal her.

At first I regularly visited my poor deranged wife in the quarters I had appointed for her care. But as time went on, she became a perpetual reproach, a memory of my error, not in marrying her (though in my shame I came to think it was an error) but in disposing of the child. She seemed a living testament that too savagely proclaimed my guilt, and I confess that in my weakness I turned away in horror of it.

The message recounting Clara's death was accompanied by the coral that Bertha held in her hands the night of the fire. An offering, I think I said it seemed. But to what or whom? No god or fate had taken her child. It was I, Edward Rochester, alone who had done this thing.

As I stood on the roof of the burning house, where I had kept my wife all but prisoner, from my inner mental flagration a saving spark of insight was born. "Bertha," I said. "Forgive me." At that moment I wanted nothing more than to be as we once were with our little child. She didn't speak a word but stared into my eyes and in the light of the flames licking upwards I saw great tears run down the folds of her once handsome cheeks. To my dying day I will never forget that countenance which I had helped to ruin. Then she gestured, as if to thrust the coral at me. As I moved to receive it she turned, the pathetic child's remembrance still clasped in her hands, ran swiftly to the edge of the parapet and threw herself down.

When Jane found me in Ferndean, in retreat from my old life, she told me that she had come because, at a moment of crisis when another man was pressing her to let him make her his own, she had heard my voice calling her name. How could I tell her how devoutly I wished she had gone to India with her stern cousin St John Rivers? The idea of marriage to her now revolted me. I pleaded my infirmities. She insisted they only made me dearer to her. I hinted at a lost virility, hoping that a natural delicacy would prevent her enquiring further; she smiled as if she understood my embarrassment and forgave me. Oh, the scourge of that forgiveness when it was not hers but another's that I needed to soothe my fighting soul!

No argument would deter Jane from her conviction we should marry and complete the folly I had begun. Worn down by her persistence, I consented. What else could I do? It was true that I had loved her but for reasons I had not then understood. I had seen in her a refuge from my own inexperience and error. I had so roundly failed one woman that it wasn't in me to seem to fail another now. She had held out against the idea of becoming my mistress. Now she held out against any idea that she should not become my wife. It was she

Plymouth Libraries
01752 305900

Self Service Receipt for Borrowed Items

Name: Mr Walter James Foster

Title: Reader, I married him: stories inspired by Jane

Item: F20203148X1234

Due Back: 08/12/22

Title: Death in Paris

Item: F20208681X1234

Due Back: 08/12/22

Title: Emmerdale girls

Item: F20211275X1234

Due Back: 08/12/22

Title: One hundred names

Item: F20806574X1234

Due Back: 08/12/22

Title: Switch bitch

Item: F20205073X1234

Due Back: 08/12/22

Total Borrowed: 5
17/11/2022 11:30:17

Thank you for using self-service

who urged the renewal of the vows that had been so dramatically interrupted. She who led me to the nearby church, where she had organised with the parson that the banns be done away with, having been read already before. Ah, that seeming slightness concealed an indomitable will.

I have come to question many things as the years pass. For one thing, I question the truth of that moment when she claimed to hear me call, for if she had heard any name across the ether it was not hers I cried yearning into the darkness but that of my lost child. From the spark of insight that emerged, phoenix-like, in my last fatal encounter with Bertha, there grew the blinding certainty that loss of that little child had bred my infatuation with Jane. With her girlish body and elfin looks she had come to seem to embody the daughter I might have had.

And I see too, as my physical vision slowly recovers, that I was not alone in the misconception of my desire. For Jane would always have preferred me as I am now, maimed, under her control. In my full health and strength I was too much a match for her. Enfeebled and disillusioned and guilt-ridden as I am, she will always hold the upper hand.

With the hazily restored sight of my one eye I observe her nightly at her desk, where she sits writing furiously. She tells me she is writing an account of her life, and I have every confidence that she will turn our story as her will would have it — herself my saviour, her fierce morality triumphant, a truly righteous heroic love conquering all. Which is why I have seen fit to write

169

down my own version of events in the hope that some future reader might ponder an alternative.

I have as little expectation of this ever being published as I am certain my young wife's account will be. Already she has written to publishers, under the name John Elton. As I have come to see from her history, the force of her conviction is of a metal that no man can easily withstand. For this account I hide behind no pseudonym. Nor do I imagine I have any prospect of being published. It is for poor Bertha's sake, and in memory of little Clara, that I write this down, in order that there be somewhere some truthful record of what they came to mean to me. When I die, I shall entrust the account to my foster child, Adele, along with Clara's coral, which I found so charred in the ashy remains of Thornfield that no one but myself will see what it had once been.

Dorset Gap

Tracy Chevalier

They would make a very odd match, like daisies and gladioli, lace and leather. Ed knew that; he wasn't stupid. Well, he was stupid in many ways, but not in that way.

He wasn't sure why he was with her today. The night before they had been to a rave in a field in Dorset, and the next morning both had ended up in a group of people who, despite hangovers and skin grainy with dried sweat from all-night dancing, had been intent on a walk to clear their heads. That plan lasted until they stopped at a pub in a tiny village and lost momentum in front of their pints. Jenn had gazed at them all, ranged around the table in various stages of stupor, then picked up the map and left. Ed watched her from the pub window, walking away along the empty country road, her wellington boots making her look like a farmer's wife. Beguiled by the bit of calf between the bottom of her dress and the top of her wellies that flashed with each stride, he pulled on his jumper and went after her.

He didn't know her well. She was the housemate of a friend, studying Eng. Lit. to his Geography, so that academically their paths at university never crossed. He had seen her on the verges of parties, clutching a plastic cup of cheap warm wine that she probably took all evening to drink, sitting in a corner of the canteen with a book propped in front of her, crossing campus with a small smile, her eyes fixed on the middle distance. She was not friendless, not at all, but she was not a joiner either. Which was why Ed had been amazed to see her squashed into a corner of the car they were taking to the rave.

Now, the morning after, he caught up with her on the road that headed into the depths of the countryside. Jenn barely glanced at him, simply nodded and kept up her even pace. Her round glasses and shapeless dress and frizzed hair signalled an indifference to her appearance that made her even more attractive. It annoyed Ed, this impulse to follow someone who didn't care, but it didn't stop him either, didn't make him turn back to the simple civility of a pint and a packet of crisps.

They walked up the little-used road out of the village and along a valley, hung on two sides with Dorset's greenest hills, a canvas where black and white cows had been spattered to give it a convincing bucolic vibe. Ed couldn't look at them too closely or his head pulsed from last night's indulgences. "Where are we going?" he decided to ask. Everything with Jenn had to be decided, measured.

Jenn gestured ahead with the map. It was incredible that she had a map out here. Last night she'd had a tent too, and a sleeping bag, and had probably got a good night's sleep. Ed had seen her dancing early in the evening, eyes closed, contained, a fraction out of time with the thumping beat. Then she'd disappeared and he'd forgotten about her in the wash of E and drink. He himself hadn't slept at all except in the car coming to the pub. He should be back in that heap of recovering ravers.

They didn't speak — it was easier not to — but walked in silence through the emerald landscape, the road unfurling before them, its steamy surface gleaming silver in the sun and hurting Ed's eyes. No cars passed. Not even a tractor.

Eventually they turned off the road onto a path that led from the valley up to a ridge. Ed had to pick his way around mud puddles that Jenn strode straight through, showing off with her confident wellies. His trainers were split and muddy and he already knew that later he would have to abandon them somewhere. He stopped to pee into a hedgerow, watering the flowers he knew none of the names of, though he expected Jenn would know and be pleased to be asked. He wouldn't ask her. Why was he following her like this, helplessly full of something — a mix of desire and hope and self-disgust?

Jenn did not wait for him, or slow down, and as the hill became steeper he fell further behind, panting, till she was out of sight. He had no cigarettes left or he would have stopped for one. His mouth was dry — E did that. Jenn would have water. Where was she?

At last he reached the top of the climb, the hill levelling out and then tipping over into a wide bowl punched into the green earth. Jenn was standing at the edge, a field planted with something or other far below, peering back and forth between the map and the vista before her. She pointed at the far horizon. "Look, you can see all the way to Poole."

But Ed had already lain flat on the grass. She gazed at him, and for a moment seemed about to continue on her way. But then she sat down, ten feet away, and took out a book from her knapsack. Jenn would be the kind of person who always had a book on the go. Ed had loved books too, until suddenly he hadn't, around age fourteen, when waves of temptation in the form of girls and drink and music and TV had crashed over and swept him away. While she read, he closed his eyes and let himself absorb the sun. He could hear sheep bleating in the distance, and birds somewhere, but little else. In the stillness his ears fizzed with last night's music.

Though he needed to, he couldn't sleep, for she was there, with her book. Eventually he opened his eyes and propped himself up on his elbows. Across the bowl, black sheep were dotted on the far hillside like fleas. "Do you have any water?" he asked. Maybe asking would bring out the motherly side of her. Besides, he was thirsty as hell.

Wordlessly she threw a bottle at him, then took up her book again.

Ed drank three-quarters of the water before stopping himself, his mother's admonishments memorable even years later ("Eddie, THINK about your brother, and me, and your dad, before you finish that bottle!"). He

174

screwed on the cap and tossed the bottle back so that it hit her leg. Jenn ignored it.

"What are you reading?"

"*Jane Eyre.* Rereading it, actually."

Ed squinted at the cover. "Brontë," he read. This rang a bell. He thought hard through his headache, his persistent, low-grade queasiness, his dehydration that the water hadn't fixed. What he dredged up, in a high whiny voice, was this:

> Heathcliff,
> It's me — Cathy,
> Come home.
> I'm so co-o-o-old!
> Let me in your windo-o-o-ow!

He was proud of his rendition, and immediately went hard, remembering the hours he'd spent as a young teenager watching the video he had stumbled across, Kate Bush dancing in her red dress with her big bright mouth and her tiny tight hips and her caressing hands. Oh yes.

"That is *Wuthering Heights.* Not *Jane Eyre.*" Jenn clipped her words hard. "Emily rather than Charlotte Brontë. There is a big difference. The biggest difference."

"Oh. You know, I always thought she was really singing 'Waterproof Eyes' rather than 'Wuthering Heights'."

That did not help, Ed knew as the words hung between them, and he had that all-too-familiar sensation of wanting to claw them from the air and stuff them back in his mouth. He would have to appease Jenn somehow, or she would take off too fast across the fields and leave him stranded in Dorset — a prospect that terrified him. It was too green and quiet and pure out here.

Already she was stuffing the book in her bag and picking up the map. "What's *Jane Eyre* about, then?" he asked, lobbing the question in her way to slow her down.

Jenn left a long pause so that he would know how deliberate her selection of words was. "A governess full of inner strength who marries a completely inappropriate man."

"Oh. Right."

They moved on, and Ed didn't ask where they were going.

Over a gate and into a wood, they walked down a path — "the Wessex Ridgeway", she'd reported, because she knew that too — lined with nettles and thistles, which narrowed and enclosed it. Then, suddenly, it fanned out into a kind of clearing, where five paths led off, some into fields, others up or down hills. Next to one of the paths a wooden post had been driven into the ground, and a box the size of a bread bin attached to it at waist height.

"Dorset Gap", Jenn read from the map. "It's a convergence of several ancient routes. Look, that's a hollow way, where the path has sunk down over hundreds of years. People have been passing each other along these paths for centuries. It makes me feel so insignificant." She smiled; it seemed insignificance was something she aspired to. She was more animated by this nondescript patch of grass than Ed had ever seen her.

He looked around, and a memory came back to him that not even a hangover could bat away.

"I've been here before!" he announced.

Jenn stared at him.

"When I was young, on a family holiday," Ed added.

Years ago, he and his younger brother had followed their parents along paths through fields and woods and farms, guided by their father wielding an Ordnance Survey map just as Jenn was. Ed had lagged behind, thwacking nettles with a stick and throwing clods of mud at cows, who responded with bovine indifference. It was rainy, and muddy, and he would rather have been back at the B & B watching TV. Even snooker — even cookery shows — would have been better than this walk. He was eleven, and bribes of chocolate and games of Animal-Vegetable-Mineral no longer worked on him the way they still did on his brother.

They had arrived at this crossroads, and Ed's parents had made for the box while he hung back, looking for something to hit with his stick. All he could find was his brother, who cried out and was ignored.

His parents had opened the box, then opened a tin inside the box and taken out a black and red school notebook. Reading it, they discovered that passing walkers wrote in it, usually something about the weather and the surroundings, and signed and dated it.

Dorset Gap glorious as always — perfect for a Boxing Day walk.

The Cooper Family, Boxing Day 1988

Had a lovely brisk walk here. Beautiful even in the rain. Picked wild garlic for salad tonight.

Derek and Tessa, 3 April 1989

Millie's 6th birthday today — she walked all the way here in her new pink boots!

Amanda, Rob, Millie + Tom, 10 August 1989

There had been pages and pages of the stuff, and Ed couldn't understand why his parents spent so much time reading back through it. Then they had insisted on signing it, writing something banal that Ed didn't even bother to read. They had made him sign it too, and that had been the start of his teenage rebellion. He had written:

Terminally bored — Dorset Cereal Killer in the making.

They hadn't noticed.

He smiled now, remembering the misspelling, the being clever without knowing it. "You'll like this," he said to Jenn, going up to the box on the post. This was the first time she would actually respond positively to him on this walk, and Ed knew he'd better exploit it. He opened the box and the tin inside, and produced a notebook with a flourish.

178

It was blue, but otherwise it might as well have been 1989 again. The comments were much the same:

We have come here on a walk on our 17th anniversary. Shame about the rain!
Bob and Betty, 25th April 1998

Could it be any lovelier here? Heavenly flowers.
Chris with Trigger off the lead, 4 May 1998

Mum and Dad made me sign this.
Robbie, 15 June 1998

The last made Ed smile. "Robbie" had been here today. Maybe he and Jenn would see him, trailing behind his parents, throwing sticks at sheep and beheading wildflowers.

He handed the notebook to Jenn, who predictably sat down and read all the way through it as if it were an exam text. Ed didn't tell her there were a couple of other notebooks in the tin, or she would have read those too. While she studied it he wandered about, taking a few steps down each path to see if something exciting lurked in a field or under a tree. Nothing did, as he knew nothing would.

Jenn looked up. "You say this existed when you were young?"

"Yep." Ed came back and stretched out next to her, taking her words as an invitation.

"How long ago was that?"

He shrugged. "Ten years? Fifteen?"

Jenn watched him. "Which was it — ten or fifteen?"

He should've guessed she would want precision. "Nine years," he chose randomly, though it happened to be right.

"I'll bet it's been going on much longer than that." Jenn was so absorbed in her thoughts she didn't notice that Ed had begun to trace her calf with a finger. "I wonder where the other notebooks are. Maybe a local farmer keeps them."

"Doesn't it just get thrown away when it's full?"

"I hope not! This is social history in the making, in its purest, most natural form."

Even when she was right, Jenn's stances were fairly exhausting. Ed continued to run his finger up and down her calf, venturing past her knee.

"Is there a pen in the tin? Never mind, I've got my own."

"You're going to sign it?" Even as he said it, Ed knew the answer. He'd known the answer since seeing the post and the tin and the notebook. He'd known it since age eleven: people liked to sign that fucker.

"Of course. It's a responsibility for every passing walker to play an active part in history." Jenn glanced at his finger on her thigh. Ed removed it.

She rummaged about in her bag, pulling out the water bottle, a cardigan, the *Jane Eyre*, an apple. When she found her pen, she sat with the notebook on her knee, thinking. She thought for so long that Ed picked up the book and began flipping through it. Even *Jane*

180

Eyre must be more interesting than lying here, waiting for Jenn to compose her magnum opus.

It wasn't. He turned towards the end, to see if the book got better. It didn't. What a lot of words.

"Your turn." Jenn held out the notebook and pen. Ed felt like he'd time-travelled back nine years.

She had written:

I am no bird; and no net ensnares me; I am a free human being with an independent will.

Jenn, 15 June 1998

"Um, what is this?"

"From *Jane Eyre*. I always sign things — guest books, visitors' books — with a quote from whatever I'm reading at the time. To give a bit of myself."

Ed frowned. "But that's *not* you — it's *Jane Eyre*."

Jenn shrugged. "Books often say what I'm thinking better than I can. Now, are you going to sign it?"

She continued to hold out the notebook, and Ed took it, suppressing a sigh. His mind was wiped completely clean of wit or profundities or anything that could possibly impress her. He couldn't even think of a song to quote, not even "Waterproof Eyes". For a second he was tempted to copy his eleven-year-old Cereal Killer quote, but even in his blankness he knew better than that.

"Hurry up," Jenn said, pushing her things back in her knapsack. "We should get back or the others might wake up at the pub and leave us stranded."

When in doubt, imitate, Ed thought. The sincerest form of flattery. He wrote. It didn't take long. Then he signed and dated it and handed it to her, suddenly pleased, and a little nervous to see her response.

She read what he'd written and began to laugh — much harder than Ed thought his words warranted. He hadn't quite meant them as a joke. She laughed so hard she squeezed her knapsack to her chest as if she were hugging a pillow, tears forming at the corners of her eyes. She was very beautiful when she laughed. It pained him.

"Oh, Ed, you are funny," she said at last.

"What? What? I wrote a line I'd read! What's funny about that?"

Jenn smiled as she deposited the notebook in the tin and shut it. "Nothing's wrong with it. Well, not nothing." She put the tin in the box and closed it. "I think you should read *Jane Eyre* sometime, that's all. Then you'll know what the line really is." She shouldered her bag and turned back up the path they'd come down.

Ed watched her, thinking maybe he would not follow, but remain at Dorset Gap with its history being written down and kept in a tin box, or in a local farmer's bottom drawer. His simple line, so simple even he could remember it — "Reader, she married me" — had joined all the other lines, banal and profound, at this crossroads.

Party Girl

Nadifa Mohamed

It wasn't always like this, you know; for ages I was the kinda girl people said no one would wanna marry. Party Girl. *Sharmuuto. Dhillo*. I've heard it all. Started when I was around thirteen and got these breasts from nowhere, I'm talking flat as anything to E-cups in a coupla months; my *hooyo* made me put on a *hijab* quicksharp, no lie. Didn't stop nothing, though. Boys and men still asking for my digits left, right and centre. Nothing to write home about, just leaaaannn Somali boys acting gangster and Jamaican boys asking for a little touch. *Hooyo* said it was my face — that I've got the kinda eyes and lips that make men think they got a chance — she even started chatting about a *niqab* and I was like, hold on, bruv, there ain't no way I'm covering my face. What am I? Some kind of Man in the Iron Mask? It wasn't anything about my face, anyway, it was those E-cups and the way my *badhi* strained against the cheap, nylon school trousers.

I started partying around fifteen, before I took my exams. Suldaan had moved in and *hooyo* was distracted with her new baby. As long as she saw me at the kitchen table doing my homework while she made dinner, she let everything else slide, maybe cos she felt guilty marrying some asylum seeker. It pissed me right off, you know? Suldaan came in with his brown, Tooting Market suitcase and started saying that it was *haram* for me to wear my normal clothes in *my own home*. I had to sit there, burning up, watching telly with my *hijab* on. Then it was my scent: I couldn't wear perfume around him, because "it ignited the libido". Please. What's he hanging around outside my room for then? When *hooyo*'s off trying to get the baby to sleep and I'm getting changed for bed. Such a goddamn *nacas*.

I ain't even playing, if he comes at me, he'll get a shank straight through his black heart. I told Mum that to her face, and she just stares at me and says, "What have I raised?"

Anyway, the partying, yeah, it was all right. Used to go to Dalston and those ends with my GBFs. A bunch of white kids with skinny jeans and daddy's credit card and us — tearing it up on our EMA and travelling home on free bus passes. We bounced into those places looking like something out of *Aladdin*, all three of us misfits bespeckled and stunting on dem. I'd cut my hair short cos it was tangling every day under the scarf and I looked more like a boy than Yusuf (who's a full-on drag queen now) with his pretty lashes and long, Princess Kaur Singh hair. Every time, and I mean ev-er-y time, Sulaiman would get falling-down drunk, thrashing about and speaking in tongues, his leather jacket left in some bar, his cheap mobile glowing in the pocket as we kept ringing. I'd have pills flowing through my veins, the stars turning into disco balls as we went out to smoke, a warmth pouring out of every inch of my skin and into the cold winter night.

I got into Oxford even with all that going on. Was on some bad come-downs during those sixth-form exams but ended up getting max on some papers. Chose English. Matriculated at the Sheldonian with a bunch of tufty-haired public school boys. Did the Beowulf thing, hated it, moved on to some proper stuff: Baldwin, Morrison, Donne. Got roughed up a bit by boys who couldn't keep their hands to themselves. Ran outta money, piled on more loan, ran outta money. Had a breakdown or something like it. Sent home, Suldaan had gone and the house was bare quiet, even the baby had become this surly, silent boy. Went back, finished what I started and got a First, thank you very much. Had missed the Milk Round so went back to London to sign on.

They tell you all this at Oxford: how you're at this great place and are gonna be great yourself but I had a hard landing. Sulaiman had bunned uni and got a job straight outta sixth form working for a French designer, so I hung out with him in his ridiculous flat in Knightsbridge and smoked and read all of the things I hadn't had a chance to.

It seemed like I blinked and a decade fell away, people had bought houses in Zone 5 and 6, had kids! Even Yusuf was busy Googling American surrogates that he couldn't afford. Madness. I had nothing but my childhood bedroom on a council estate that no one seemed to leave and a pocketful of antidepressants.

It was the best of times, it was the worst of times; jokes, it was just the worst. You could say that I was looking for someone to make it all better, but that doesn't really go where it needs to go, it was more that I needed someone (but not quite anyone) to make the rest of my life worth living. "The mind is its own place, and in itself can make a heaven of hell, a hell of heaven," as Milton said, and my cosy, dole-given, curtains-closed heaven was pure hell. I did the internet thing and felt I was searching through a catalogue of undiscovered serial killers. I went to a few clubs with Yusuf but the music was not my own any more. Sitting on a barstool, bass speakers hammering at my head, I held a few too many yellow pills in my hand and thought about calling it quits. *Halas.*

I don't know why it took me so long but I realised that inside me was Hiroshima, Dresden, Hargeisa. I found my mother's depression pills and we were on the same shit, the same doses; it was brutal. Even the boy (now a wasteman of epic proportions) was self-medicating, smoking enough skunk to fumigate us the hell outta there. We were all in small pieces that didn't fit together; too many countries, too many scars, too many secrets inside us. I sat down on my mother's bed, her thin back facing me, speaking to the sad green wall more than to her and I just said, "It's gotta change, *hooyo*, we're not dead yet."

We're not dead yet. We're not dead yet. *I'm* not dead yet. That became my mantra, my prayer.

I started running, found a pair of my old ghetto trainers and jogged around the deer park, trying to shed the bloat that my bohemian indolence had piled on me. I chucked the pills. Finally began to put words on paper and to ease the pressure that had clouded my mind. The writing and running made me euphoric, almost too much; I started texting everyone, saying how good I felt, how I was going to write a masterpiece. People thought I was on speed or something but it was just me, all the cogs and wheels and pistons working again. Yusuf trained me in how to look like a woman, he dragged me up and even put a long weave on my head; we blew the last of my money on a blitzkrieg around Topshop. I was good to go, he said. Small enough, plain enough and broke enough for most men to wanna date.

For all my mum's talk about me being a *dhillo*, I straight-up *feared* talking to men, if they weren't gay something made me tense up and die a little. I hated seeing myself mirrored in their eyes, with all that clarity and opacity. I stood in bars, clothed but naked, looking from their eyes to my feet and back again. Still there was the longing to contend with: the heavy, bloody, chemical urge to consume another body and spit out its bones in a new child. How do you make a stranger so intimate when they could so easily destroy you? How did women do that every day? How did *hooyo* do that with Suldaan and, even before that, with my father? How? How? How?

I found out.

It was his smell.

I had never known anything like it.

He had come to our door asking for help, like a jinn in one of Shahrazad's tales, holding out a piece of paper with an address written on it. Forming his fingers into a mock phone by his ear, "Can I borrow?"

He had shoulder-length black hair and a smile that belonged to the devil. A guitar slung across his back and shoes that had seen a century of dust.

I could hear my mum's feet on the landing upstairs, taking the position she always did when strangers knocked on our door. I looked at the note and saw the address written was on our block.

"It's just nearby," I said, "there," pointing as he padded on to our synthetic carpet, the plastic runner squeaking under his feet, the guitar chiming against the narrow walls. His smell was not of cologne or detergent but neither was it sweat or grime, it was the honey of lilacs hanging over brick walls.

I instinctively blocked his way in, and gestured for him to go back outside.

"What does he want?" *hooyo* called down. "Is he from the council?"

He backed out with his silhouette lit up in the dim light, the breeze blowing in and through me; he stopped on the doorstep and stared at me. I thought he was about to eff and blind at me but he just stared and then went, "You are very beautiful" — no sarcasm, no laughing, completely serious. I stood there, dumb look on my pillow-creased face, my hair all tangled, a dirty sweatshirt on, and then slammed the door in his face.

He moved in a few doors down, into one of the raucous flats filled with scrappy migrants. His accent was difficult to place, his face even more so. We sat on the railings as my mother watched from the window.

He read my writing and I listened to his songs. He busked so all of his money was in coins, silver and gold that spilled from his pockets and into my hands; he danced too, in a shamanic way that made his eyes glint. I took the weave out and kicked off the high heels; I knew he didn't need them. I wrote and wrote and wrote, somehow both animated and doped by him, I wrote long sentences that looped around themselves like bees following a scent.

I took down the dark curtains in my room and let the light in. I told *hooyo* that I forgave her and let the light in. I took him in my arms and let the light in.

Transference

Esther Freud

"Nothing's going to happen," he said, standing and striding towards the door. At least that's how I pictured it when I thought it over later — but it couldn't have been that way because the next time he spoke he was sitting in his chair. "It's not as if we're going to jump into bed together." He was under the window then, so close our knees were almost touching, although in reality he can't have moved because a moment later he was still there, facing into the room, the low glass table between us.

I'd gone to him for help with my obsessive thinking. I was fixated on my boyfriend, his coldness, his resistance to getting married, and the discovery, still fresh, of his unfaithfulness. "Why don't I just leave?" I sobbed through my first session. But instead of leaving, I spent hours running over past events, bewailing my passivity, recasting myself as the fiery, outspoken woman I wished I was. I'd sit at my desk, my work neglected, and re-enact how it might have been — standing up to him, storming out, throwing my possessions into the car and driving off. How powerful I felt when I was speaking the truth. But that was inside my head. On the outside nothing had changed.

"It's a torment," I told him. "Like being in some kind of trap. He says he loves me, but . . ." I cried and gulped water, tissues and tumblers helpfully lined up, while he looked at me in a sympathetic way and waited. It didn't take long before I started up again, listing the endless cycle of events that made up that week's sorrows, stopping only to blow my nose and swat away new tears. "I'm so embarrassed," I said eventually, rising up for air. "This isn't who I want to be."

That's the first time I sensed that he'd come closer, although of course he hadn't moved. "I don't mind," he said.

I know *you* don't mind. It's *me* that minds. I'm embarrassed for myself. But I didn't say these things, because that's why I was there. I didn't, couldn't say.

Each week I dragged myself to see him, crossing London from west to north, walking through terraced streets, compiling lists of things we might discuss — longing, regret, forgiveness, marriage. But as soon as I was in his room, had removed my coat and then, with some embarrassment, another layer — for it was always hot — I forgot about the lists. Instead I started on the story. It was as if I had to get it out — the poison silting up in me — on and on, if only I could stop, or at least fall silent for long enough to give him a moment to respond. But the next week there was always more. "I'm just going to have to tell you everything, and then, I promise, I'll pause for breath." And I'd start — each event in order — what I'd said, how my boyfriend had

192

reacted, my threats, his promises, all recreated with my exquisite memory.

And then, one day, finally I stopped, and I looked at him and smiled. I was smiling at him and he at me, and we held the look for what felt like an indecently long time. "That was a beautiful moment," he said. I nodded. He didn't look the type to use the word beautiful. Not that I'd ever really looked at him. Just accepted his presence, moving as it did around the room, so that when I remembered things he'd said, questions he'd raised, he seemed always to be in a different position. Like sex, I thought. And I packed that thought away.

That was the week I had the dream. I woke from it. A light lit up inside me. We'd been sitting in a train carriage, our feet touching across a cushioned seat, our backs against the panels of the walls. There was a current of love running round us, a visible light that formed a circle. And, as if for the first time, I could see him. His hair, the green that seams through copper, the flecks of grey, the close shave of his face, and something I had never noticed, his top lip which disappeared when he smiled. I leaned across and kissed him.

All day the light stayed on in me. And all that night. I was kinder to my boyfriend. Thought only once or twice of the hurt of his transgressions. I hummed, and turned a crazy pirouette in the middle of the kitchen, and although I ate my meals as usual, my body felt buoyant.

On the day of my next session I was stricken with nerves. This is ridiculous, I told myself, last week I would have been hard-pressed to describe him to a stranger, and now, even before he appeared in the doorway, his image was electric. I sat down and he sat down. He looked reserved, his eyes guarded, his face tired, his hair savagely cut. I started tentatively — how I'd been wondering what my relationship was based on, whether I even wanted to get married at all. "I've been thinking a lot about love," I told him, keeping the dream to myself. "What love really means."

"I've been thinking a lot about you," he said, and he moved his hand to his heart. Or did he? And the terrible thing is I'll never know, or what he might have said next, because I interrupted him.

"When I said I've been thinking a lot about love" — I was surprised to find that I was angry — "I meant the love in this room," and I drew a circle with my hand to encompass all the places we had been. What happened then is still unclear — I'd give a lot to switch it with all the things I forensically remember — but I must have looked stricken because he asked, "Why are you so challenged?"

Why? Of course I'm challenged! My therapist is confessing he's in love with me. Or is he? I was too cowardly to ask. And anyway, what would be the least disturbing answer: Yes? Or no?

I had to dig deep, and when I spoke I used words I didn't even know I knew. "The way you look at me, the empathy with which you listen to my troubles, the thread of light between us, that's what I want in my life. And that's what I can't imagine that I'll ever have."

He nodded wisely, sagely. As if he was, after all, a therapist and not a man.

We talked about empathy. About love. About what was possible between two people. And then I asked: "What happened? It didn't used to be like this in here."

He smiled, that beautiful lip-disappearing smile. "You started to glow," he said, "and I saw you, and I wanted you to know that you are loved."

I might have moaned. Or put my head in my hands. But I did neither. He saw me anyway. "It's all right." And that's when he said it. "Nothing's going to happen. It's not as if we're going to jump into bed together."

Whoaaa! My heels were digging in. You're so ahead of me. A few days ago you were no more human to me than a stuffed bear and now we're talking about sex! And dismissing it. Although I dismissed the dismissing part. One step at a time.

That day on my way home I missed my Tube connection, and when it was my stop I failed to get off. The light from my dream was blazing, turned up to full, and my head, my heart, the blood that ran through each and every vein, were roaring. My boyfriend was out. He'd gone away on a work trip, and later, after I'd twisted and turned and failed to sleep, I was grateful for that.

The next day I wasn't glowing. I looked at myself in the mirror. What the . . . ? And unable to concentrate on work, I took the bus to Hampstead Heath and set off on a walk. Sometimes it seems most people in North London are therapists, or training to be therapists, and it wasn't long before I bumped into a friend from university, meandering along after her dog, who had, in the years since I'd seen her, retrained as a couples counsellor. I asked her how her work was going and then, as if it meant nothing to me, about the relationship she had with her . . . what did she call them . . . patients? "What are the boundaries?" I asked. "Are you allowed to say that you've been thinking about someone outside of the session?" And I told her how, some weeks before, I'd sighed and said I didn't want the session to end, and he'd leaned his then quite ordinary head towards me, and said, "No, neither do I."

A look of alarm flashed over her face. She was wrestling, I could see it, with her dual role of therapist and friend. "Sounds unorthodox for sure."

I tried her with some more, and her eyebrows shot up. Quickly I stepped in to defend him. "Maybe he's just very skilled?" I offered. "For the first time in years I'm thinking about things that make me happy — for the first time in God knows how long, I feel attractive."

"Yes . . ." She wasn't sure, and later that day she emailed me guidelines on sexual boundaries in the therapeutic workplace.

I didn't read them. I hate instructions. And I didn't want to discover anything that might make me cancel my next session. But as the days passed I became increasingly disturbed. The two of us in that room, meshing, moving, so that I had to remind myself of the photograph he kept in my eyeline, a portrait of his children, a perfect boy and girl, and the references he'd made, in earlier, less glowy times, to his wife.

I could hardly sleep, was struggling to eat. I felt responsible — if I wasn't strong enough to go back and see him he'd know he'd gone too far. I must relax, I told myself. For him! And I booked myself a massage.

"Your pulses." The masseuse kept her fingers on my wrist. "They're jumping all over the place." So I told her the whole story. I couldn't help myself, although I reassured her too, that nothing, obviously, was going to happen.

"Not necessarily." She waited while I kicked off my shoes, and when I'd lain down on the low bed, she confided how her own father, an analyst himself, had ditched her mother for a woman who'd come to him for help. "To be fair," she sighed, "she was an awful lot younger, richer and really, if I'm honest, nicer than my mother." I would have laughed, as she did, but she had hold of my neck, and she was stretching it. "They stayed together for ten years and then when he retired, it was as if the scales fell from her eyes and she accused him of taking advantage. Her feelings for him were surely transference and should have stayed that way."

"Ouch," I protested as she pressed her thumbs into the tightness of my jaw.

"Eventually she sought advice, they both did, from a senior rabbi, but it wasn't long before she'd run off with the rabbi and six months later they were married. Turn over now, and I'll see what's up with your poor shoulders."

When I got home, reeling and uncoiled, I looked up transference.

Transference is a common aspect of the therapeutic process. It is a phenomenon characterised by unconscious redirection of feelings from one person to another and under most circumstances should be discussed and examined and moved through with the therapist. Unless, for instance, you have a phobia of spiders, and this particular person reminds you so much of an ex-lover that you're in danger of setting off for a dangerous trip into the rainforest untreated. In which case — change therapists!

My boyfriend called while I was reading and guiltily I closed my laptop and listened to his news. He was in Berlin, had secured the contract he'd been chasing, although in order to be certain of it, he'd have to stay on for one more week. He loved me, he said, and missed me, and for the first time in a long while the little voice inside my head didn't add any bitter or cynical remarks.

That night I had supper with a friend. She had married early and now had teenage children, about whom, just for tonight, she was eager to forget. "White wine?" She flagged down a waiter and ordered a bottle. She had a lot to tell. Her husband was being transferred to Seattle, and although she was worried about leaving her house, the children's school, her dearest friends, she was excited too. "And you?" She looked at me with pity. The last time I'd seen her, I was raw with the wounds of my discovery — a text message, white on the black screen of my boyfriend's phone, its yearning, sexually explicit tone, impossible to ignore.

"I'm well," I told her, and I couldn't help myself, I blushed.

"Oh my God." Her eyes widened. "You're fucking someone new!"

"No!" I protested, and I waited while our glasses were filled, although I knew I'd have to tell her. About the dream. The kiss. The glowing words of love. "Obviously," I ended, "nothing is going to happen."

But she laughed. "Why not?" She was alive with it. "Who cares about ethics? It may be destiny, the way you two were supposed to meet."

"No, no," I tried to interrupt her, to tell her about the stoop of his shoulders, the soft slope of his paunch, his wife!

She was having none of it. "Maybe you'll run away together." Her eyes were bright with the vicariousness of my living. "And I for one will be delighted. After seven years with . . ." she stopped herself. "You deserve to be happy in love."

She poured us both more wine and as she did I thought of her husband, boring, older, let's face it, practically bald, and how content she had always seemed with him. Had I been blinded by my boyfriend's easy charm, his energy, had I been struggling all these years along the wrong path? "I do think about him ninety per cent of the time," I gave her what she wanted, and she raised her arm and signalled for more wine.

As we drank, chattering our way into the future, I thought of the therapist and how his face changed as he looked at me — a soft look, a sort of melting, and my heart flipped over like a fish.

There were flowers in the room when I next entered. Had there ever been flowers before? And beside the flowers there was a photograph of his wife.

"So, how are you?" he asked when, after some long minutes, I still hadn't spoken.

"I'm not sure where to start." I felt a cold sweat collecting, the eyes of his wife resting on me, amused, and it occurred to me, all I had done was swap one object of obsession for another. "My work's going well," I tried. I'd hardly mentioned my work to him, but it was true, through all of the recent turmoil, new commissions had been flooding in. He smiled his encouragement and, glad to feel him closer, I told him about my new designs. "I'm branching into wallpaper, I've created a line with hearts and wheels," and I stopped then, because I saw how this creation had been inspired by my dream.

"Yes?" He was waiting.

"Transference." I swallowed. "I looked it up."

His smile remained. "And what did you find?"

"Well . . ." I tried to tell him about the spiders and the rainforest, in the hope that he would laugh.

"Transference and counter-transference happen all the time," he said. "Romantic, erotic . . ." I shook my head. "Therapy is all about the relationship."

I told him then, about the train, the circle of light, how our feet were touching, everything in fact, except the kiss. He withdrew a little, as people do when you admit to having encountered them in dreams, and I braced myself, expecting him to get up and move away. But he stayed in his chair. "It's the strangest thing," I was talking to myself now. "Last winter when I discovered . . . that text . . . it felt as if my heart was broken, but now . . ." and I saw it had been true for some time, "it feels as if my heart has broken open."

His lip disappeared — his smile was so wide — and my insides melted with the strength of what was possible. "Thank you," I said, and to steady myself I glanced up at his wife.

That night my boyfriend returned from his trip. "I missed you." He twined his arms around my waist, and without taking off his coat he lifted me up and carried me through to the bedroom.

"No," I said quietly when he put me down, "I'm sorry, I just—"

"*I'm* sorry," he interrupted, and when I dared to look at him, to look into his face, I saw that he was scared. "I want you to know . . ." His voice was very low, his face pale. "If you want me I'm yours."

"Is this a proposal?" I bit my lip.

"I've changed," he said. And I thought how much, how often, I'd wanted to hear those words.

"Thank you." I took his hand. "I'll have to think about it." But I didn't tell him, not yet anyway, that it was me who'd changed.

That next session I had almost nothing to say. I listened while the therapist talked and I smiled at him. The mistake we make, the masseuse had told me, once my pulses had eventually stilled, is to think that love must be about possession. You can love someone in a pure way. You can hold them in your heart. And nothing has to happen.

The Mash-Up

Linda Grant

The wedding was perfect, up to a point.

Because we were what Ali called a mash-up couple, we had to find a way of celebrating our marriage with a nod to both families, a ceremony that would make them feel their traditions were respected and that neither side had the upper hand. These things can turn ugly if not handled properly, with slights and sulks and stormings out and long-borne grievances and grudges stumbling to the surface like aggrieved old drunks. At least on my side of the family. My grandmother has not spoken to my aunt Dolly for forty-three years, since she was not placed at the top table at Elaine's wedding.

We went online and found a character called Rabbi Larry Peirera. He was prepared to conduct a wedding ceremony of our own devising, like those websites Ali used where you could customise your Nikes. Rabbi Larry, as he told us to call him, was an endearing fellow, a little mushroom of a man with a black boyfriend. When we met with him for the first time, at a bar in Shoreditch, we spent several ice-breaking minutes discussing the symbolism of our three sets of tats and he told us wonderful stories that started funny, and ended in heartbreak, of the long-ago centuries in the Sephardic world where Jews and Muslims lived side by side. "But I'm not a Muslim," Ali reminded him. "I'm *Persian*."

"Of course," Rabbi Larry said. "Indeed, the grave of our Queen Esther is in your lands." Then he ordered coffee martinis and we planned our wedding.

I explained that my parents were what you call three-times-a-year Jews, the type who go to synagogue for the High Holy Days, driving from home till they get two blocks away, then discreetly parking out of sight. "Out of respect for the rabbi," Rabbi Larry said. "Of course. And why not? Let hypocrites be hypocrites if that's what makes them comfortable. There's enough trouble in this world without waging war on wonderful people like your parents."

On those occasions my mother would wear an unbecoming hat, my father would wrap his tallis around his shoulders and hold his siddur as if he knew what the words meant. Looking down on him from high in the ladies' gallery, you could tell from the expression on his face, that pinched look he got, that he was thinking about business, about cheap Chinese imports and the demand for quality being met these days with blank stares.

We wanted to shake all that up, make something modern. "Like our globalised world," said Ali, who is a business analyst at Bloomberg.

He explained to Rabbi Larry that his parents were what they call militantly secular. Richard Dawkins was their hero. "What a fellow," they'd say. "At home they'd torture and murder him, but here he is allowed to say what he likes and nobody does a thing." The family had got out of Iran in 1983, leaving behind a mansion in Tehran and a whole valley somewhere beyond the city. At home they had been religious the way my parents were religious, Ali's grandmother in miniskirts and spike heels drinking cocktails at downtown hotels, fasting at Ramadan ("good for the figure"). Once they got to Pittsburgh and set up the dry-cleaning businesses, they started hating Islam. When the Twin Towers were attacked they said, "We're not Arabs, you know, those barbarians, we're *Persians*."

They insisted on no trace of Islam at our wedding ceremony, but there were certain Persian traditions such as the women of the two families coming together to grind sugar over a canopy above the bride and groom's heads to sweeten their lives. These elements could be present, they suggested.

Ali and I were getting married in Stoke Newington Town Hall. The place had a large enough banqueting suite to accommodate the thirty-four Persians who were flying over as well as the Israeli contingent, my mother's cousins who moved there in the seventies, attracted by kibbutz life. "From peasants to peasants in two generations," my grandfather had said scathingly, not comprehending why anyone would give up the good life in Manchester to pick oranges under a scorching sun. The kids of these cousins all worked in the field of algorithms.

The Persians and the Israelis came down on the family meal the night before the wedding like wolves on the fold. "What is a fold?" asked Ali. "I think it's where they keep sheep, or something," I said. In case there were any pork-free eaters in the crowd, the buffet consisted of a lot of lamb in various guises. Our families were big eaters. Both sides arrived wearing abundant gold jewellery, and they felt to each other, my mother said, like long-lost relatives, except the Persians took to the dance floor at the drop of a hat and they were all amazing dancers, whereas Jews, as everyone knows, ain't got no rhythm and are clumsy on our feet. We took them through the order of service for the big day, and everyone agreed that Rabbi Larry had done a great job. There was going to be the traditional Persian knife dance. "Don't cut yourself!" cried my aunt.

We spent the night apart, me at my friend Emily's house, Ali at our flat. My dress was Valentino, a very simple column, white, cape-back, which my uncle Phil got me at cost. No veil, just flowers in my hair. Ali bought a Paul Smith suit. Our wedding outfits hung shrouded in the wardrobe. Soon we would be the people who wore wedding clothes, then we would be married and in that future we imagined there would be no clouds, for we were beautifully suited to each other, I was the small noisy inquisitive bossy one, while Ali was quietly neurotic and thoughtful. We held each other's self-destructive tendencies in check.

First we had the short civil ceremony at Clissold House, in front of a small group of close family and friends. We said the words, we signed the register, then we walked hand in hand across the park to the town hall and sailed in, bridesmaids and groomsmen flowing behind us. Rabbi Larry was waiting to meet us by the canopy, looking pleasingly rabbinical. He had prepared some beautiful readings, from the Song of Solomon and the Persian poet Hafez. We were married; I had married him, the love of my life.

But before the food was brought out, and the speeches, and the first dance, the final symbolic act of our marriage took place, the little Jewish ritual. Rabbi Larry had had a special wine glass commissioned that was inscribed with both our initials. He took a folded handkerchief from his pocket and held it up as if he were about to perform a conjuring trick, then he wrapped it around the glass and laid it on the floor. Ali trod on the glass; he smashed it. Then he let out a piercing scream, which was rounded off by a kind of ululation. "Fuck fuck fuck, oh God help me!" I looked down at his foot. A long shard had pierced the thin leather of his shoe.

Rabbi Larry cried out, "I never saw this happen — this never happened to me before!"

"To *you*?" I said. "What's happening to *you*? Look at Ali, he's going to bleed to death! Help him, someone. For Christ's sake, will someone please do something!"

There were five doctors in the house, who all came running. The consultation was quick. "He needs to go to hospital," said Dr Stephanie Weinstock, my mother's sister's daughter, the dermatologist specialising in psoriasis who is married to Anthony Weinstock, the orthopaedics man who specialises in ankle replacement. The Persian doctors agreed, strenuously. "He must go to the emergency room, get an ambulance, quick, quick!"

"Come on, darling," I said. "Take my arm."

"No, I'll go with him," said his mother, Mamak, who was wearing a striking turquoise floor-length gown with sparkly straps. "He needs a mother's love, poor darling."

"She's right," said my mother, in a Donna Karan suit, the pair of them looking as though they were attending completely different functions. "He'll be back in an hour, don't worry, we'll have the meal and hold off on the speeches till he gets back. You can't leave the guests by themselves, it doesn't look right."

I was crying. "Darling," I said, "what have we done to you? I'm sorry I'm sorry I'm sorry."

"Don't worry," Ali said. "I just need a few stitches and another pair of shoes. I'll be right back. Stay here."

He waited in A&E for five hours. They bandaged him up and gave him some pills. "I'm going home," he texted me, just before eleven. "I'm exhausted. I guess you're still holding the fort."

In those hours trouble had broken out in the town hall. The Persians were starting to question this barbaric ritual. Ali's uncle Firouz wanted to know how many times this had happened. One of the Israeli cousins said she'd been to a wedding years ago when this happened — a black day, like circumcisions sometimes not working out the way they were supposed to. The men all screamed. One of my second cousins, Ari ben Oren, tried to divert them by going into a scholarly explanation for the origins of the glass-smashing ritual, explaining to them how this was supposed to symbolise the destruction of the Temple. "I thought we agreed no religion?" Fashid, Ari's father reminded him.

But with the mention of the Temple, the conversation slid into a discussion of Middle East politics.

When large groups of opinionated, intelligent people, particularly men, come together, if the talk is not safely diverted to football, then unfortunately politics and specifically international relations are a topic on which everyone has a heated opinion.

Gradually the wedding party broke down into warring factions. Somehow they had got on to the Iraq war; I wasn't following the arguments but voices were raised. I tried to go round to everyone with my glassy smile and apologise for the delay in Ali's return. Some hysteric on his side of the family wondered if his condition had not somehow taken a turn for the worse: maybe he had blood poisoning, maybe his foot had to be amputated. She had heard of such a case. Rabbi Larry had disappeared. The wedding was in a state of suspended animation. The food was eaten, but no speeches, no first dance, or anyone dancing.

When I got home Ali's mother was lying on what was supposed to be our marital bed, holding his hand while he slept. His foot was heavily bandaged.

"How is he?"

"It was a terrible time. The doctors were no good, in my opinion."

I stood there in my wedding dress.

"Best if I spend the night here," she said. "My poor baby needs me."

"But I'm his *wife*."

She shrugged. And under her breath she said something that sounded like, "We'll see."

There is a saying that when a wedding is perfect, nothing that follows can match it. Everything is a letdown after that occasion which you put all your work and planning into, never thinking of the long years of married life that will follow the marriage itself, the wailing kids, the tight finances, the joys and sorrows of being a lifelong couple resisting all the extracurricular temptations. Better for a wedding to go a little wrong; better, even, for it to be a disaster, for it foreshadows all the times that are to come. Marriage is not a romantic fantasy, it's hard work.

This is what my mother told me the following day, and yet Ali and I have been divorced now two years, which is nineteen months longer than we were married.

A friend of mine went to another wedding presided over by Rabbi Larry. "The bride was locked in the toilet and couldn't get out," she said. "The whole thing was held up an hour while they found a janitor to release her."

Say what you like, in my opinion Rabbi Larry is a fucking jinx.

The Self-Seeding Sycamore

Lionel Shriver

Jeannette had no idea that plants could engender so much hatred.

For years, she'd left the garden to Wyndham. Weekends outdoors provided an antidote to the windowless stasis of his lab. Though their plot was sizable only by London standards, she'd humoured him. (Whatever was there to do? A little watering during dry spells, a ten-minute run of the hand mower round the lawn.) Having begrudged the dear man neither his solitude nor his superfluous pottering, she treasured snapshots of her husband in muddied khaki trousers, bent over a bed, doing heaven-knew-what with a characteristically intent expression. Now, of course, she knew exactly what he'd been doing. How much he'd spared her.

While still cosseted by mutual spousal existence, she'd scanned with indifference bitter first-person articles about how fiercely people avoid the bereaved — a revelation her own friends had amply illustrated for a year or more. She didn't blame them. Unintentionally, she and Wyndham had fallen into the heedlessly hermetic unit of two that's so off-putting from the outside. If she didn't need friends then, she'd no right to demand their solicitations now. Besides, she'd grown less compelling to herself. A widow of fifty-seven had both too much story left, and not enough. It was narratively awkward: an ellipsis of perhaps thirty years, during which nothing big would happen. Only little things, most of them crap.

The big story that was over wasn't interesting, either. Pancreatic: swift and dreadful. Yet the pro forma tale did include one poignant detail. Two years ago, she and Wyndham took early retirement, he from private biochemical research, she from her job as a buyer for Debenhams. Some colleagues had quietly disapproved, and soon no one would be allowed to stop working at fifty-five, but to Jeannette and Wyndham that argued for a leap through the closing window. They'd not found each other until their forties, and had made extravagant travel plans for while they were still in rude health. The reasoning was sound; the arithmetic, not. The diagnosis arrived a mere ten weeks after Wyndham's farewell party.

She hadn't kept track of whether fifty-seven was the new forty-seven, or thirty-five, or sixty-four — but in any event whatever age she'd reached was not the age she was. Not long ago, she and Wyndham had mourned his every strand that clogged the plughole, each new crease in her neck when she glanced down. Now? She could not get older fast enough.

Convinced that a garden took care of itself — it grew, bloomed, browned and without prodding renewed the cycle — other than hiring a boy to mow, for the year following Wyndham's death she left the back to its devices. In truth, she missed the sharpness of those first few months, whose high drama would have been impossible to maintain without its sliding into a humiliating fakery, a performance for herself. While still free-flowing and unforced, the grief had been so immersive, so rich and pure and concentrated, with the opacity of Cabernet, that it verged on pleasure. Yet from the start the anguish had been spiked with an awful foreknowledge that the keenness of her loss would blunt, leading to a second loss: a loss of loss. Some soft, muffled bufferedness was bound to take over, as if she were buttressed by excess packaging. Unlike the searing period, with its skipped meals and feverish lie-ins, a bufferedness could last forever, and probably would.

Sure enough, the stab ebbed to ache; a torturous residual presence gave way to absence. Jeannette took refuge in self-sufficiency. She would take nothing (besides that reduced-rate pension), and expect nothing. There must have been millions of such Britons: perfectly neutral social quantities, mutely shopping and tidying up. She would take care of herself, as the garden did.

So late this April, she was surprised to note on an aimless stroll beyond the slug-trailed patio, simply to escape the house — which had never felt suffocating when she shared it — that flowering shrubs past their prime were pooping mounds of rotting pink blossoms, under which matted grass skulked, dying or dead, a urinary yellow. Ineffectually, she raked the piles of petals with her fingers off the moribund lawn, in idle amazement that flowers could kill. The silky mulch had a nice heavy wetness, reminiscent of her cheeks after an inadvisable third glass of wine. Its original perfume mixed with an aroma deader and flatter, like sweet but fading memories intermingling with her present *self-sufficiency*.

She surveyed the beds on either side. Pooping flowers were the least of it. Unafflicted by Wyndham's "superfluous" attentions, the ceanothus had bushed out in scraggly extrusions like an unbarbered Afro, blocking the stone path to the tool shed and poking her in the eye. Ivy had choked the herbs; the ferns drooped with snails. Weeds snarled around Wyndham's languishing plants. The lawn had bare patches from peeing foxes, vermin she'd been too apathetic to shoo. She couldn't speak for the human sphere, but apparently in the botanical world, without the constant intercession of a benevolent higher power, evil triumphed.

At first anxious about uprooting her husband's beloved something-or-others, Jeannette soon mastered the gardener's rubric: anything that grows fast and well is malevolent. Weeding, she was tortured by a cliché that circled her head like a successful advertisement jingle: *Nature abhors a vacuum*. She came to match each invader with a uniquely flavoured dislike. Burrowing into the mortar of the property line's brick wall, a pretend-attractive plant with small devious leaves inspired an impatient disgust, especially when she failed to rip out the root system (more or less always): the crafty, low-lying wallflower would be back in a week. Allowed in the passivity of her grieving to rise six feet high, a gangling daisy-like species with disproportionately small, stupid yellow flowers had spread thick white ropes of lateral roots so quickly and so thickly that in another month's time the towering, insipid plants would have taken over the world. This aversion was laced with fear; she pursued their extermination with the grim, stoical thoroughness of genocide. Indeed, through late-life gardening she discovered in herself a murderous side. In this laying of waste, the institution of her private scorched earth policy, she came closer than she had in seventeen months to joy.

Yet Jeannette reserved her most extravagant loathing for clusters of innocent-looking seedlings that seemed to erupt in concert on a single day, as if obeying a battle plan. Oh, on its own, a single sample of this anonymous item seemed innocuous and easily vanquished. A mere three inches high, two bright never-mind-me leaves splayed on a spindly stem. But when snatched from the ground, lo, the tiny flagpole had sunk into her property a good four inches below — and virtually overnight.

Besides which, any organism in sufficient quantity is gross. Bulging clusters of these seedlings, pushing against one another in their blind, ignorant bunching, sprouted en masse through the bark cover around the tool shed. The impertinent would-be trees cropped up in the lightless murk below the shrubs. They perforated the lawn every two inches. They penetrated the ivy that had killed the chives, and threatened the ivy, too.

Thus by May, her every hour in the garden was devoted to stripping out mocking bouquets that foisted themselves around the trunk of the wisteria, squeezed between the slats of the compost box, and prised the tool shed's baseboards from its frame. Daily, she massacred seedlings by the *thousands*, creating whole burial mounds of the shrivelled fallen, and still they came. The slaughter recalled a certain kind of asymmetrical warfare, whereby a better supplied, more technologically sophisticated army is overrun by forces in rags with sticks, the adversary's greatest weapon its leadership's utter obliviousness to casualties on a staggering scale.

Any child soldier she failed to slay right away would stake a territorial claim. Within days an overlooked seedling jagged out in aggressive, multipronged foliage with the rough nap and variegation of *real tree leaves*. The fragile stem woodened to sturdy stalk; the taproot plummeted and grew clinging hairs. Her attempts at jerking these interlopers from the ground (the stem always broke) were no more effective than the Home Office's feeble efforts to deport asylum seekers.

No mystery, the source of the assault. On the opposite side of the party wall, a monster of a tree rose three storeys high, its trunk only a few inches from the brick, ensuring that nearly half its branches extended over her own garden. It was a charmless thing, blocking light from the herb bed, and already grown pregnant with *more seedpods*, its branches sagging from the weight of their great ghastly clumps. Crazed eruptions of tiny fibrous pods outnumbered its leaves to such an

216

extent that the tree looked shredded. So eclipsing did her antipathy for this verdant vandal grow that she failed to note: this was more than she had felt towards any living thing, one way or another, since Wyndham's flatline.

A vastly more beguiling tree, to which Wyndham had been partial, their flaming Japanese maple was growing inexplicably lifeless and bare, so Jeannette booked an appointment with a tree surgeon. He wasn't much comfort — "The poor tree's time has come, missus" — but so long as he was at hand, she pointed to the ogre overhead, obnoxiously thriving. "Speaking of trees whose time ought to have come," she said, "what's *that*?"

The surgeon grinned. "A self-seeding sycamore."

The name rang a bell. Wyndham must have mumbled it once or twice. It pained her that her patient husband had eradicated half a million seedlings every spring with so little complaint. What other suffering had he disguised, especially in those last months?

"A volunteer," he went on. "*Nobody* plants a self-seeding sycamore on purpose. It's a pest tree." He looked it up and down, as if measuring it for a coffin. "Three-fifty, and I'll cut it down for you."

The house on her eastern side was owned by a man she gathered from misdelivered post was called Burt Cuss. It was an ugly name, like a one-two punch. Perhaps also in his fifties, he had a hulking, furious bearing, and either he seldom left the house or for extended periods he wasn't there. Sightings were rare. In all seasons, she'd only spotted him in a black crew-neck tee, black jeans, neo-Nazi boots, and a buzz cut. She'd never spoken to him — which should have been unusual, but in London wasn't. She and Wyndham had speculated about their neighbour — as one does. Given the biceps and hard stomach, her husband assessed the man as ex-Army. Jeannette surmised he was divorced. Soon after Burt moved in, he'd burned a pile of papers out the back, in which she'd spied photographs. Irrationally, she was a little afraid of him. If only because they *hadn't* spoken, she rushed inside in the uncommon instance that he ventured into his own garden — if you could call it that.

Burt's garden was subject to near-total neglect. It hadn't been landscaped in the slightest. Other than the malicious sycamore right at the back, its only plant life was scrub grass, which grew a foot high before Burt, no more than twice a year, thwacked it to jaundiced nubs with a scythe. Nearer the house, bits of furniture slumped in the rain. Plastic bags that blew on to the long narrow plot would flap there for weeks.

Most Londoners would have sold their first-borns into slavery for fertile terra firma a fraction of that size, a canvas begging to be painted with azaleas, and in times past the dismal waste ground had aroused her dismay. From the master bedroom on the first floor, she had a panoramic view of this unsightly patch, which might even have dropped adjoining property values a tad. Yet now that she'd seized on the tree surgeon's offer — to be spared that malignancy of seedlings every spring, £350 was a bargain — suddenly her

218

neighbour's obliviousness to horticulture seemed a stroke of good fortune.

In her retired, socially neutral incarnation, Jeannette had to steel herself to interact with anyone; she could go days without saying a word, and even the encounter with the tree surgeon had been draining. She'd lost the knack of small talk. But a firm purpose was fortifying.

It felt odd to knock formally on the front door when she gawked daily at her neighbour's unkempt inner sanctum. The peephole cover swung. Multiple locks.

"Right?" he said gruffly, in the usual uniform. Up close, his eyes were green.

"I'm sorry, we've never been—"

"You're in ninety-two," he cut her off, jerking his head towards her house.

But of course: while you're supposing about neighbours, they're supposing about you. "Jeannette Dickson." He nodded curtly, keeping his own name to himself. "I was hoping we might talk about your tree."

"What about it?" It was astonishing Burt was even aware of having a tree.

"I hate it." No self-respecting Briton had any business harbouring such ferocious feelings about a plant, and she feared she'd cast herself as a kook.

"What'd that tree ever do to you?"

"More than you'd expect," she said, trying to sound reasonable. "Its seedlings. They erupt by the thousands. I spend hours and hours pulling them up."

"Sounds terrible," he said, and the deadpan grated.

"I grant it's not like being strafed by an invading army" — martial imagery was fresh in her mind, and

Wyndham's conjecture that the man was ex-military had morphed from speculation to fact — "though I now have a feel for the experience of being taken over by aliens. The point is, I'd be willing to pay to have it cut down."

"Sounds a bother. What's in it for me?"

A matter to which she had dedicated too little preparatory thought. "You must have at least as bad a problem with seedlings yourself."

"Problem I ain't even noticed can't be much of a problem."

"Well, allowing me to eliminate that tree would be neighbourly. I doubt mine is the only property on this street to which your sycamore is exporting scads of unwanted seedlings, and other homeowners in the area would be grateful as well. We'd both have more light, and your own, ah, *garden* would feel larger and more open." It was the best she could do, on the spot.

"No sale. Rather have my privacy."

She was getting flustered. He stood before her too squarely, blocking the door in an unfriendly fashion, arms folded, forearms rippling. The T-shirt was tight, his pectorals formidable. She wondered how a man who seemed rarely to go outdoors had got that tan. He was a brute, monosyllabic and sullen, nothing like Wyndham, who was tall and lanky, with a sly humour he saved for her; not big on exercise, beyond the pottering, but sinewy, with no waste on him, which made the end come faster, with so few reserves on which to draw. If also not a big talker, he was brilliant, they all said so at the lab, unlike this animal, and when Wyndham did say something he'd made it count.

"My tree surgeon says no one would deliberately plant such a 'pest tree'—"

"*Your* tree surgeon?"

"Why's that funny?"

"I don't even have a GP."

"What I meant was, that's the opinion of an expert."

"Darling," Burt said. "I been through this rigmarole before, and you lot got your answer. Ask your husband."

The surprises were two: that this neighbour had done only nominal supposing about the residents of number ninety-two, having failed to notice its population had halved; and that Wyndham had tried to negotiate this very solution, to no avail.

"I'm afraid my husband passed away, eighteen months ago." Ergo, *here I am, still grieving, and I'm spending all my time ripping up your flipping seedlings.*

But Burt didn't easily embarrass. "Tough luck," he said dispassionately.

"Could you consider my proposal? I'd make all the arrangements. Please? As a favour. It would mean so much to me."

"Lady, I spent seventeen years doing *favours* for a bird not so different from yourself, and in the end it didn't mean nothing to her at all."

He shut the door in her face. Confirmation: divorced.

The following few days, Jeannette spent more than one tiresome afternoon in a state of suppressed rage, grumbling about that prick next door while prising single sycamore seedlings from a busy cover of woodbine, something like plucking individual grey hairs from a heavy beard with tweezers. Meantime, incredibly, seedlings she'd already uprooted and left to wither were still struggling their wounded roots back into the bark cover and once again obeying their prime directive to become Earth's most odious trees. Good God, it was like watching privates who'd had their limbs blown off drag bloody torsos across the battlefield and pick up guns with their teeth.

Yet when Jeannette peered discreetly over the party wall, she could not discern, in Burt's foot-high scrub grass, *any seedlings at all*. The immunity was biologically infeasible.

Armed with a sheaf of printouts, she knocked on Burt's door for Round Two.

"Don't tell me," he said. "I'm to dismantle my upper floor, so you get more sun in your sitting room."

"It's all over the internet." Jeannette brandished the sheaf. "On blogs, social media, on botanical websites. Everyone detests those trees. Even in forests, they take over and destroy the habitat—"

"Speaking of trees," he interrupted, giving her a onceover. "You've *spruced up*."

She blushed. True, ever since Wyndham died she'd been rather careless in the sartorial department, and this afternoon had taken advantage of a snappy wardrobe from years as a Debenhams buyer who was encouraged to bring home samples. The hasty makeover was merely more strategy: to be presentable, to seem together and sane, a neighbour anyone would want to please. So, fine: she'd washed her hair.

"They're not even native to Britain," Jeannette carried on. "It's an invasive species from the Continent. Sycamores have only been here a few hundred years."

"The toffs on *Downton Abbey* have only been in Britain 'a few hundred years'."

Jeannette frowned. "You don't seem like the costume drama type."

"So what do I seem like?"

Awkwardness made her honest. "Someone who does loads of press-ups."

That won her a half-smile, a first, perhaps a prelude to a full smile, which she precluded by pressing her case. "If you'd simply take a look at these . . ." She held out the sheets of A4. "There's a uniform consensus . . . We'd be doing a community service."

"You're a terrier, you are. Know the type. Just wear you down. Don't work no more, not on me."

Before he had a chance to shut the door again, she burst out, "Nearly half of that tree is on my side of the property line. I've checked with the council: I'm within my legal rights to cut off any of that sycamore that's sticking over the wall!"

He shrugged and said, "Be my guest," perhaps missing her parting shot, "It'll look ridiculous!" As if he cared.

Unfortunately, when she contacted the tree surgeon again, allowing that the actual owner of the sycamore was uncooperative, he turned down the radical pruning job by text: *Dodgy in evry wy. Physicly difficlt + any idea hw ugly disputes ovr evn wee shrbs in ths cntry gt, btw neibrs? Rd th papr? Ppl gt killd ovr less! Stying out of it.*

Very well. But she was not simply rolling over. The alternative was year upon numbing year, toiling away as an ever more elderly pensioner in the gardening equivalent of the salt mines to strip away another crop of seedlings, budding with idiot hopefulness, perking and poking and flopping about with garish green naïveté. Unless she took a stand, each year her futile Sisyphean extermination would be undertaken in a spirit of submission and impotence.

First off, she would demonstrate the extent of what Burt refused to label a problem. Thus after yet another mass murder of seedlings by the log store — an empty structure that made her feel wistful and remiss, for she hadn't reordered fuel for the wood burner, around which she and Wyndham had lingered through many a toasty winter evening — Jeannette gathered the hairy pile of crushed blades and dangling taproots, marched to Burt's front door, and deposited the offering on his step with a note: "Sorry, I believe these belong to you." Within minutes — he could have heard her scuttle away, and she was braced for a blast of blue invective — a belly laugh carried to her patio, round, resonant, and loose.

Jeannette rifled the tool shed the next morning. Even if Wyndham had kept a chainsaw, which it seems he didn't, she'd have been too afraid of the monstrosity to use it. But she did dig out a long trusty handsaw, whose rudimentary technology she understood, and which in a moment of inattention was unlikely to amputate her arm. Besides, the identifying "rip-cut teeth cross-cut" on its cardboard sleeve sounded suitably violent.

The sky-blue shorts with decorative pockets she wore for the project that afternoon were sensible for a warm spell in June, though they were nearly new, and showed off legs little veined and rather shapely for a woman her age. The crisp yellow crop top was also airy and cool; at Debenhams, she'd always maintained that good styling needn't be impractical. Drawing the sword of vengeance from its scabbard, she climbed from bench to wall, then scrambled on to the roof of the log store (already shaggy with helicopter seedpods, lying in wait for next year). From here she enjoyed ready access to a fat lower branch of the sycamore, right where it thrust presumptuously across her property. Gripping the branch with her other hand for balance, she traced a cut with the tips of the teeth a few daring inches into Burt Cuss's scruffy domain. The blade juddered.

By the time she'd established a starter notch, she was sweating; the yellow crop top would soon be a write-off. A handsaw seemed unfitting for green wood, which continually grabbed at its teeth and brought each wobbly stroke to a standstill. After half an hour of rasping, and stopping to catch her breath, she'd got not an inch through a branch whose diameter ran to half a foot, and whose demeanour remained placid, if not contemptuous. At this rate, she'd be sawing sycamore branches in all weathers for the next year. Already, her upper arm ached, and she'd developed a blister on her right forefinger.

What she needed was the smallest symbolic satisfaction. That meant removing one full branch to start with — much more doable if she climbed further up into the tree to attack a higher, thinner limb. Aiming for a vulnerable-looking bough ten feet overhead, Jeannette dusted off skills from a tomboy childhood, planting a pink plimsoll firmly into the Y where the branch at which she'd hacked so ineffectually met the trunk.

Goodness, she must have been a brave little girl. When ascending many a tree to nearly its summit on family holidays in the Lake District, she didn't remember feeling this terrified. Executing a few more shaky manoeuvres, struggling both to pull herself up and to keep hold of the saw, Jeannette remembered from painting the loo ceiling during the first footloose fortnight of retirement: fear destroys balance. Committed to this folly, she decided it was good to keep forcing yourself to do something hard, even if that was the sort of *Saga*-style resolution that marked you as decrepit. By the time she'd hoisted herself to within striking distance of the target branch, she was getting her confidence — or at least she'd stopped shaking.

Braced against the trunk, she got purchase on the bough — nevertheless two inches thick. Her elbow kept running into a branch behind her, preventing a full stroke. The project grew so consumingly tedious that she lost all trace of vertigo. At last she made headway: the cut opened up from the weight of the flagging bough. With a crack, the bottom remnant splintered. What a pity that she'd been keeping steady by gripping the severed side of the branch.

He kept the sitting room dark, with curtains drawn, though on a long summer's day it was still bright at 9 p.m.

"I should really go home," she said weakly from the sofa.

"Rubbish, you can't walk," Burt said, bringing whisky. "Keep that leg elevated."

There was the broken ankle, a cracked rib, a sprained right wrist, and naturally she was pretty scratched up. "Mortified" didn't begin to cover it.

He wasn't ex-Army, but a medic for the Red Cross, who flew out at a moment's notice to Haiti or Sierra Leone. A medic certainly made for a more providential neighbour than a retired women's clothing buyer who was a fool. The moment she fell, he had streaked out, then crudely splinted her ankle with duct tape and sections of the *Independent* (not, as she'd have expected, *The Sun*). At a lope, he carried her several streets to their local clinic. Those expert administrations as she woozed in his overgrown grass were hazy, but she did remember the black T-shirt bunched under her head, its distinctive musk, and the bumpy journey to the clinic was vivid. Jeannette hadn't felt the clasp of a man's arms for nineteen months. Pain or no, the sensation was thrilling.

Burt interrupted her reverie about the many daily activities this former "social neutrality" would now have trouble doing for herself. "You'll need help. Got kids?"

"No," Jeannette said. "Wyndham and I did not *self-seed*." The shorts were soiled, silly and too exposing, and she was grateful for the sheet he'd brought her, even in the heat.

"I feel part responsible," he said, nipping at his drink. "Should have stopped you when I first spotted you climbing that wall. With a *handsaw*, for fuck's sake. Figured I'd let you learn your lesson. Thought it was funny."

"I suppose it *was* funny."

"So what was the plan? You'd never have lopped more than a branch or two."

"Over time, I was hoping to cut off enough to kill it."

"But what's so bloody important about a few little plants? You're bigger than them."

"*Few?*" She turned away, groping, unsure of the why of it herself. "I told you, I hate them. So mindlessly cheerful and impossible to discourage. Just starting out in life. Willing to give it a go, even in bark chips. Then the mess of them. They're rioting, insane. Running roughshod over all my husband's tending and discipline. Invading, uninvited, *out of control*. And I feel an obligation to honour Wyndham's creation, *in memoriam*, to not let the garden go to hell in a handbasket on my watch. I only found out recently how much effort a garden is, how much work he must have

228

done, which I was blithely unaware of, or even scoffed at. Besides. Also. There's something horrible. The replication. The burgeoning is grotesque. I can kill them in the thousands, but I still won't win over them as a mass. I know they're so much smaller than I, but together, as a profusion, they're bigger, and they make me feel helpless and defeated all over again." It was the fatigue, and shock, and the blurring of the painkillers, but the plethora of personification must have verified the verdict: without question, a kook.

"And you?" she added feebly. "What's so important about that tree? I haven't sensed any love lost."

"Had my fill of female wilfulness, I reckon," he said. "Wilfulness begets wilfulness. Spirals, and never ends well."

"Doesn't it?" she asked with a smile, as he freshened a drink they both knew conflicted with the advisory on her prescription.

After sharing his takeaway, he insisted she settle for the night on his sofa. She slept hard and long, stirring only at a loud, high-pitched buzz outside. The council, ironically, must have been finally pruning the London planes along the pavement.

Rising at midday with chagrin, Jeannette hobbled with her NHS crutch out of the back double doors. She knew her way around. The houses on this stretch were identical.

Right at the back, Burt was splitting the last of the big logs, using the stump of the self-seeding sycamore as a chopping block. In wonderment, she could see through the slats: rising on her side of the party wall, the log store was nearly full, its contents neatly stacked. An offering — or was it a proposal? As she approached, he remembered to put on his chainsaw's safety catch. Off to the right, fat fluffy twigs of felled pod clusters piled bonfire high.

After landing a decisive blow on the wedge with his sledgehammer, Burt announced gruffly, "Sycamore seasons fast, and burns hot."

"If Wyndham is to be believed," she returned, "so do I."

When he was not away treating cholera patients, they would recline in the glow of incinerating sycamore in her wood burner, watching the concluding Christmas special of *Downton Abbey*, and later the repeats — though Burt drew the line at *Poldark*, which he ridiculed as a sappy bodice-ripper, and she accused him of being jealous of the lead. They would stay in separate houses; the arrangement maintained a courtliness, an asking, that they came to cherish. Every spring, the seedlings returned. According to the Royal Horticultural Society website, the sycamore lays a seed bed that will recrudesce for years. But it had laid her own bed also. *Nature abhors a vacuum.*

The Orphan Exchange

Audrey Niffenegger

When I was ten years old my mother and father died in the war and I was sent to the local Orphan Exchange. We lived in a small city in the north of the country and this Orphan Exchange was not a prosperous or well-situated institution. It stood by itself in a narrow valley that was prone to flooding, lacked protective trees and was vulnerable to passing planes and drones. Its original patrons were generous but as time went on they had been replaced by others whose charity was less open-handed and more self-satisfied. Then the war came and everything became scarce. I do not really remember the time before the war, but I dream about it occasionally. In the dreams I have something sweet to eat, perhaps a ripe peach or a little cake, and I eat and eat and no one disturbs me; I eat until I wake, still unsatisfied.

I arrived at the Orphan Exchange on a winter night in the back of a jeep. The building was strangely beautiful in the dark; bombs had chewed its upper storeys so that it stood massive and black with lacy edges against the starry night sky. Tallow lamps lit a few windows. The girls were in bed and the NGO worker who'd brought me handed me over to the matron quietly, as though I was contraband, and left without a backward glance. The matron led me by flashlight into the gymnasium, which was full of cots; I wondered if the whole school slept here. I later discovered that there were dormitories but on the night I arrived there had been a plague of rats upstairs and the girls had all been granted the special favour of sleeping in the gym. I was given a cot and thin bedding and left alone with eighty unfamiliar girls who breathed quietly or harshly in the cold gym. I lay awake for a long time listening to them before falling into wary intermittent sleep.

In daylight the Orphan Exchange was a bomb-crumbled mess, patched and jerry-rigged with any old thing. Some rooms had blue tarpaulin ceilings, some had plastic where windows should have been. In the classrooms during lessons the sound of water dripping could always be heard, even if it hadn't rained, and the plaster walls and ceilings bubbled and bulged.

Breakfast that first morning was nasty burned porridge and all the girls ate a bite or two and then put down their spoons. The girl sitting next to me whispered that the food was always horrible, "almost inedible and never enough". I was used to hunger but this seemed to be a policy of the school, that we should not have enough of the terrible stale bread or fake orange juice to ever satisfy us. I was small for my age and the portions were too little even for me; the older girls often got desperate and stole food from us younger girls. Later that day a tall girl took my lunch, which was half an apple and a piece of hard cheese. I ran after her, grabbed her arm and twisted until she cried out and dropped my food. Then I stepped on her foot as hard as I could and went off to sit by myself. I ate quickly and glared at anyone who came near me.

The Orphan Exchange was not impressive and I was not impressed. But it didn't matter what I thought about it because I had nowhere else to be. I was not an endearing child. My mother's brother's wife was my only living relative and she didn't want me. The other girls were in similar straits. It was better not to ask a girl why she was there. We were all curious and superstitious so it was OK if someone told you her story but not OK to ask. You might bring her bad luck on to yourself if you asked. Mr Brocklehurst, the superintendent, might send you on a bad exchange, or you might fall ill. The girls there were constantly sick: typhus, TB and pneumonia haunted the Orphan Exchange.

Our hair was cut short as a defence against lice and vanity. They cut my hair on the second day and I cried a little because it had been the only pretty thing about me. I was small and plain; if I wasn't smiling people asked me *What's wrong?* so that I seemed to be complaining even if I was only wondering what was for dinner. All my long black braids fell to the floor and the matron gathered them to sell to the wig makers. Nothing was ever wasted then.

After my hair had been sacrificed and I had dried my tears I went like a little shorn dark lamb to find my classroom. I had tested far above my grade level in reading, history and writing. Both of my parents were university professors, our flat was full of books and none had been denied me. Ms Temple, the headmistress, tested me in her small chilly office and when I put down my pencil she said, "You still have half an hour left," and picked up my test paper. She looked at it, looked at me, and gave me a different (and somewhat more difficult) test. When I handed that one to her she raised her eyebrows and gave me a third test, which gave me a little trouble.

Ms Temple said, "If I place you at this level you will be with the oldest girls in the school. Would you rather be with girls your own age?"

"I would rather not be bored," I said.

She smiled and wrote a note and sealed it in an envelope. She wrote a room number on the envelope and said, "You may join the first class. Give this to Ms Scatcherd."

So I was searching for this room, envelope in hand. Sometimes I dream about this moment: I am standing in the long dismal hallway, all the other girls are in class, I hear the murmur of lessons. I put my hand on the doorknob and hesitate, because inside the classroom a woman suddenly shouts, "You stupid, stupid girl! Stand there, I don't want to hear another word."

In the dream I always wake up before I can see her. But that day I opened the door and saw a girl standing calmly at the front of the class, gazing over the heads of the students with a slight smile on her face. It was an inward-directed smile, as though she could see something pleasant the rest of us could not. She was tall and very pale blonde and though we were all dressed the same, in grey wool and black cotton, she looked as though she had chosen these clothes, as though she was an actress playing the part of an orphan and when the scene was over she would laugh and have a coffee and a cigarette and flirt with the director of the movie, of which she was obviously the heroine.

I walked to the front of the class and handed my envelope to the teacher, who read Ms Temple's note and waved me to a seat at the back. I watched the girl standing there smiling to herself until the bell rang and we all filed out of the classroom and went to our meagre lunch.

Afterwards we were shooed outdoors into the frozen rubble-strewn yard that had once been a garden. I found the disgraced girl sitting in a niche in the garden wall, out of sight of the break monitor. She was reading a book.

I stood near her and she ignored me. "What are you reading?" I asked.

"A book," she answered without looking up.

"Which one?"

She handed it to me. It was in Russian. I gave it back to her.

"Where are you from?" I asked.

"You ask too many questions."

"OK." I turned to go.

"What's your name?" she asked.

"Jane."

"Mine is Helen. How old are you?"

"Ten."

"I am fourteen. I came here six years ago."

"Before the war?"

"It was a real school then."

"And you've been here all this time? You weren't exchanged?"

"I was exchanged, but then I was sent back here, and no one has asked for me since then." She smiled but her expression was grim.

I did not understand the nature of the exchanges then, so I pretended that I knew what she meant. But she saw that I didn't know. "You're too young," said Helen. "They won't send you anywhere for a while yet."

"Where do they send us?"

Helen shrugged. "Different places. I was sent to a pharmaceutical company, to be a guinea pig. But my father got upset when I wasn't here, and they had to return me."

"If you have a father why are you here and not at home?"

"My mother died and my father remarried. His new wife didn't want me there, so here I am." The bell rang and Helen stood up. "Are you coming?"

"Helen, wait — why do they send us? What do they get in exchange?"

"I don't know, Jane. Don't ask so many questions."

I followed her back to class.

In the afternoon it was as though nothing unusual had happened in the morning: Helen sat in the second row and the teacher joked with her and the other students. I discovered as the days went on that it was not out of the ordinary for this teacher to lose her temper, and the girls regarded her as mercurial but interesting; they bore her eccentricities patiently.

"Why do you let her treat you that way?" I asked Helen a few weeks later. "Why are they all so cruel?" It was break and we were sitting in the cold yard, on the steps of the ruined terrace. There were signs of spring: trickles of water inside the walls of the building, a change in the air. By then I was somewhat resigned to the routines of the Orphan Exchange. But I didn't understand why the teachers were so erratic or why several of them had singled Helen out for extra abuse. That morning Ms Scatcherd had beaten Helen on the shoulders with a switch; she accused Helen of "day-dreaming". I was holding a snowball against the welts now, trying to alleviate the swelling.

"Perhaps they don't get enough to eat, either," said Helen. "Ms Scatcherd is always more sane after lunch."

"But why is she so mean to you? You're one of the best students. You never give her any trouble."

"I think the teachers are angry with me. Or afraid? No one ever came back from an exchange before, and they know they can't get rid of me now because my father would find out."

"But why are they afraid?" I asked. "Was it so bad?"

"It was strange, but not too bad. We had better food there. I think they were testing cold medicine; they kept giving me nasal sprays. But I was only gone for a week, and the drug trial I was assigned to was supposed to go on for a year. So I never found out exactly what they gave me and they didn't explain anything." Helen reached over to take the snowball from me. She added fresh snow and handed it back. "That feels good." The bell rang, Helen covered her shoulders and we went back to class.

As spring came, conditions improved at the Orphan Exchange. There were food deliveries from newly reconquered territories in the southlands. We were given vitamins and aid workers arrived with powdered milk and books. My hair grew out slowly (never before or after that time have my hair and fingernails grown so slowly!) and I felt a little more familiar to myself.

But something was wrong with Helen. She had a fever and a headache, she was tired; then a weird rash appeared on her face and spread all over her body. One morning she threw up her breakfast.

"You have to go to the infirmary," I said.

Helen shook her head. "Better not," she said.

But I made her go. We stood at the door of the infirmary. It had once been a kitchen and though the ovens and refrigerators had been removed to another part of the building and beds and medical equipment stood at rigid angles to the walls, there were still traces — the fume hood, the hatch for passing plates from kitchen to servers — that somehow gave a suggestion of cannibalism in the accidental conjunction of the culinary and the medical.

Helen and I stood in the corridor peering through the narrow window in the door. Helen knocked and for a while no one answered. Eventually the nurse came up behind us and we jumped as though we'd been caught misbehaving.

When the nurse saw that it was Helen she said, "Come in, quickly," and then she stopped me as I tried to follow. "Are you sick, too?" she asked.

"I don't think so," I said.

"Go back to class, then, we'll take care of your friend."

I protested but finally Helen said, "Go ahead, Jane, I'll be OK." So I left her there.

Perhaps I only imagined that the teachers conspired to keep me away from Helen. After class I tried to go to the infirmary but the maths teacher demanded that I go over a test we'd taken three days before; then it was time for dinner and then Ms Temple asked me to run an errand for her. I went to bed in a doubtful frame of mind. When all the girls were at last asleep I crept out of the dormitory and made my way in my nightgown, barefoot through the cold corridors, terrified. When I came to the infirmary the nurse wasn't there and there was only one other girl, a very young child who slept tightly curled in her crib, her thumb half in her mouth.

Helen was sitting up in bed. Even in the half-light I could see that her face was covered in red blotches. I climbed in with her and she drew the covers over both of us. She was feverish; I went and brought her a cold pack and got back into bed.

"Don't leave me, Jane," she said.

"I won't," I whispered. We fell asleep spooned together like little cats.

I woke up in my own bed the next morning.

I dressed hurriedly and ran to see Helen before breakfast. Her bed was empty and the other girl was still asleep. The nurse came in wearing her coat and gloves, followed by Ms Temple.

"Where is she?" I cried.

"She's gone," said Ms Temple.

"She's dead?"

Ms Temple hesitated. "Yes. I'm so sorry, Jane."

"But where is she?"

"We sent her back to her family."

And that was that. Helen was gone. I grieved her stubbornly, publicly, slowly. Years went by and my grief became private and steady. The war dragged on.

When I was fifteen I was exchanged. I was lucky: instead of being a guinea pig like Helen had been, or a sex worker or a scullery maid like some other girls, I was sent to an enormous house in the middle of nowhere to be an au pair for a girl named Adele who spoke only French. The dad was seldom at home and the mum was ill; she was kept in seclusion in a suite at the top of the house and I was warned not to speak to her. It was a strange household but the servants were kind and there was an enormous library; Adele and I used to spend days there reading, drawing, eating cheese and fruit and junk food (Pringles, Snickers, Coke — the dad had connections, I had never seen so much decadent food). We spoke mostly French and I even managed to become a little plump. It was easy to forget that half the world was trying to annihilate the other half. We seldom saw drones there; the sky was empty and huge. Time passed, the war sputtered out and finally ended, Adele grew up and was about to go to university and I found myself free and at my own disposal for the first time in my life.

I owned nothing, but Adele wrote me a reference and signed her dad's name. She gave me enough money to get by for a little while. I stuffed a backpack with food and left feeling pleasantly unencumbered.

I took a train to the city I had lived in as a child. It was barely recognisable to me; none of my old landmarks had survived. It was wonderful to walk in the city by myself under the midday sky without fear. I found a bombed house in our old neighbourhood that had a few intact rooms and I slept there. Every day I walked around the city, knowing I ought to look for work but reluctant to speak to anyone. On the third day I was walking near the devastated business district when someone called my name.

I turned and it was Helen. Beautiful Helen, confident Helen — she was ravaged now, disease had made her old, had robbed her of her golden hair and her clear skin, she was pocked and stooped — but she was my Helen and she was alive.

For a moment I was too surprised to react and I saw that she was ashamed and thought I didn't recognise her. Then I ran to her and embraced her and we cried.

We bought coffee and buns from a food truck and sat together on a bench in a park. "What happened?" I asked.

"They were testing biological weapons," said Helen. "They gave me smallpox and then my father wanted me returned to the Orphan Exchange and they gave me the antidote, but it didn't quite work. That's why the teachers didn't want me there. So when I got sick I was sent back to the lab, because I was contagious." Helen sighed. "I'm so relieved to see you, I was afraid I might have infected you."

"I'm OK. I guess I was lucky."

"I thought they were testing cold remedies." She looked away. "Am I hideous, Jane?"

"Not to me."

"Liar."

"Helen," I said, "did you ever find out — what did they exchange us for? What did they get? Money? Food?"

She said, "All they got was protection. I mean, in exchange for us, the place did not get bombed. So the other girls were protected in exchange for a few of us being handed over to the horror show."

"So they got nothing in exchange for us."

"Or everything — life."

"You are so calm about it." My eyes welled with tears.

"I'm alive. So are you." She leaned over and kissed me. I kissed her back.

We had found each other and we stayed together. We got boring jobs, we moved into a tiny flat above a bakery and we made a home together. When it eventually became legal, Reader, I married her. It was enough; it is enough. We walk together in the evenings through the peaceful city, hand in hand, not speaking much, moving slowly, our thoughts drifting until it is time to turn towards home. My Helen. I wouldn't exchange her for anything in the world.

Double Men

Namwali Serpell

A friendship that fails to negotiate dogs and chickens is doomed to wither, even a friendship that has weathered decades of hardship and tedium. Mama Lota and Nanjela had raised children together; performed birth and death rites in tandem; carried loads, light and heavy, as one. Now that there were no men left in their households, they depended on each other, hooked their everydays, the tasks of tending to body and home. In a small field, they grew enough greens, beans, potatoes, cassava, yams, groundnuts and maize to feed themselves, and kept the surplus in Mama Lota's storehouse. They gave the damaged but edible leftovers to widows even less fortunate than they.

Mama Lota bought the dogs because the storehouse had been robbed again. This time, she'd caught them in the act. She'd burst through the door with furious shouts, her *chitenge* haphazard, her barely-there hair uncovered, light spoking erratically from the lantern she held aloft. The boys fled, crawling from her hailstorm, except for one boy who, Mama Lota speculated later to Nanjela, must have been raised by a bitter woman who beat him too hard and too often. His lackeys scurried pitiably around him but this boy alone stood, lengthening up like a thread of smoke, his fist wrapped around a stone Mama Lota had thrown. He spat and threw it back. It struck her above her left eye, knocked her over, knocked her out and turned her eyebrow into a red smear that healed later into a purple cross, which everyone said made sense since her husband, long deceased, had been a pastor.

Those thieving boys had broken in through the one small window in the storehouse across from the locked entrance. When Mama Lota toppled across the threshold, they ran away through the door she'd burst through, ran right over her body, their pockets and hands full of all they planned to sell. And just for the sake of it, they stole the lantern that had tumbled from her hand.

This was why Mama Lota had sent her nephew to purchase the Doberman Pinschers. Not because of the stolen food, nor the requited stone, nor even the wound it had opened. It was this pettiness of taking her lamp, which her husband had received as a boy from a *muzungu* hunter he'd fetched game for, and which he had polished every night of their marriage, whistling pleasantly through the gap in his front teeth. Mama Lota liked to remember him this way: nearby, his mouth and hands occupied. And now the glass and metal thing that reminded her of a lost person — it, too, was gone.

"They can't even use it," Mama Lota complained in her high, soft voice as she poured Nanjela a cup of tea a few days later. "Where will they find the paraffin?"

"Heysh, these boys," Nanjela replied in a trembly baritone, glancing at the bandage over her friend's eye.

They were in Mama Lota's kitchen, sitting on a pair of rickety chairs inherited from the church when Pastor Chisongo died. The women watched the steam untangle above their teacups, shaking their heads at the old, familiar nightmare: able-bodied males with nothing to lose.

A ferocious noise scraped through the window — a snarling, snatching sound. Nanjela started. The dogs were quarrelling. "But is it good to have these . . . doublemen around?" She shuddered. "They're like demons."

"The Doberman breed is good for protection. I picked the angriest ones!" Mama Lota smiled, then frowned. "I'm not going to suffer for some stupid child who throws stones at his elders. And just *takes*." She sucked her teeth.

"I don't know," Nanjela shook her head. "I think they're eating our chickens."

The Dobermans were indeed rapacious. They had rather sensibly begun to supplement the leftovers Mama Lota gave them with mice and birds and snakes — and yes, the occasional chicken from the coop behind the storehouse. The fonder they became of her, the more broken little corpses would the two young dogs lay at Mama Lota's feet. She'd pick the carrion gifts off her steps with a grimace and scold the grinning beasts. "Foolish monkeys," she'd frown, then smile, patting them on their warm, flat, black foreheads as they wagged the knots where their tails had been.

But they were not foolish. That was a sentimental view to take about such vicious creatures. Nanjela discovered just how vicious the very next morning. She had gone to visit Mama Lota to plan the bonding ceremony, the elaborate two-week affair that would preface the wedding. Nanjela's daughter, Nayendi, was to marry Mama Lota's nephew, Lukundo. The old friends were finally going to join their families. This was the wedding for which they had been saving chickens.

As Nanjela headed to Mama Lota's that fateful morning, she tried to consider the match objectively. After Nayendi had graduated with top marks from her boarding school, she'd taken a position at a bank in town. It was a prestigious but lonely job, one that had soon forced the girl to reach out for companionship. A distant cousin, Mary, had introduced Nayendi to Lukundo, who had dropped out of school to work as a mechanic. Only after they had fallen in love had they realised that his aunty and her mother were the closest of friends. At least this is what cousin Mary, the matchmaker, claimed. Nanjela wasn't sure how far to trust this relative, with her underwear for clothing and make-up like a badly iced cake. But Nanjela couldn't deny that Nayendi had done well to find such a handsome, prosperous husband. And what a boon that he was Mama Lota's nephew!

"*Odi!* Anybody home?"

Mama Lota's metal gate, peppered with rust holes, whistled in the breeze. Beyond it, nothing stirred but for a pair of doves in the avocado tree, deep in a saddest song competition. Mama Lota, a late riser, was

248

probably still asleep. Nanjela opened the gate and stepped quietly towards the house to wake her. Then she saw, and remembered, the new dogs. They were untied, dozing by the door, the red dust around them scoured with paw prints. One stirred, an ear snapping up like a sail, then down again. Nanjela closed her eyes, crossed herself thrice, and recited a prayer to her ancestors. When she opened her eyes, both dogs had risen, eyes and teeth glinting, ears at full mast.

Nanjela turned and ran. The dogs leapt after her. They did not bark and she did not scream and the morning was eerily quiet as she raced back through Mama Lota's gate and down the road. She was lurching through her own gate when one of the dogs yanked at her wrapper. Shouting *"Futsek!"* she slammed the gate across his body. He yelped and darted back, her wrapper still hanging from his jaws, dragging in the dust. She locked the gate and backed away from the wooden slats, which shook with the force of the doubleman throwing himself against it.

Reduced to her underwear and her heartbeat, Nanjela stumbled inside. Trembling, she bathed and changed into a new wrapper. She sat for a while and prayed. She tried to continue her day: cooking, eating, sewing Nayendi's white wedding dress, cooking, eating, sleeping. But when she rose the next morning, a picture rose with her: the dogs, silent furies; her small body struggling at the gate; the dragging *chitenge*; her white bloomers incandescent with shame.

She sat on her veranda, listlessly washing her feet. She could feel rather than see the sun emerging behind the smoke from the charcoal pits. Birds snipped the morning quiet into ribbons of sound. Women with buckets of water on their heads drifted down the road, chatting softly. Mothers and daughters. Nanjela watched them bitterly. Her own daughter was coming home today. The bonding ceremony would begin, and she and Mama Lota would become sisters. But none of this eased her. Nanjela felt sure everyone had seen, that the story of her bloomers was spinning through the village, gathering laughter. If only the dog had killed her. Or bitten her leg. Better pity than jokes.

She might have laughed it off herself if she'd been able to sit with her friend and drink tea and talk it over. But they were all too busy with the thrum of the imminent wedding. In a few hours, Nanjela would have to dress up to meet her future son-in-law, who would kneel before her, offering food in exchange for her wisdom. She had in fact already met Lukundo, a few weeks ago, staggering insouciantly as Mama Lota's demonic dogs pulled him along, straining at their leashes. Lukundo was tall like his aunty, and wore town clothes so casual they had to be expensive. He had a smattering of pimple scars and one of those big, shiny smiles that made Nanjela shake her head. Yes, indeed. Nayendi had done well for herself.

Nayendi, with her terrible, indisputable goodness! Nanjela felt a pang for the little girl she'd once had — the naughty busybody who had once set fire to the curtains, just to see. That was long ago, though, long before Nayendi had started carrying herself like a new wife, doing all her chores, saving her small moneys for

250

school fees. Nanjela knew this undue rectitude had to do with her first-born daughter Anjela, who had renamed her mother for life, only to die of tuberculosis. Such a slight. A cough, a spot of blood. Sorrow. It was after her sister died that Nayendi had started trying to be two daughters in one. But there was something arrogant — wasn't there? — in the idea that she could be enough for her mother, could make up for the hole that Anjela's death had made in Nanjela's chest, a hole like a hole in the ground too big to fill, a hole you could only ever cover up and maybe make a trap with.

There she was now, the perfect daughter, standing by the gate, waiting for Nanjela instead of shouting into the yard like any other relative. Nayendi was wearing a decent skirt suit that had somehow escaped the dust from the road. She had always managed to avoid the dirt, even as a child. Goodness, but Nayendi was pretty now, her skin smooth and reddish like groundnut skin. It was nearly almost tiring how decent and pretty she was. Although the smile Nanjela hid behind her hand as she walked towards her daughter was genuine, her spirits sank when she saw the leather suitcase at Nayendi's side: brown and spotless and just the right size. It was nearly almost unbearable.

And so when Nayendi tried on her wedding dress for the very first time, its maker, her mother, was not with her as she turned like a fan in front of the spotted mirror. Mama Lota was with her instead. The older woman could barely make out the girl's serious face and the dress, a thin white cloud. It was dark in Mama Lota's bedroom, the avocado tree outside the window casting a thick weave of shadow within. Nayendi squinted, stepping forward to evaluate herself. Sighing at what she saw, she glanced back up to her neatly cornrowed hair, and only then did she seem to notice Mama Lota's face hovering over her shoulder in the mirror.

Mama Lota smiled, but only to let the girl know she was not alone. Mama Lota disliked looking in the mirror, much less smiling into it. One of her eyes always drooped and the hitch of her smile puckered the wrong cheek. It felt thin, too, her smile, more so today because something was missing. Nanjela. Why was her old friend brooding? Nanjela wasn't lingering at meals or flattering the in-laws. She'd declined to advise the couple, refused to help with the cooking. When Mama Lota asked her, "What is happening here?" Nanjela demurred sulkily. She would leave the bonding ceremony to Mama Lota.

"I'm old. I'm tired," she said. "I just want to take care of the grandchildren."

"*Ah-ah!* And what about your own daughter? Who will take care of her?"

And here was her answer, Mama Lota thought, peering at the nervous ghost in the mirror. Nayendi. Still a child practically, the hunger in her eyes like a baby eyeing a nipple. The bride looked at the reflection of Mama Lota's eyes and began to explain about the Western-style dress. Mama Lota laughed and took the girl by the shoulders and turned her around so they could see each other truly. "Nayendi, Nayendi. My husband was a pastor. I know all about white dresses!"

252

There was a knock on the door. A child came in and knelt down and breathlessly declared: "They're here." Mama Lota hastened from the room, closing the door behind her, leaving Nayendi to change out of the white dress into the *chitenge* outfit she'd wear for the traditional ceremonies.

Tonight, there'd be a feast! Mama Lota thrilled. Chickens to be plucked! Groundnuts to be shelled! Thumbs to be recruited! Mama Lota was electric with the stuff of preparation. She felt as though she were in charge of a fleet of *kapenta* canoes, accounting for the wind and the waves, shouting orders for boats to be washed and nets to be gathered and bait lights to be lit. All those slippery silvery fish would tumble into their laps, eventually, even if they lost a few in the mud. She would see even those, would scoop up even those, feed them to her lovely new dogs. Yes, Mama Lota had always kept her eye on everyone and everything. Perhaps it came with being so tall.

And yet she barely noticed when her nephew Lukundo left the candlelit living room that dusky evening just as the final ceremony began. A dozen married couples, ranging in age from thirty to eighty, were sitting in a circle around the couple kneeling on the floor. The experienced spouses were all nodding their heads like flowers in a rain shower, concurring with the advice that intoned from one corner of the room or another. In the gentle lull of consensus, Mama Lota hardly blinked when Lukundo hunched his way out of the room. Probably going to the outhouse, she thought, fingering the scab on her eyebrow, still damp at the edges and smelling like an *ngwe* coin. Mama Lota tried to focus as an old man droned on about the importance of sharing, no matter how little you have. Even when there is only one peanut left, the man said, even a peanut can be halved.

Meanwhile, as these parables echoed on without her, Nanjela was keeping her promise to care for the grandchildren. She stalked the yards of the adjacent houses, yanking toddlers out of danger, pushing the little monsters off each other, spanking those too slow or too stupid to get away. It was exhausting. She'd only ever had two daughters, and the chaos of even these three children, for instance, each arguing a different version of who'd done what to whom and why, was too much. Was there no one who had been watching, no one who could tell her what had really happened? The children shrugged. Nanjela sent them off to bed, shaking her head at their lunacy.

She floated along the edges of the yard, avoiding the elders and the children, avoiding the dogs and her daughter's hungry eyes. Night fell. Under the trees, moonlight lay like the tatters of a veil. Nanjela found herself near the storehouse. Broken glass from the robbery still lay on the ground, the splinters flashing broken light. A dim yellowish glow gaped from the hole where the window had been. Had those thieving boys returned? She could hear nothing but the grating sound of insects courting each other. Nanjela moved closer, stood on her tiptoes and peered in through the blank window. The first thing she saw was a disc of light quivering on the floor. It was an electric torch, and something was moving violently beside it.

The insects creaked on and the wind picked up and Nanjela stared and stared until she made out a head bobbing in and out of the light. She had been looking for half a minute when a sobbing sound rose up and a shadow shifted and the thin shiny seam of a hair-weave glistened like a snake. It was Mary. The man shifted — the rocking lovers were seated, facing each other now — and Nanjela caught a glimpse of his back, still studded with the pimples he'd managed to clear from his face. Idiot boy, Nanjela spat to the ground. Idiot girl. Does she have no loyalty?

As if Nanjela had conjured Nayendi with the thought, there her daughter was, opening the door to the storehouse, standing across from the window through which Nanjela was spying. The lovers froze. Nayendi stood, staring at them. Then her eyes darted around the clasped figures and caught her mother's eyes and held them. Nanjela felt the urge to run but she knew her old knees wouldn't take her far. This moment of seeing felt even more private than the smell of sex in the room. Nanjela looked down first. She was heartbroken for her daughter, who would be heartbroken for shame, who knew nothing, Nanjela thought, of the willingness to be hurt that marriage breeds in you: how at first you pull back your palm from the slap, but over time simply wince and look away, and eventually just hold your hand out, patient as a beggar, resigned. When Nanjela looked back up, her daughter was gone, and she could see Mary's face full on now, chin tipped to the moonlight, radiant with laughter.

By the time Mama Lota arrived at the scene — having grown suspicious that both groom and bride had left the bonding ceremony — clothes were back on and pacts had been exchanged. But Mama Lota knew. She looked pointedly at Nanjela and asked, "What is happening here?" Nanjela took her friend's hand in hers and told the truth. The older women both realised that even at this point, no one else had to know about this dramatic betrayal. The wedding guests were drunk on food and beer and marital amnesia. No one had noticed anything amiss.

Mama Lota found the bride sitting under the avocado tree, weeping. One of the tied-up dogs was by her side, licking her hand with animal compassion. Mama Lota levered herself to the ground and put an arm around her. Nayendi looked up and said, "Tell him yes, tell him yes. Tell him yes, I'd marry him." Mama Lota sighed and patted her dog on the head. Eventually, they all went up to Mama Lota's bedroom, the oblivious elders still intoning below. Lukundo sat by the dresser, his head in his hands. A bored Mary leaned against the spotted mirror. The old women knelt on the ground beside each other. Nayendi sat on the edge of the bed, nodding down at her hands in her lap.

"Tell him yes," she said again and again, as if he weren't there. Awed by her, ashamed of her, tired, the others remained silent as she persisted. All for nought. Lukundo left before they could marry. He left that hot, close bedroom and packed his things and just as the sun cracked the pale shell of the sky, he walked off down the village road, leaving the wedding to collapse in on itself.

Mama Lota and Nanjela never speak of that night except in the most roundabout way, sucking their teeth at the good that begets evil, shaking their heads at the evil that begets good. How is it, for example, Nanjela often wonders to her friend, that the child conceived that dreadful night, or perhaps a short while earlier, had turned out so well in the end?

"*Ah-ah*. But we're the ones who raised him," Mama Lota chuckles.

"Yes, but that one is a demon and that other one is a vulture. How did they make such a good boy?"

And so it goes. One despairs; the other reassures. Nanjela steps sprightly beside her lanky friend as they tend their small field of crops. Mama Lota has grown shorter over the years, bending like a crane. The evening of their heights has brought them closer, as has the shared undertaking that began one morning a year after the wedding that never was.

Mama Lota and Nanjela, stepping outside after an amiable debate over the relative merits of mobile phones, had found one of the doublemen licking something under the avocado tree. Nanjela got there first. She took a deep breath and smacked the dog firmly on the nose. He wandered off, accustomed by now to her disdain. Nanjela gently picked up the mewling, swaddled creature. Three or four months old by the look of it and — she checked — a boy.

Mama Lota approached. "What is this?"

"*Shh-shh-shh*," Nanjela said with warning eyes, pressing the baby's face to her chest to calm him. Mama Lota stood by, fists on her hips, impatient. Only when he was quiet did one friend lower her arms to present to the other the child's untouched face, familiar as a reflection.

"Look," said Nanjela. "Look who it is."

Robinson Crusoe
at the Waterpark

Elizabeth McCracken

They had come to Galveston, the boy and his fathers, to look at the ocean and chaw on saltwater taffy, but Galveston was solid November fog. As they drove down Seawall Boulevard, the Pleasure Pier emerged from the mist like a ghost ship: first the multicoloured lights of the rollercoaster and Ferris wheel, then an enormous sign that read, *BUBBA GUMP SHRIMP CO*.

"Good God," said Bruno, the older father, the *old* one. The sky was mild as a milk-glass hen. He would have said this aloud but nobody else in the car would know what milk glass was. Instead he tried, "I hate the seaside. Where are we going?"

"You know where," said Ernest, the younger father, who was driving.

Bruno had understood — when he fell in love with a young man, when they bought a house together, when he agreed to having children (one child at least) — that his life would become narrower and deeper, fewer trips to Europe, more moments of surprising headlong love. He had never imagined that family life would mean this: a visit to an indoor German-themed waterpark in

Galveston, Texas. The fog had done it. They were headed to a location called Schlitterbahn, where there was an artificial river, for their river-obsessed son.

"You'll feel at home," said Ernest consolingly. "Being German-themed yourself."

"Darling, I'm German-*flavoured*. German-scented. Only my mother."

"A mother counts double," said Ernest.

Bruno inclined his head towards their son — born to a surrogate, with an anonymous donor egg — in the back seat. They had forbidden him video games, so the boy had fallen in thrall to a pocket calculator, which he carried everywhere, calculating nothing: he could count, reliably, to six. "Well," Bruno said.

"I mean, *your* mother," Ernest said. "Your particular mother."

But that was something Bruno and their son had in common. Bruno had an adoptive German-born mother, and a presumably biological English mother who had left him at a public library in Manchester, England. Not in the book deposit, as he liked to claim, but in the ladies' room. In this way Bruno and the boy had the same mother: Anonymous. As in anthologies of poetry, she was the most prolific in human history. This particular Anonymous — Anonymous Manchester — had left him behind like a love letter to strangers; his parents had adopted him; his parents had divorced; his mother brought him to America. That was his provenance. He catalogued manuscripts for an auction house in Houston, other people's love letters, other people's diaries. Provenance was everything, and nothing. The point was not to stay whence you came, but to move along spectacularly and record every stop.

Still, he did hate the seaside. His beloved worked as a PR person for a technology company that specialised in something called Cloud Services, but Bruno was a person of paper, and the ocean was his enemy. The seaside turned books blowsy and loose. It threw sand everywhere. Its trashy restaurants left you blemished, oil-spotted. It drowned children, according to Bruno's mother. She had few fears but drowning was one, and she had handed it down to her only son, like an ancestral christening gown that every generation was photographed in.

The fog made them drive slowly, as though not to break their car upon it. A wedding party walked towards them along the beach: bride, groom, six blue-clad bridesmaids, two men in tuxes, all of them overweight, one whippet-thin photographer walking backwards. The lactic light made them look peculiarly buoyant on the sand. Above them, a line of large khaki birds flew parallel to the ocean, heads ducked to avoid the clouds.

"Pelicans!" said Ernest, and then, in a hopeful, accusatory voice, "A wedding."

"Pelicans?" said Bruno. "Surely not." But there they were, single file and exact, military even, with the smug look of all pelicans. "Pelicans flock!"

"Well, sure," said Ernest. "What did you think?"

"I thought they were freelancers," said Bruno. "Pelicans!"

"They looked like brother and sister," said Ernest, "the bride and her groom. Like salt and pepper shakers."

"They did," said Bruno.

The three people in the car, on the other hand, looked nothing alike, though strangers could see they belonged together. Strangers were always trying to perform the spiritual arithmetic: the tall paunchy goateed near-senior citizen, the short hirsute broad-shouldered young man, the otherworldly child, who called now, from the back seat, in his thrillingly husky voice, his dreams filled with artificial rivers, "Schlitterbomb!"

"*Bahn*," said Ernest, and Bruno said, "That's right, darling, Schlitterbomb."

Ernest and Bruno had not married, not legally and not, as Ernest would have liked, in a church, or in a friend's backyard, or on a beach. Bruno did not believe in weddings, though he'd been married once, once for fifteen years, to a woman. He'd been the young husband then. Now when Ernest brought marriage up, Bruno said, "I'm an old hippie," which was true insofar as he, unlike Ernest, had been alive in the 1960s and had done some drugs.

Why marry, after all. The boy stirring in the back seat *was* their marriage, even though, from the first, it was Ernest who had summoned him up, first as a dream and then as a plan and then as a to-do list. It was Ernest who wanted a child, and then specified a biological one, who found the donor egg, and the surrogate, and then offered to Bruno what seemed like a compromise: they could mix their sperm together. "Oh God, how revolting," said Bruno, and Ernest pointed out gently that it wouldn't exactly be the first — "But not in a laboratory," said Bruno, who ordinarily was the one with a sense of humour. And so the boy was Ernest's child by blood, and Bruno's by legal adoption. Ernest was Daddy and Bruno was Pop; Ernest believed in vows, Bruno in facts and deeds. The important fact was four years old. The fact was named Cody. The fact had never-cut red hair that hung to his shoulders and was so fair-skinned as to be combustible. Every day he was slathered in sunscreen; the first freckle would be a tragedy Ernest might never recover from. God knew when they'd manage a first haircut. When Cody and Bruno were out in the world together, they were generally taken for grandfather and granddaughter and this thorough wrongness incensed Ernest, though Bruno had learned over the years not to take the mistakes of others too seriously, not when his own mistakes required so much analysis. He couldn't explain to Ernest the real trouble with a wedding: Ernest's terrible taste, which he, Bruno, would have to go along with, and smile, and declare himself happy. "I like peach," Ernest would say, displaying a napkin. Or, "My family loves disco music." Or, "We could have Beef Wellington."

Once upon a time, Bruno had had opinions about everything — the politics of Eastern Europe, baby clothes, how airline stewardesses should comport themselves, interior decoration. Then: Ernest. Ernest, from a happy Cuban-American family, had grown up going to Disney World for vacations and watching sports on television and buying clothing in actual shopping malls. Ernest had quite the worst taste Bruno had ever encountered. Up-to-date, American taste. For instance: Bruno had never imagined that a person he loved could admire, never mind long for, the abomination that was an open-plan house. Proper houses had doors, had walls, had secrets. But as they watched real estate programmes for tips on buying — neither had ever owned property, Ernest because he was young and Bruno because he was lazy — he was horrified to hear Ernest say, "Now see, that's perfect. You can see everything from the kitchen."

"Do you know who else likes to see everything from the kitchen?" Bruno asked. "The Devil. Hell is entirely without doors."

"Heaven doesn't *need* doors," said Ernest.

Then Bruno had to remind himself that Ernest actually believed in heaven and hell, at least a little. So he said of the interior decorator on the television, "Look at that fool. I'm to trust him to arrange my furniture when he can't even wear a hat at a convincing angle?" Look at that fool, yes, he thought to himself, of himself. That old fool would live in a panopticon, for love of Ernest.

And so Bruno decided to treat his opinions like a childhood collection — decorative spoons, matchbooks — something comprehensive and useless. Put it all away, beneath the bed. Let Ernest decide; let Bruno feel superior. Now they owned a house in Houston,

Texas, where when you walked in the front door you could see the kitchen, the dishes in the sink, the nook with the small offering to the gods that was the child's breakfast: a stem end of baguette, split and spread with jam. The playroom, the backyard, all the ways you could bolt.

Bruno had given up a lot for Ernest. He would not tolerate a wedding.

Schlitterbahn was an enormous medical military arachnoid construction, candy-coloured tube slides corkscrewing out of barracks. In the summer it was open to the air; in November, half the park was closed, and half covered against the weather. Bruno had looked up details on his phone; now he said aloud the fake German names in the most authentic German accent he could conjure, the voice of his mother. "*Blastenhoff,*" he said. "*Wasserfest. Surfenburg.*"

No matter what you renounced in this life, fate would provide the parody. At the Schlitterbahn box office they had to offer their wrists, and in a quiet ceremony they were braceleted, married to the park. The outdoor attractions — that was the word, *attractions* — were closed, but there were plenty of indoor attractions. "Most of my own attractions have been indoors," said Bruno to the young officiant, a plump woman with calligraphed eyebrows, who brandished another bracelet and asked if they wanted splash cash. "Do we?" asked Bruno. "Yes," said Ernest. He shifted Cody on one hip. The boy had already put on his orange goggles, and he rubbed like a robot cat against Ernest's ear. "Honey, ouch," said Ernest. "You take it, Gravy." He stepped aside so that Bruno could offer his wrist to the young woman a second time.

"I'm a good swimmer," the boy told her.

"Are you? That's great!"

"Well," said Bruno.

"I *am*," the boy insisted. The rule of the household was to encourage, but Bruno wanted to say, *No, sweetheart, you're an awful swimmer. You suck.* One of the things he hadn't realised before having a child: how many ways there were to die of self-confidence.

In the locker room they crammed their clothing into a minuscule cubbyhole. Only in a bathing suit did Ernest seem un-American: dark, furred, in a pair of unfashionably short but devastating red swim trunks, a 1960s movie idol from another country. Not a Frankie or a Bobby — a Francesco, a Roberto. "Handsome," said Bruno, accusingly, but Ernest shook his head.

"Ah well," said Bruno, and started to pull on his navy swimming shirt.

"You don't need that," said Ernest. "It's all inside."

"*I* need it," said Bruno, touching his stomach.

"I want a river," said Cody, shivering in his lime green tights — ankle-length, to protect him from the sun and cold both.

"And so you shall have one," said Bruno.

"What's its name?" said Cody.

"I don't know."

"Río Balsas? Douro?"

"The Darling," said Bruno. "That's your river."

Bruno took one hand, Ernest the other. They could feel the current flow through their little conductor.

The boy and his rivers. At this, and only this, he was a prodigy. He was slow to walk, to talk, to eat solid food. He still wore a diaper at night, requested another diaper once a day to move his bowels, which he would only do in the kitchen, next to the cupboard with the lazy Susan. Bruno, according to his mother, had been entirely toilet-trained at one and a half, but Cody would be a kindergartener before the process was done. "It's the sign of a genius," said one of the mothers at preschool. "Coincidentally," Bruno had answered, "also the sign of an idiot." What the mother had meant was it could still go either way; they were not yet at the fork in the road between *gifted* and *special*. But this mother had children who were toilet-trained at ordinary ages, who hit every milestone in excellent time. Modern parenthood: other parents examined your children for deficiencies so they could augur their own child's future from your child's psychic entrails.

They wandered down a Plexiglas corridor, in and out of the warmth that fell from the overhead heat lamps. At a dead end a Gothicky arrow captioned with Gothicky letters pointed right, to something called *Faust und Furious*.

"Well," said Ernest. "He was German, wasn't he? Faust?"

After a moment Bruno said, "*Technically*."

Eventually they found a room filled with children and their parents, a pirate ship run aground in a shallow pool, hordes of insufficiently dressed strangers.

The variety of swimming costumes! Chubby women in two-piece costumes, middle-aged women in waterproof dresses, men in flowered trunks, Speedos, ankle-length pants. And the navels: sinkholes, champagne corks, thumbprints. Bruno's own belly button was inward; so was Ernest's; the boy's a little love-knot, a souvenir of the day he'd been delivered to them.

Children flew down slides and splash-landed. Parents stood watching, or walked babies through the water, or lay on deck chairs as though sunbathing beneath the corrugated roof. Two lifeguards in pointless sunglasses wandered around mid-shin in the water, clutching long foam rescue devices to their abdomens.

The boy started to run in.

"Walking feet!" called Ernest. "Careful, honey." He turned to Bruno. "Was this a terrible idea?"

"This was your idea."

"We should get him a lifejacket."

"It's one foot of water."

"You can drown in three inches."

"I know all the ways you can drown," said Bruno.

"Yes," said Ernest, "I'm sorry."

They looked back. The boy was already gone.

Dead, Bruno decided. He felt this any time he couldn't locate Cody for more than a minute, even in games of hide and goseek, when the boy wouldn't answer his name: an absolute conviction that he was now looking for a corpse. This was something he had never told Ernest, who believed Bruno too laissez-faire to do any real parenting. Ernest was reasonable, logical, in his worry. He had a sense of proportion. For Bruno, there was nothing between uncertainty and catastrophe. That was his secret.

"Where is he?" he asked Ernest now.

"He's somewhere—"

They ran sloshily through the water. Behind the pirate ship was a smaller slide shaped like a cheerful gape-mouthed frog, and here they found the boy sliding down the frog's great tongue. The goggles gave him the look of a scientist testing gravity.

They perched on the edge of the pool and watched the frog as it vomited toddlers. Toddlers, and Cody, who went up the steps along the frog's spine and down its tongue as though practising for later: that exactitude and joylessness. The air seemed made of shrieking and flesh. Bruno was grateful for his swim shirt, which hid his gut. He had the urge to reach out with bent fingers and just brush the inside hem of Ernest's swim trunks, imperceptibly, though it wouldn't be imperceptible to Ernest, and Ernest wouldn't approve.

He did it anyhow.

"Gravy," said Ernest. But he hooked one pinky into Bruno's Schlitterbahn bracelet and gave it a fond tug.

Then Cody was at their knees. "I want my river," he said. "I want to tube on my river."

"Of course," said Bruno, and Cody smiled again. His teeth were even, loosely strung. Bruno had always been appalled by parents who lamented the passing of their children's youth. *If you could just keep them this age!* And what would be the result? A child like a bound foot, a bonsai tree.

O Cody and his milk teeth: just a little longer, please.

The fact was Bruno was no better than anyone: he knew they'd got the best one. The *best* child, the most beautiful and distinct. The red hair out of nowhere, the ability to hail a waitress across a restaurant. The love of maps, and of birds, the obsession with Charlie Chaplin. The native slapstick. The way he liked to caress with his shoulders and the side of his head. His animal nature. Yes, he loved birds but he wanted to take them out of the sky, too. Sometimes Bruno worried that this was an inheritance from him, how they both wanted everything they loved twitching under the weight of one big paw.

A pair of double doors took them outside into the chill, where a heated pool spun steam from its surface, as though it were the source of Galveston's fog, on one side a bar advertising Bud Light. A middle-aged woman sat on one of the half-sunk barstools and tipped blue fluid into her mouth from a statuesque glass.

"A bar," said Ernest, in a voice of wonder, he who had given up bars for parenthood. (Bruno had given them up longer ago, for other reasons.)

"Have a drink," Bruno said.

"Really?"

"Why not? We're on vacation."

They stepped, the three of them, into the slapping heat of the pool. The bartender was a young man, with dark skin and dreadlocks, perhaps hired to match the island theme. He was dry, the bar itself a well that kept back the water. "Under eighteens got to be on the other side," he said, in a Texan accent. He indicated a beaded rope stretched across the middle of the pool. "I'm sorry, guys," he said.

270

"Oh well," said Ernest, turning around.

"Sit," said Bruno. "Shall we find the river, Code? While Daddy rests and has a drink."

"Yes," said Cody seriously, as though he'd been arguing this for hours.

"No," said Ernest.

"Have a margarita," said Bruno, who knew that to be granted permission was a kind of love for the long-partnered. Nothing major, not quitting your job to be an artist, not travelling solo for six months. A drink. Another slice of cake. A half-hour of foolish pleasure in bed with somebody else. The love of children was said to be unconditional, but it was nothing but conditions. *I don't love you any more!* Cody might shout, when refused more television, and Ernest — the disciplinarian and therefore the spurned — would say, *You don't mean it.* But Bruno was a man of the world, Bruno could see that it was exactly true, just as in another hour it would be exactly false. That was the alarming thing about some people, how their love was like the beaded rope across the pool: the substance was continuous, but it was only the beads that kept it afloat. Some people could put love down and pick it back up and not know why your feelings were hurt by the loveless intervals, which in the end made no difference.

"Are you sure?" Ernest asked.

"What a nice grandpa!" said the lady at the bar. Her sunhat appeared, like its owner, intoxicated but doing its best.

"Not really," said Bruno.

"I'm just being friendly," the woman said, in a menacing voice.

"Me, too," said Bruno. To Ernest, he said, "Sit and have a drink. For God's sake, when were you last alone?"

Ernest took a seat around the corner from the woman, who swivelled on her stool to watch him pass. "I won't know what to do with myself," he said, and then shyly, gesturing at Bruno's wrist, "You've got the money."

"Of course!" He waded back into the pool. "Stay there, Cody."

"Cold," said Cody, and shivered dramatically. "Let's go to the river."

"You're doing *great*," Bruno said warmly. "Now, how does this work?"

The bartender took his wrist with a tender familiarity, a secret handshake, a pulse-taking. Just in case Bruno hadn't caught his meaning, the bartender winked, in a cousinly way. He moved Bruno's wrist past the register, which beeped.

"You could buy *me* a drink," said the woman. Her glass was empty; her teeth were blue. "It's Thanksgiving. It's Thanksgiving *tomorrow*. I'm drunk."

"I know," said Bruno.

"Really?" said the woman.

"This isn't, as I believe we say, my first rodeo. And for the lady." He nodded at the bartender, but perhaps he only longed for another gentle handling of his wrist, the beep that acknowledged a transaction. There it was. "Magic!"

"There's a transponder," Ernest explained. "It keeps track."

"Cloud Services," said Bruno.

"I don't think so," said the bartender.

"Cloud Services," said Bruno, more seriously, and Ernest said, "Yes."

Back inside, around the corner, some poor soul in a dachshund costume, talked — no, silently communed — with a tube-topped woman and her crewcutted pre-teen son. The dachshund costume wore a collar with an enormous tag that said, *Schatzie!* Its mouth was open in a terrible permanent smile, filled in with a black net grill. Behind the grill glittered a pair of human eyes. Bruno tried to meet them. It was as misbegotten a creature as Hieronymus Bosch ever dreamt up.

They turned on to a bridge, and looked over, and there it was: the river. Families floated along on single inner tubes, or on figure-eight-shaped inner tubes built for two. In Texas, *tube* was a verb, meaning to ride upon one. The chlorinated air smelled of infection being held just at bay.

"River," said Cody.

The bridge led eventually to an artificial beach. The river was circular. On the right families pushed off on their journey; on the left, they staggered out, pulling their inner tubes behind them. Bruno had the sensation that he experienced, every now and then, of having washed up himself on some shore, with no memory of his passage — not just how he got here, Schlitterbahn,

Galveston, Texas, but his life, in which he lived with a man and had a child and loved both.

He found a double inner tube from a stack near the water, a doughnut on one side and on the other a ring with a plastic floor that said, *BABY SEAT. MAX WEIGHT 25 POUNDS*. He had no idea how much the boy weighed. That was Ernest's department. Look at him, skinny thing, his ribcage an upturned rowboat. They waded in, and Bruno lifted Cody into the baby seat so he faced forward, could hold on to the handles on either side. They pushed out and the current took them. Bruno heaved his torso up and grabbed the tube on either side of the boy. They went around a corner, past a palm tree and a flotilla of fully dressed women in *hijabs* floating together.

He had the unnerving, recurring feeling that he'd forgotten to remove his watch, but it was only the shackles of the waterpark around his wrists. Half the people in the artificial river were swimming it, a whirl of limbs, no vessels. Boys, mostly, of all ethnicities, pink and umber and tawny and brown and sienna. It seemed as though there'd been a shipment of boys, and their boat had crashed, and here were the survivors. *The Raft of the Medusa* at the Waterpark. There were a lot of them, shouting in terrifying pleasure at each other. The water got rougher. Bruno reached around Cody and grabbed the rings. "Are you all right?" No answer. He realised with alarm that this was a terrible mistake. Impossible to know how deep the water was. Deep enough to buffet them along. A baby seat? Who would take a baby on something like this? They ran over one of the swimming boys, who popped up choking, laughing.

Bruno knew all the ways you could drown because his mother had told him, and because of Eleanor, now ten years dead, his wife for fifteen years, Eleanor of the psychiatrists and misdiagnoses, Eleanor whom he loved as well as he'd ever imagined loving anyone, until he met Ernest, when he realised his essential trouble might also have been a question of extraordinary misdiagnosis, though he only had himself to blame. Eleanor, had she been alive, would have made fun of Ernest, not because he was a man (which might have thrilled her) but because he was *conventional*. A terrible insult, from Eleanor. To not know Faust was the fiction and Goethe the German! They had never had children because she had a horror of a living thing inside her body; she said she couldn't believe that modern science hadn't figured out a less barbaric way to reproduce. One that might allow you to drink as much as you liked, for instance: the studies were just coming out, then, that suggested in utero alcohol was a bad idea. (So why, he imagined her saying now, surveying the Schlitterbahn crowds, did children ever since seem to be getting *stupider*?) She was the author of most of Bruno's opinions. Holding them was his way of keeping her alive; not insisting on them was his way of doing the same for himself. She had started to lose her memory. Could be early Alzheimer's, her doctor said, or arteriosclerosis, or more likely alcoholic insult to the brain, and Bruno hadn't cared: you don't worry about arson or faulty wiring till *after* the structure has burned to the ground.

She'd died in the bathtub, drowned, full of vodka and Valium. Maybe she'd forgotten how many she'd taken. Maybe she'd merely remembered the full measure of what she'd forgotten. Surely, said Ernest, when they fell in love a year later, you knew all along about yourself, you liked men. Bruno could only say, *I was waiting for you*.

He and Eleanor had been married in a sad ritual. Her parents were dead; his mother, who was only ten years older than Eleanor, had hated her immediately. Eleanor had bought a white dress, because Bruno had told her that his mother cared about such things. His mother had laughed in her face. "Well," said Eleanor, afterwards, "we'll never do *that* again, thank God."

The current picked up. The banks of the river were made of tile. The palisades were tiled as well, and studded with more bored lifeguards, standing like unemployed goats. He looked up and longed for the pelicans of the morning, their competence and precision. His biceps ached from holding on. He couldn't see Cody's face. At the next turn, a young park employee stood up to his waist in the crashing water. His job was to catch inner tubes as they threatened to bash into a wall, to send them in the right direction. How could so badly designed a thing exist at a place meant for children? Bruno paddled his feet. He wanted to avoid the guy, but instead they knocked right into him. "Sorry!" he shouted, and then they were shoved away, in the opposite direction, in front of the wave machine.

Now they were surrounded by loose boys and empty bobbing inner tubes. "Hold tight!" he commanded Cody, as he heard a wave behind them. A woman in a neon-pink swimming dress clung to a single inner tube. Clawed at it. They hadn't seen this stretch of river from the bridge. Every few seconds some hidden mechanism slapped out a wave, which then lifted the flotsam — people, tubes, goggles, swim shoes — and dropped the flotsam, and smacked the flotsam on the head. Even artificial rivers are careless, Cody.

Survivors of the Whaleship *Essex* at the Waterpark. The *Lusitania* at the Waterpark. *The Poseidon Adventure* at the Waterpark.

He'd thought he hadn't wanted children because Eleanor hadn't wanted them. He *hadn't* wanted them for that reason. But of course it was that Eleanor was already forty when they'd married and she'd convinced herself she was too old. Perhaps he was too old, too, but here was his heartbreaker, screaming as they bounced along.

"Are you all right?"

The boy nodded the back of his head. You could hear the waves from the wave machine behind you before they lifted you up. That was good. They were just one turn from the beach. Now Bruno was holding Cody's right wrist to the starboard handle of the inner tube. Every wave threatened to scupper them. What would happen then? Would it jolt a lifeguard into action? Would the boy be picked up by the passengers of another tube? Sucked into the filtration system? Bruno thought of Ernest drinking at the swim-up bar, Ernest who would never forgive himself, though he would forgive Bruno, and that would be the worst thing that could ever happen to either one of them. No, not the worst thing. Of course not.

A bullying wave pushed the edge of their raft, tipped them, rushed overhead, and swept Cody away.

Above the river the burghers of Schlitterbahn saw the flash of pale flesh, the hair that streamed behind as though a cephalopodic defence, *Stay away*. The last inhabitant of the lost city of Atlantis, washed into the waters of Torrent River — that was its name. A little boy, surrounded and then eclipsed by the bigger boys, the wild boys of the German-themed waterpark. "Look out!" shouted a blue-tongued woman from the bridge, but she was drunk, and already the other people doubted what they had seen, and besides, so what? Those feral boys would take him in. They never went home, those boys, they lived here, they circled and circled, howling and laughing and dreaming of home.

"Cody!" Bruno shouted. "Cody!"

The boys found the body, and lifted it up, and then there was his darling's face, panicked, one hand out, and Bruno snagged it, and they were back in each other's arms, bumping up on to the incline of the concrete beach. Cody coughed. He was alive. Not a lifeguard had shifted. They were surrounded by wild delight, shrieking, flesh, stove by a whale, but safe.

Not till they had staggered out — not on to dry land, there was nothing, nothing, nothing dry in all Schlitterbahn — did Bruno realise that the water had stripped the swimming tights right off, that Cody now stood, naked, just as God had made him — though of course God hadn't been anywhere near Cody's conception, an event Ernest called a miracle. Surely the opposite, Bruno had thought. Ordinarily he hated God getting credit for Science's good work. Yet here the boy was, the narrow naked awkward miracle.

"Jesus," said a voice. A man, this new model they now made, tremendously fat from the hips up, an epidermic barrel, skinny as a kid from the hips down, such a precarious construction it hurt Bruno to look at him. "Cover that kid up!"

Their towels were back by the pirate ship. Bruno took off his shirt, and draped it over his son, to make him decent.

At the Wasserfest Bar, Ernest stirred the slush at the bottom of his drink. O Schlitterbahn! The freckled, the fat, the hairy, the veiny, the chubby girls in bikinis, the umbilically pierced, the expertly tattooed, the amateurishly scrawled on, the beautiful, the grotesque, all the Boolean overlap: Ernest thought he'd never felt so tender towards the variety of human bodies. He loved them all. Every bathing suit was an act of bravery.

"Yes," he said to the bartender, whose name was Romeo, "I'd like another," and then there was his family: Bruno with water dripping from his beard, Cody wrapped in some black cape which he now flung off, saying, "Daddy! Daddy! I capsized! I capsized! I was saved!"

"You're naked!"

"Naked!" said Cody.

"Marry me," said Bruno, galumphing in.

Notes on the Contributors

Joanna Briscoe is the author of five novels, including the bestselling *Sleep With Me* (Bloomsbury), published in eleven countries and adapted as an ITV drama by Andrew Davies. She has had several stories published in anthologies and broadcast on Radio 4, has written for all the national newspapers, and worked as a columnist and literary critic for the *Guardian*. Her sixth novel, *When Nobody's Looking*, will be published by Bloomsbury UK and US in spring 2017. She lives in London with her family. Joanna Briscoe first read *Jane Eyre* while growing up on the moors in Devon, and her favourite section is when Jane is at Lowood.

Tracy Chevalier is the author of eight novels, including *At the Edge of the Orchard*, *The Last Runaway*, *Remarkable Creatures* and the international bestseller *Girl with a Pearl Earring*. She first read *Jane Eyre* when studying for her English Literature BA at Oberlin College. Her favourite part is when Jane has to sleep rough for a few days until she finds refuge with the Rivers family.

Born in Dublin in 1969, now based in Canada, **Emma Donoghue** is an award-winning writer of novels both contemporary and historical, short stories, literary history, and drama for radio, stage and screen. She is best known for *Room* (2010) and her film adaptation of the novel (2015). Revisiting one of the favourites of her adolescence, *Jane Eyre*, she wrote the introduction to the Folio Society's new edition, describing it as a book that "made the world take a nobody seriously" — a goal that animates all Donoghue's own work. Her next novel, *The Wonder*, about an Irish girl in the 1850s who seems to live without eating, comes out in September 2016. www.emmadonoghue.com

Helen Dunmore was the first winner of the Orange Prize and is also an acclaimed children's author and poet. Her novel, *The Lie*, was shortlisted for the Walter Scott Prize for Historical Fiction and the 2015 RSL Ondaatje Prize. Helen Dunmore's fiction and poetry is translated into more than thirty languages and she is a Fellow of the Royal Society of Literature. Her latest novel is *Exposure*, published by Random House UK and Grove. She loves the many layers of Jane Eyre's character: her fiery intelligence, her battling spirit as she takes on a world which tries to crush her, her wit and her audacity. But Jane Eyre can be stealthy too, and that is what drives Helen's story.

Esther Freud trained as an actress before writing her first novel, *Hideous Kinky*, which was shortlisted for the John Llewellyn Rhys prize and made into a film starring Kate Winslet. After her second novel, *Peerless Flats*, she was chosen as one of *Granta's* Best of Young British Novelists. Her other books include *The Sea House* and *Lucky Break*, and her most recent, *Mr Mac and Me*, was shortlisted for the New Angle Prize and was the winner of the East Anglian Book Awards best novel. She contributes regularly to newspapers and magazines, and teaches creative writing for the Faber Academy. She first read *Jane Eyre* as a teenager, and although it remains one of her favourite novels, she accepts its influence over her early life wasn't always healthy, especially when, as a lovelorn fourteen year old, she hung out of her window, convinced that someone, somewhere was calling to her.

Jane Gardam is an acclaimed novelist who excels in the short story form. She has twice been awarded the Whitbread/Costa Prize for Best Novel of the Year and she also holds a Heywood Hill Literary Prize for a lifetime's contribution to the enjoyment of literature. She was awarded an OBE in 2009. Her most recent novel, *Last Friends*, was shortlisted for the Folio Prize, and Jane is a recent recipient of the Charleston-Chichester Award, the only award to recognise longstanding creativity and achievement in the short story genre.

Linda Grant is the author of six novels and four works of non-fiction. Her second novel, *When I Lived in Modern Times*, won the Orange Prize for Fiction. *The Clothes on Their Backs* was shortlisted for the Man

Booker Prize. Her family memoir, *Remind Me Who I Am, Again*, won the Mind Book of the Year and the Age Concern Book of the Year. She lives in London. Linda Grant's copy of *Jane Eyre* is a navy blue hardback with the Latin motto of her school embossed in gold on the cover. It was awarded for winning the Rosa B Chambers prize for Reading Aloud, an accomplishment which finally found an application at literary festivals.

Kirsty Gunn has written five works of fiction as well as three short story collections, and, most recently, a long essay about her interest in and connection to Katherine Mansfield. Her most recent collection of short stories, *Infidelities*, published in 2014, was shortlisted for the Frank O'Connor Award and won the Edge Hill Prize. She is Professor of Writing Practice and Study at the University of Dundee and lives in London and Scotland with her husband and two daughters. She has known *Jane Eyre* since she was nine and continues to think about her. In that way — as is the case with all truly realised fictional characters — Jane is a contemporary.

Tessa Hadley is the author of six highly praised novels, *Accidents in the Home*, which was shortlisted for the *Guardian* First Book Award, *Everything Will be All Right*, *The Master Bedroom*, *The London Train*, *Clever Girl* and *The Past*. She is also the author of two collections of stories, *Sunstroke* and *Married Love*. She lives in London and is Professor of Creative

Writing at Bath Spa University. Her stories appear regularly in the *New Yorker* and other magazines. She cannot remember the first time she read *Jane Eyre*, but it must have gone in deep, and it's never stopped working. And whenever she's cleaning she remembers Jane and Hannah getting Moor House ready for Christmas.

Sarah Hall was born in Cumbria in 1974. She is the prize-winning author of five novels — *Haweswater, The Electric Michelangelo, The Carhullan Army, How to Paint a Dead Man* and *The Wolf Border* — as well as *The Beautiful Indifference*, a collection of short stories which won the Portico and Edge Hill prizes. The first story in the collection, "Butchers Perfume", was shortlisted for the BBC National Short Story Award, a prize she won in 2013 with "Mrs Fox".

Susan Hill is the author of sixty books. Titles include *I'm the King of the Castle, The Woman in Black, Strange Meeting, The Beacon* as well as the Simon Serrailler detective series. *The Woman in Black* is the basis for the UK's second-longest-running stage play ever, and a major film starring Daniel Radcliffe. She has never read *Jane Eyre*.

Elizabeth McCracken is the author of five books: *Here's Your Hat What's Your Hurry* (stories), the novels *The Giant's House* and *Niagara Falls All Over Again*, the memoir *An Exact Replica of a Figment of My Imagination*, and the most recent collection

Thunderstruck & Other Stories, which won the 2015 Story Prize. A former public librarian, she is now a faculty member at the University of Texas, Austin. She didn't read *Jane Eyre* until she was in her mid-thirties. Her absent-mindedness about reading it meant the amazing gift of a great book that she had nearly no misconceptions about: she sat on a rented sofa in rural Denmark, and fell in love with it.

Nadifa Mohamed was born in Hargeisa in 1981. Her first novel, *Black Mamba Boy*, won the Betty Trask Prize, was longlisted for the Orange Prize, and was shortlisted for the *Guardian* First Book Award, the John Llewellyn Rhys Prize, the Dylan Thomas Prize, and the PEN Open Book Award. In 2013 she was selected as one of *Granta*'s Best of Young British Novelists. Her second novel, *The Orchard of Lost Souls*, was published in 2013 and won a Somerset Maugham Prize; it was longlisted for the Dylan Thomas Prize and shortlisted for the Hurston/Wright Legacy Award.

Audrey Niffenegger is a visual artist and a guide at Highgate Cemetery. In addition to the bestselling novels *The Time Traveler's Wife* and *Her Fearful Symmetry*, she is the author of four illustrated novels, *The Three Incestuous Sisters*, *The Adventuress*, *The Night Bookmobile*, and *Raven Girl*, which was also adapted into a ballet by the Royal Ballet, Covent Garden. She lives in Chicago and London.

Patricia Park is the author of the debut novel *Re Jane* (Viking/Penguin Random House), a modern-day interpretation of *Jane Eyre* set in New York and Seoul. She was a Fulbright scholar and has written for the *New York Times, Guardian, Salon, Daily Beast* and others. A self-proclaimed "Eyre-head", Park first read Brontë's classic as a twelve-year-old in Queens, NY, and has since wondered what if, Reader, she *hadn't* married him. Park is at work on her second novel, set in Buenos Aires.

Francine Prose is a novelist and critic whose most recent book, *Peggy Guggenheim: The Shock of the Modern*, was published by Yale University Press. Her previous books include the novels *Lovers at the Chameleon Club, Paris, 1932, My New American Life, Goldengrove, A Changed Man* and *Blue Angel*, which was a finalist for the 2001 National Book Award, and the non-fiction *New York Times* bestseller *Reading Like A Writer: A Guide for People Who Love Books and for Those Who Want to Write Them*. She writes frequently for the *New York Times Book Review* and the *New York Review of Books*. She lives in New York City.

Namwali Serpell was born in Zambia in 1980 and is associate professor of English at UC Berkeley. Her work has appeared in *Tin House, n + 1, McSweeney's, The Believer*, the *San Francisco Chronicle* and the *Guardian*. She received a Rona Jaffe Foundation Writers' Award; was selected as one of the Africa 39, a

Hay Festival Project to identify the 39 best African writers under 40; appeared in *The Best American Short Stories 2009*; was shortlisted for the Caine Prize for African Writing in 2010, and won the Caine Prize in 2015. On reading *Jane Eyre*, she says: "I first read it in one long, fevered sitting that took me through the night to a grey, rainy morning. It was 1995 and I was back in Zambia for a year of secondary school. Perhaps that's why my story commingles these two versions of home: my country and the wild landscape of letters into which I so often escape. Jane has always seemed my spiritual double."

Elif Shafak is Turkey's most-read woman writer and an award-winning novelist. She writes both in English and in Turkish, and has published fourteen books, nine of which are novels, including *The Bastard of Istanbul*, *The Forty Rules of Love*, *Honour*, *The Architect's Apprentice* and her genre-crossing memoir *Black Milk*. Shafak blends Western and Eastern traditions of storytelling, bringing out the voices of women, minorities, subcultures, immigrants and global souls. Defying clichés and transcending boundaries, her work draws on different cultures and cities, and reflects a strong interest in history, philosophy, culture, mysticism, Sufism and gender equality. www.elifshafak.com

Lionel Shriver's novels include the National Book Award finalist *So Much for That*, the *New York Times* bestseller *The Post-Birthday World*, the international bestseller *We Need to Talk About Kevin* and the

Sunday Times bestseller *Big Brother*. She won the BBC National Short Story Award in 2014. Her journalism has appeared in the *Guardian* and the *New York Times*, the *Wall Street Journal* and many other publications. She lives in London and Brooklyn, New York. Her twelfth book *The Mandibles: A Family, 2029–2047* is forthcoming in 2016. Shriver has not read *Jane Eyre* since her teens, and admits sheepishly to dependency on multiple mini-series to refresh her memory — having avidly watched more than one.

Salley Vickers is the author of eight novels, including *Miss Garnet's Angel* and *The Cleaner of Chartres*, and two collections of stories, most recently *The Boy Who Could See Death*. Her books explore themes of art, psychology and other dimensions and she allies herself with an old tradition of storytelling. Salley Vickers won her first ever school prize when she was thirteen for an essay on Emily Brontë, and has remained a devotee of the Brontës ever since. They feature in *Cousins*, her latest novel published by Viking in summer 2016.

Evie Wyld is a prize-winning author living in south London. Included in Granta's 2013 list of Best of Young British Novelists as well as the *Daily Telegraph*'s Best Writers Under 40, Evie was the winner of the 2014 EU Prize for Literature. Her first novel *After the Fire, A Still Small Voice* won the John Llewellyn Rhys Prize and a Betty Trask Award. Her second, *All the Birds, Singing*, won the Encore Award, Jerwood Fiction Uncovered Award and Miles Franklin Award. It was also shortlisted for the Costa Novel Award and longlisted for the Baileys Women's Prize. Evie's graphic memoir about her childhood obsession with sharks, *Everything Is Teeth*, was published in August 2015 and illustrated by London artist Joe Sumner.

A Note on Charlotte Brontë

Charlotte Brontë was born in Yorkshire on 21 April 1816, the third of six children of Patrick and Maria Brontë. In 1820 the family moved to Haworth, a small village on the moors where Patrick became curate to the church. Charlotte lived most of her life in Haworth, apart from short stints at boarding school and as a governess working for other families, as well as two years studying and teaching in Brussels.

Her mother died in 1821, and her two elder sisters in 1824, leaving her the oldest of four. She, her sisters Emily and Anne, and her brother Branwell were very close, and primarily self-taught. As adolescents they began to write, making up stories about fantasy lands. In particular, Charlotte and Branwell invented and wrote about the kingdom of Angria.

None of the siblings married, but went out to teach or tutor or work as governesses, inevitably returning home. An idea to open a school at Haworth was the impetus for Charlotte and Emily to go to Brussels to improve their French. There Charlotte fell in love with her married teacher, Constantin Heger, and subsequently wrote about this experience in the posthumously published *The Professor*, and in her last novel, *Villette*. The Haworth school plan never attracted enough students and the plan was abandoned.

In 1845 Charlotte discovered a cache of poems Emily had written, and determined that they should be published, along with poems by herself and Anne. They managed to find a small publisher to bring out *Poems by Currer, Ellis and Acton Bell* — the curious androgynous names the sisters took to disguise themselves — but the volume only sold two copies. The sisters were reinfected with the writing bug from their youth, however, and all three began to work on novels, often sitting together in the dining room to write, and reading out their words to one another at night.

Emily's *Wuthering Heights* and Anne's *Agnes Grey* were published with little fanfare in 1847. Charlotte's first — *The Professor* — was rejected by publishers, but when she sent in *Jane Eyre*, based in part on her time at boarding school and as a governess, a publisher knew it had a winner, and on publication late that year it became a bestseller.

The public tried to guess who "Currer Bell" was. When a theory began to circulate that one person had written all of the novels, Charlotte and Anne travelled to London to reveal themselves to Charlotte's publisher to prove that "Currer" and "Acton" were two different people. (Emily was too retiring to go with them.) The publisher, George Smith, was astonished to discover that the author of *Jane Eyre* was a small, shy woman, but he and his mother took her in and encouraged her to meet members of the literary world, including

William Thackeray, one of Charlotte's favourite writers. He famously held a dinner party that she attended, where she sat mute, refusing to blossom into a witty guest, and Thackeray left the party for his club, not to return! Charlotte also met and became friends with other writers, including Harriet Martineau and Elizabeth Gaskell; the latter published a biography of Charlotte after her death.

In 1848 and 1849, within the space of eight months, Charlotte lost Branwell, Emily and Anne — the two sisters to the tuberculosis rife in Haworth, Branwell to alcoholism. Still she managed to continue to write, producing and publishing *Shirley* (1849) and *Villette* (1853). In 1854 she married Arthur Bell Nicholls, her father's curate, who had pursued her despite her father's objections. Charlotte was only to enjoy less than a year of marriage before she died, pregnant, possibly of dehydration and malnourishment from severe morning sickness, or from the typhus that struck down an old family servant.

Other titles published by Ulverscroft:

THE FIRST PHONE CALL FROM HEAVEN

Mitch Albom

In the small town of Coldwater, Michigan, a handful of bereaved residents start receiving phone calls from beyond the grave. Some call it a miracle; others are convinced it's a hoax. Regardless of opinion, one thing is certain: Coldwater is now on the map. People are flocking to this tiny, remote town to be part of this amazing phenomenon . . . Sully Harding's wife died while he was in prison, and he now cares for his young son — who carries around a toy cell phone, believing his mommy is going to call him from heaven. But Sully soon discovers some curious facts: the calls only come in on a Friday, and each recipient happens to have the same cell phone plan. Something isn't adding up, and Sully is determined to keep digging until he uncovers the truth . . .

A PROPER FAMILY HOLIDAY

Chrissie Manby

Sisters Chelsea and Ronnie Benson haven't spoken to each other in two years. When their mother announces she wants the whole family to go on a week-long holiday in Lanzarote for her sixtieth birthday, both dread the excursion for different reasons. Sophisticated singleton Chelsea, a fashion journalist, would rather not revisit the "chips with everything" world she left behind when she moved to London. Ronnie, now a mother of two, is feeling fat and frumpy: the last thing she wants is to strip down to a swimsuit alongside her super-thin, super-chic sis. The week begins badly and gets worse, as underlying tensions and secrets are exposed. And then their mother drops a bombshell on the group. Will the holiday bring the sisters closer, or blow the Benson family apart?